D0978810

PAPER ANGELS

Also by Billy Coffey

Snow Day

PAPER ANGELS

A Novel

Billy Coffey

Faith Words

New York   Boston   Nashville

FaithWords
Hachette Book Group
237 Park Avenue
New York, NY 10017

www.faithwords.com

The FaithWords name and logo are trademarks of
Hachette Book Group, Inc.
FaithWords is a division of Hachette Book Group, Inc.

The publisher is not responsible for websites (or their content) that
are not owned by the publisher.

First Edition: November 2011
10 9 8 7 6 5 4 3 2 1
Printed in the United States of America

Library of Congress Cataloging-in-Publication Data
Coffey, Billy
Paper angels / Billy Coffey.—1st ed.
p. cm.
ISBN 978-0-446-56823-4
1. Guardian Angels—Fiction. I. Title.
PS3603.O3165P37 2011
813'.6—dc22

2011011096

CONTENTS

Contents

PAPER ANGELS

It is not known precisely where angels dwell—whether in the air, the void, or the planets. It has not been God's pleasure that we should be informed of their abode.

—Voltaire

1

In the Black

It was a point of pride to the citizens of Mattingly, Virginia, that our town was the most boring twenty square miles on the planet. The running joke was that Mayor Jim Willis should have that printed on a sign at the town limits for everyone to see. Something simple and honest, just as we all were— *Welcome to Mattingly, Where Nothing Ever Happens.* What had happened the previous weekend had never occurred in our town, and thank God for that. That's why the headline in the following Monday's *Gazette* was the size normally reserved for catastrophes and political elections (which, to Mattingly folk, were usually one and the same). ONE DEAD, ONE SOUGHT IN GAS STATION ROBBERY, the banner read. The subtitle— SHOCKING ACT LEAVES OWNER HOSPITALIZED—summarized the 893 words of the piece that took up the entire front page and most of page two as well.

It was much later that I read the article and the two dozen or so others written over the weeks and months after the incident. I still have them pasted into a scrapbook that sits on the shelf in my living room. The facts of the story are all there, the who and what and when. Not the why, though. Like most things in this life, the why came later.

At the time I was giving no thought to headlines or justice. I was in the black then, left to wander through a strange land spread out inside me, an in-between place that was not as bad as hell but not as good as heaven. Confusion and unconsciousness didn't imprison me as much as they provided comfort. They were another bandage to cover another wound that could have just as easily festered into death. Many of the townspeople trickled in and out of my room during that time. They sat with me and prayed for me and gave their own account of what had happened. I heard them as if we were on opposite sides of a closed door, not clear but understood well enough. I found the near death that gripped me no different than the near life I had lived. I said nothing to my neighbors and gave no indication I was aware of their presence. I felt a pain worse than that of my flesh, a pain even now I doubt can be fully spoken.

When I finally awoke it was to a different sort of darkness, this one lighter but colder. Emptier, even. The lights above me dimmed and rippled. Everything felt heavy, like I was being held underwater. Noises entered through an open door to the hallway—phones rang, voices gossiped. Labored coughs echoed from a distant room. Shadows walked past. Then my nurse appeared to officially welcome me back to the world.

Kimberly Simms was a regular in my gas station. She stopped by every morning for her bottle of juice and a newspaper, both of which she said she never finished because work got in the way. A pretty brunette just two years out of college, she already carried the strong soul and slumped posture that seemed a requirement in the health-care profession. I always thought doctors and nurses were soldiers in a war where often a stalemate was the closest thing to a win.

"Well now," she said, "my night's starting off right. Nice to see you in the land of the living."

I looked up at her, which was all I could do. Anything more seemed impossible. "Wish I could say the same," I answered, and then smiled in an attempt to make Kim believe I was kidding. "What time is it?"

"Little after seven in the evening. You've been out quite a while, Andy. Days. Thought I was gonna have to start going to the Texaco every morning."

"Timmy'd like that," I told her.

"He's already been by." She moved closer to check my monitors and me with the easy grace of practice. "Trust me, he wouldn't like it. Poor guy was a wreck. How are you feeling?"

"Barbequed."

It was her turn to smile, a small grin that couldn't help but grow into a soft laugh despite herself. For years I'd seen Kimberly Simms the customer, the young girl who visited me every morning and whom I'd known since she was in pigtails and carrying around her dolly. She was a kind soul even then, and it was no small feat that she had managed to hold on to that kindness through her teenage years and now into life as an adult. Yet in that hospital room I saw for the first time the girl I'd known as the woman she had become. No wonder the young guys in town were jumping over themselves for the chance to put a ring on her finger. For the moment, Owen Harlow was the lead horse in that race. He and Kim had been dating for about seven months.

"We'll take care of your burns," she said. "You're now my official project. Well, you and Mr. Alexander down the hall. I'm not letting either one of you out of my sight."

I tried to lift my head. Gravity took hold and pulled it back to the pillow. Streaks of silver light shot across my eyes. Kim pushed a button to raise the upper part of my bed and asked me not to move.

"Keeping an eye on me shouldn't be that much of a problem," I said. "I don't feel like I'll be up and running anytime soon."

"Don't you worry," she said. "We've bandaged up your face and your right hand. Your burns weren't as bad as they could've been, which is very good. But you have a pretty good bump on your noggin, and that's not so good. The doctor will stop by a little later on. He'll talk over some things with you and we'll change your bandages. You'll be seeing some other people too, specialists and whatnot. I'll make sure you're fixed up good as new, Andy."

"I know you will."

Kim's smile turned into a look of concern that bordered on

remorse. She cleared her throat in the hope it would make it easier to say, "Jake wanted me to call him as soon as you woke up, night or day. Guess I'll go do that."

"No," I said. "Please don't. I don't want to talk to Jake right now."

"I know you don't, Andy." She put her hand on my shoulder. "But it's part of his job. He needs to get a statement from you as soon as you're able. He's got the tape from that video camera you put up, but he's still gotta talk to you. Whole town's in an uproar over what happened, especially since one of them's still on the loose."

I smiled and shook my head. A few years ago my insurance guy told me I had to put one of those video cameras in the store. Some kind of new regulation or something. I'd laughed at him, mostly because the only thing it'd be good for was watching me sit there by the register all day. Turned out I was wrong about that.

"Just give me a bit, Kim," I told her. "Please? No need to bother the sheriff until tomorrow. I won't be forgetting what happened anytime soon. I just don't want to talk about it right now."

The thoughtfulness that ruled Kim's personality was now working against her. I could see the emotions scuffling in her eyes. Which was more important, her job or her friend?

"I'll get in trouble, Andy. You don't want that, do you?"

"No," I said. "No, I don't want that. 'Course, I coulda said the same when a certain sixteen-year-old girl ran outta gas up near Happy Hollow and asked a certain owner of a gas station to help her out so her daddy didn't catch her out where she wasn't supposed to be."

"You're never going to let me forget that, are you?" Kim's shoulders slumped as she said that, proof that sometimes our sins don't just find us out, they find us out again and again.

I shrugged and managed a grin. "Not if it comes in handy."

"Okay," she sighed, "I suppose I can bend the rules a bit. But only if that makes us even."

"Even Steven. Thank you, Kimmie."

She took a step back and regarded me. "Are you in any pain?"

"Some," I said. Which was a lie. But it was nothing I couldn't handle and nothing Kim or anyone else could fix.

"We have some pretty strong meds going into you, so they'll help. Might make you a bit loopy, but I don't think you'll mind." She gave me a wink that either said she was kidding or she was not. "You up for some food? Might do you some good."

"No, but thanks. Not very hungry right now."

"Okay. You get some rest then. I'll be right outside, and I'll check on you in a bit. In the meantime, you just hit the button there if you need me."

I nodded. Tried, anyway.

Kim gave me a last squeeze on the shoulder and lowered my bed, then moved toward the door. She stopped just before leaving and turned toward me. The dim lights seemed to focus on the tears in her eyes. "I'm sorry, Andy," she said. "I truly am. This shouldn't happen to anyone, and especially someone like you. I just don't..." Kim tried to finish her sentence, but she couldn't find anything to add that would make things better.

"Thanks, Kim. And don't feel bad. I don't understand much right now, either."

She offered a weak smile and walked out toward the direction of a pained and elderly cough from a nearby room. I settled into my pillow and let my eyes gaze upward. My thoughts dwelled on all the other people who had over the years found themselves in this bed. People separated by age and beliefs and circumstance, but who had all found a common bond in staring at that very ceiling and repeating the same words I'd just said.

I don't understand.

Instead of letting myself try, I let the medicine sink me back into unconsciousness.

2

Elizabeth

When I woke again, evening had given way to darkness and night had settled in. My head felt like old leather that had been stretched and then pinned under the sun to harden. I was swollen from the neck up, held together by tape, gauze, and a thin layer of ointment I assumed was supposed to soothe my skin but only made me feel like it was crawling. Kim had said they would change my bandages the next morning. I began counting the hours.

A horrible thought came to me then, one that in the midst of the shock and darkness I had not considered. I inched my hands toward my face. Bandages began at my chin and ended at the top of my head, leaving me with openings at my eyes, nose, and mouth to exercise my senses. Poetic, I supposed, that I would become the invisible man. I pushed down harder on my face. Then my head.

Nothing. I felt nothing.

The fire had incinerated my beard and hair.

There are times in life when so many big things pile up that it takes only one small thing to tumble them all. Realizing I'd lost the hair I'd had my entire life and the beard I'd worn almost as long was that small thing. The guy who torched me had failed to kill me, but he had succeeded in rendering me naked before the world. I would have preferred the former to the latter.

"It'll grow back, Andy. If you want it to, that is."

I jerked my head to my left and winced as skin wrinkled

around my neck. There in the wooden chair not three feet from my bed sat a woman. A denim shirt rested untucked over her faded khaki pants. Long brown hair was held in a pony-tail by what looked like a leather tie. A thin strand of gray had escaped to the front of her right ear, wanting nothing to do with its less experienced kin. She watched me with her legs crossed, exposing a thick pair of nurse's shoes that hung un-tied from her feet. The one propped in the air made a smooth circular motion, as if she were waiting for something to hap-pen.

I tried to clear my eyes. "Caroline?" I asked.

"No," the woman answered. "Who's Caroline?"

She shifted her weight to the left and scraped against the vinyl seat, watching me with a look of someone who had seen too much but chose to hope anyway. Her gaze then turned downward to a folded piece of paper in her left hand. She pulled a pair of scissors from her shirt pocket and began cut-ting.

I watched as small white slivers fell onto a wooden keep-sake box that sat balanced on her lap. The hinges looked worn and rusted by age, and the wood—I could make out the look of oak even in the shadows—had been worn smooth. Pock-marks and dings decorated the sides and top, marks of use rather than decoration. It was not a large container but nei-ther was it small, just enough for whatever means most. Such boxes were common in the South and often passed down from one generation to another. I had one myself. Actually, one very similar to that one. Very similar indeed.

"Where'd you get that?" I said.

"There now," she said. "That wasn't so hard, was it?"

"What?" I asked.

"Talking. From what I understand, getting you to do that has been quite a chore since you got here. But you spoke a little with Kim. That's a good start."

I followed her eyes through the cracked door toward the hallway. Kim was sitting at the nurse's station talking on the phone. I couldn't tell what she was saying, but her words were clipped and to the point. I heard an exasperated "Owen" and thought of the few dozen young men in town who would love to know there might be trouble in paradise. She looked up in our direction and then down, covering her forehead with a hand.

I turned back to the woman beside me. "You give me that box," I told her. "You don't have any business with that. That's *mine.*"

"I didn't peek," she said. "Promise."

The slivers continued to fall, one, three, seven.

"Stop that," I said.

She did. Both the paper and the scissors disappeared into her shirt pocket. She looked at me again, waiting.

"Where'd you get that box?" I asked.

She motioned to the table with her eyes and said, "It was sitting right there when I got here. Someone must have dropped it off for you."

Jabber, I thought. *It had to have been Jabber.*

"Well, it was left for me," I said. "Not you."

I rubbed my hand against my leg to try and calm the imaginary needles that pricked it. The woman leaned forward in her chair and placed her hands on the box. "You're right," she said. "I'm sorry, Andy. I just needed to borrow it."

"So you could do what?"

"Get you to talk."

I balled a fist and took a deep breath. The pain of both calmed me. I looked through the door again at Kim. She sat watching us.

"Who are you?" I asked.

"My name is Elizabeth Engle." She stuck her hand out as she said it. Mine remained at my leg. "You can call me Elizabeth."

"Well it's very nice to meet you, Ms. Engle. Now would you please do me the courtesy of returning *my property* to the table here and explain what you're doing in *my* room? Or would you rather I push this here button and have Kimmie kick you out?"

"Oh, Kim wouldn't kick me out," she said. "I'm here for you, Andy. You're my job."

I snorted through the gauze around my mouth. "And what job is that? Sneaking into patients' rooms, rummaging through their stuff, and then scarin' them half to death?"

"I snuck in because I didn't want to wake you," she said, raising one finger, "and I apologize for making you jump"— two fingers—"and I said I didn't peek"—three fingers.

Elizabeth rose from her chair and returned my box to the table. She set it down carefully, almost reverently, and patted the top of it twice. Then she returned to her seat beside me and leaned forward.

"What do you want?" I asked.

"To make you feel better."

"You a doctor?"

"No, not really."

Elizabeth left her answer vague. A wave of nausea washed over me. As if being Kentucky Fried Chickened wasn't enough, now I had to have my brains scrambled, too.

"You're a shrink," I said.

"More adviser than shrink."

"Well I don't need an adviser, I just need to go home."

"You will," she said, "when you're ready. Which isn't quite yet. There are wounds no one sees, Andy. It's the job of the doctors and nurses to mend the ones that are visible, and it's my job to mend the ones that aren't."

"I have invisible wounds, huh?" I asked. "That you're gonna mend?"

"Yes."

"And how are you gonna do that?"

"By listening to you."

"You're gonna sit there and listen to me and play with your scissors and paper?"

"That's right," she said.

I grunted. "You're crazy, lady. I'm not in the mood for any New Age psycho bull. I don't share my feelings, and I'm not gonna get in touch with my inner self. I don't wet the bed, I don't dream of my mama, and there is no way, no way on God's *earth*, that I'm gonna talk to you about why I'm here."

I expected her to say something smart, something gooey with kindness and understanding, but Elizabeth said nothing. She simply reached forward and gently put her hand on my own.

"You don't have to talk about any of that, Andy," Elizabeth said. "You can just talk about whatever you want. I promise."

When she smiled it was a beam that fell on me like cool rain on a hot day, the sort of shower that makes you lean your head back and stretch out your arms so you can gather in as much of it as you can. A rare smile. Caroline's smile. And in that moment Elizabeth managed the impossible. She melted me and yet held together what little of my heart was still alive. I had never seen this woman, didn't know her, and yet I felt as though she had always known me. I would have been frightened to death if it hadn't felt so good.

But just as quickly as she had drawn me out, my hurt drew me back in. The anger that had gripped me refused to let go and dug its claws into what was left of my flesh, reminding me that I was right to feel its hotness. That I *deserved* it. That it was *mine*.

I drew my hand away from hers. "There's nothing you can do for me," I said. "I'm not going to talk to you."

"Yes, there is," she said, "and yes, you will. Who's Caroline?"

"That's none of your business," I said. "I appreciate you stopping by, Elizabeth, but I don't want you here. I don't want *me* here. All I want to do is be left alone until someone tells me I can leave."

"Well, see, that's the thing." Elizabeth straightened herself and crossed her legs again. "Turns out I have a lot of say in how long you stay here. Those invisible wounds can be pesky."

"That's bull," I said.

"You really think so?" Elizabeth smiled again, teasing me. "Try me. I'll keep you here until the Rapture if I have to."

I started to offer the sort of bullish grunt men are famous for, the kind that saves them the trouble of actually having to say *Who do you think you're talking to?* But at that moment Elizabeth took hold of my hand again and squeezed, and the snort I was about to offer lodged itself halfway up my throat and refused to budge. A mild panic began to build. Half of me saw her as just someone else to keep at arm's length. The other half, the half that not only let her take my hand again but keep it this time, whispered that her presence could be all that was keeping me tethered to whatever hope was left in my life.

Then I considered what had happened and whose fault it was. His—the Old Man's. And God's by proxy. But I decided that I shared much of that fault, not through my actions but through my trust. For letting Eric inside.

I turned away from her and looked at the wall in front of me. For the next hour neither of us spoke. Elizabeth returned to her paper and scissors. I was tired and angry and hurt. Elizabeth didn't need to be a counselor to see that. What she didn't see, what she couldn't, was why. When I finally spoke, it was more out of surrender than acceptance.

"We talk about only what I want to," I said without looking at her. "And if you tick me off or try to ask me stuff that's none of your business, I'll throw you out of here myself. I wasn't much of a sharer before, and I ain't one now. Especially to strangers. I'll do what I have to just to get back home and away from here. But I'd rather stay mad because I have good reason to be mad, and I'd rather feel guilty because I should feel guilty. Those are my choices to make."

Elizabeth shrugged. "Deal."

Silence again. More staring and cutting.

"What now?" I asked.

Elizabeth set her scissors and paper aside and pointed to the box on the table. "How about that?" she asked. "Seems pretty special. Might be a good idea to start with what you think really matters before we go talking about what you think doesn't."

I looked at her and shook my head. "No offense, but that's one of those things that ain't your business. It wouldn't make much sense to you."

"It doesn't have to make much sense to me, it just has to make sense to you."

I was about to refuse again but then heard a noise from down the hallway, a small echo that both mixed with and stood out from the calm commotion of chatter and ringing phones. Someone was whistling. I thought at first it was my imagination, a consequence of returning to the world. But it persisted, grew louder as it approached.

"Do you hear that?" I asked her.

"Hear what?"

The melody was both oddly familiar and not, like a memory that had yet to occur. I knew that song. No, I thought, not song. Hymn. One I'd last heard sung by my grandmother nearly fifty years ago—

> *Shall we meet beyond the river,*
> *In the clime where angels dwell?*
> *Shall we meet where friendship never*
> *Saddest tales of sorrow tell?*

The whistling stopped and morphed into a shadow that loomed just outside the doorway. For a moment I thought Death itself had come for me. "Mercydeath" is what came into my head, though I had no idea what that meant. But the face that peeked around the corner was not Death. It was worse.

The Old Man walked through the door and leaned against the foot of my bed, then let out a slow and painful exhale. His faded hospital gown was just one prop among the many I'd known. I supposed he had designed that one in order to offer me some sense of unity, like the people I once saw on television who had shaved their heads in support of their cancer-stricken loved ones. He dragged an IV line behind him, though the pole it should have been connected to and the solution bag that should have hung from it were missing. A visitor name tag was stuck to the gown in the middle of his chest. OLD MAN had been written on it in blue crayon.

"Hiya, Andy," he said.

Fury that had wedged in a dark place inside me for three days kindled then sparked.

"I'm sorry it had to be like this," he said, "but I'm not sorry that it had to be. Do you understand?"

"No," I muttered. "No...I...don't."

"Andy?" asked Elizabeth. "Are you okay?"

Her words were mere echoes in my mind, another voice from the other side of the door. The Old Man looked at her and then to me.

"I know you're mad," he said, "and I know you're hurt."

"Andy?" came the echo.

"I need you to trust me one more time. I've never given you cause to doubt me before, have I?"

"Andy, who are you talking to?"

"Everything I've shown you from then until now, every little thing, comes down to this."

"—Andy," I heard Elizabeth say, *"I need you to—"*

"—listen to me," the Old Man finished. "I need you to let this lady—"

"—help you," said Elizabeth. *"Whatever's happened, you still have—"*

"—now. That's what matters. God sent her."

"Stop it," I moaned. "Please just stop."

Elizabeth took her hand from mine and muttered an echoless "I'm sorry."

"No," I told Elizabeth, then I reached out for her hand without realizing I had done so. "Not you. Not...it's *him*." I pointed a trembling finger of my bandaged hand toward the end of my bed. *"You* did this," I shouted to him. "This is *your* fault. Where *were* you?"

Elizabeth returned her hand. "Andy," she said, "please try to relax. You'll bring Kim back in here, and I need you to stay with me. Okay?"

The Old Man said nothing, and in that silence was an absence of more than mere words. His presence seemed gone as well—the humor, the lightness, the sometimes unbearable ease. Instead I saw in his eyes a satisfied weariness, the sort that would come by traveling a long road and finding a peace in the walking. This, I considered, was his final lesson to me— that life was not as much one beautiful lesson after another as it was a succession of hard places that must be endured. What beauty and ease we searched for in this world would be found not in open fields or along peaceful shores, but in the crags and crevices of the mountains we climbed.

"It's time for me to go, Andy," he said, "but don't worry. This isn't good-bye. You'll see me soon."

The Old Man turned away and continued his stroll down the hallway, among the living and the dead and the both.

"Come back here," I pleaded, but all I could manage was a whisper that could carry no farther than Elizabeth's ears.

I covered my face with my hand and sobbed. Elizabeth took my head in her free hand and guided me into her shoulder.

"Andy," she whispered, "tell me who was there."

"I can't," I whispered.

"Yes, you can."

You still have now. That's what matters.

No. Nothing mattered. Not now.

Trust me one more time.

Never again.

God sent her.

God.

I felt Elizabeth's warmth, the soft touch that somehow held me tight. It had been years since I'd last felt a touch like that. Not since Caroline. Lovely Caroline. She was gone now, there but gone, close and yet worlds away. Like everyone else. After all that time, I thought I had accepted that. I thought it was good and I was fine, but it wasn't and I wasn't. What I once had had now been taken away. All that was left was the warm embrace of a woman who reminded me of what could have been but never was.

"Tell me," Elizabeth tried again.

It was then, my soul broken, that I shared my secret. Finally and fully after all those years. Told to neither confidant nor friend, but to a stranger who held my brokenness against herself.

"My angel," I said.

3

The Box

I sunk my head deeper into Elizabeth's shoulder, shocked at my own confession. I could only hope that somehow the words had come out muffled against her shoulder, that just as I'd spoken them the phone had rung or the air had kicked on and she hadn't heard me. That way, she would ask me to repeat it, and I could say something else. Anything else. But Elizabeth had heard me. She'd heard me clear.

"Oh," she said, "is that all?"

She chuckled at her own wit and gently patted my head. The sensation was not unlike being hit with a sledgehammer. Evidently all the tape and gauze served more as a barrier for germs than any real sort of protection. But I neither flinched nor uttered a word of protest. I would have endured that pain for eternity and a day if it meant I could stay right where I was.

Elizabeth released me and returned to her seat, careful to keep her hand on mine. There was nothing flirtatious in that small act, no hint of romance or desire. But it was magic just the same.

"You gonna take me to the rubber room now?" I asked.

"Sorry, no. It's occupied at the moment by a guy who thinks he sees the Tooth Fairy."

The heaviness between us was shooed away by laughter. It was the one thing I needed and the one thing I didn't expect.

"All the same," I said, "maybe you should reserve some space."

"Why's that? Do you think that's where you belong?"

I shrugged. "You're the counselor. I can guess you don't hear a lot of folks saying they see imaginary people."

Elizabeth raised her eyebrows and asked, "Is that what he is to you? Imaginary?"

"I know it ain't normal."

"Normal?" Elizabeth followed the word with a soft laugh. "Well, I guess that depends on who you are. Some people would think you'd had your brain baked along with your head. Others would give you a clap on the back and ask what took you so long to share the obvious. It's all about what you believe."

"Didn't know what I believed was important," I said.

"What a person believes is the only thing that's important."

"Then what do you believe?"

Her eyes widened. It was a question I don't think Elizabeth had anticipated. With her free hand she stroked the wrinkle that had appeared in her khakis. "That's a question you can ask if I'm ever in that bed and you're ever in this chair."

"Ah," I said. "Gotcha. Me patient, you doctor."

Elizabeth nodded.

"Well, Doc," I said, finally comfortable enough to settle back into my bed, "congratulations. You've managed to get something out of me no one ever has."

"I think there's more than one thing no one's managed to get out of you," she said. "But for now, let's concentrate on this one thing. So this 'angel' has been around for a while?"

I let out a very long and very slow exhale. "Yes," I said. I was determined to keep my answers short as long as I could, testing to see if this new ground I was walking upon was solid or quicksand.

"When did you first see . . . it?"

"Him," I corrected.

"Right, sorry. When did you first see *him*?"

There was a part of me that still begged for quietness. Enough had been said already, more would only lead to trouble. Elizabeth must have sensed my wariness, because at that moment she said, "It takes a lot of courage to open some of the doors in life, Andy. It takes even more courage to walk through them."

Maybe that was true and maybe not, but I was pretty sure I wasn't in much shape at the moment to either open *or* walk through a door. I had been beaten and burned, poked and prodded. I had been educated. Not just in the nastiness of the world, but in the suddenness of it. I'd lived most of my years in a town where nothing much ever changed, and yet in the span of five minutes everything had. The Andy Sommerville who went to work three days ago and had nothing to worry about except a loose nozzle on the gas pump was gone. I didn't know who or what had replaced him, and I didn't know how to find out.

I need you to listen to me. I need you to let this lady help you.

The Old Man had said that. The same Old Man who had said so many other things over the years. Who had kept me as much company as I'd ever known and encouraged me and made sure I kept to...well, maybe not the straight and narrow, but the closest thing to it. And though at that moment I despised him with a hatred only the Devil himself could appreciate, he had never been wrong. Not once.

"My parents died when I was ten," I told her. "It was my daddy's fault. He was a drunk, and a mean one at that. I remember hiding behind the couch while he beat my mama with his belt because she'd taken his drinking money to buy me clothes. I hated him. He was the worst man I've ever known.

"One day he comes home from work and starts drinkin' like usual, and he runs out of beer. Says he's driving to the store. Mama says, 'No you're not, you're too drunk.' So he makes her drive him. I wanted to go, too. The thought of being alone made me scared. But Mama said no, that they'd be right back." I paused, not sure how to finish the rest, and then decided to go ahead and say it. "Guess she didn't do a good enough job driving, because when they left the store he was behind the wheel. He ran a red light and got T-boned by a beer truck. Can you imagine that? My drunk dad gets hit by a beer truck."

Elizabeth said nothing.

"Both of 'em died right off. Least I got that. They didn't hurt. That was all saved up for me, I guess."

"What happened to you?"

"We were living up in Richmond then. I loved that city. So big and bustling. It swallowed me up, and I liked that feeling. But I couldn't stay after that. The only kin I had left were my grandparents on Mama's side who lived here in Mattingly. They came for the funeral and then brought me back here with them. Been here ever since."

"I'm sorry," Elizabeth said, and she said nothing more. That alone endeared her to me. Life was full of tragedy and there was no reasoning with it. Sometimes *I'm sorry* is all you can say because it's all you should say. That was when I thought my new ground was solid.

"It was tough," I told her. "Real tough. I got settled well enough on the outside—got to school and made friends and all that—but on the inside I was broken.

"I turned eleven about a month after I got here. My grandparents decided to go all out to try and make me feel better. Like I was a part of something, you know? They wanted to make their family and their town my own, so they threw a party and invited all my friends. That was a great day, it really was. But deep down I knew I couldn't be given more than what had been taken away, and I think everyone else knew that, too."

"Nice of them to try," she said.

I nodded. "It was, and I loved them for it. But all it did was prove to me that I'd lost everything. I was in bed that night staring up at the ceiling, and I got an idea. I figured that Daddy took my mama away from me, but God must have allowed it. I didn't deserve that to happen to me. So I figured by all rights God should send me someone else. Not someone to replace Mama—no one could do that—but someone who could help

me just the same. Someone who could understand. So I got
out of bed, went to the window, and looked up at the Big Dipper."

"The Big Dipper?"

"Mama always said the second star from the end of the handle was the door to heaven. 'That's where the answers to our
prayers come from,' she'd say. To this day I don't know where
she got that, but I was willing to give it a shot. I think I'd have
tried anything at that point. It was hanging right there in the
sky, right for me. I stood there and looked at that star for the
longest time. Then I prayed. Prayed like I'd never prayed before. And when I said my amen . . ."

"What?" Elizabeth asked.

I cleared my throat. "When I said my amen, that
star . . . winked. I swear it did. It was there like normal one second, and then all of a sudden it sorta puffed up and shined
and then shrank right back down again. I thought it was my
eyes playing tricks on me. I don't know. Maybe that's exactly
what it was. I was hurtin'. Sometimes when you're hurtin' you
see things that aren't so."

Elizabeth looked down and smiled at the wrinkle she was
smoothing out. The way she did it, so calm and smooth, en-
chanted me. "And how long did you have to wait for your
answer?" she asked.

"Not long. I woke up later that night and rolled over, and he
was just standing there by the window staring at me."

"What did he look like?"

"Just normal, I guess. Old. No wings or halo or anything like
that. He said, 'Hiya, Andy.' He just stood there for a bit, and he
was gone. I thought I was dreaming until I saw him again the
next day. He started his thing right after that."

"His thing?"

"Yeah," I said with a shrug. "Don't really know how else to
put it. He just kinda . . . shows up. From time to time."

"Why?" Elizabeth asked. "Is there a reason?"

"I don't know. He tells me stuff. Tells me to pay attention

to something or gives me advice. Sometimes it's a warning."
I said those words and trailed off, thinking of the one warning he never bothered to offer. "He seems to get a kick out of it. No one can see him, but sometimes he'll be dressed different or doing something to try and blend in. Sometimes it's a costume or a suit, sometimes not. He always wears a bracelet on his wrist, though. Always. Thin and black. Silk, I think. It's nothing fancy. Actually looks pretty cheap to me, but I can tell it means a lot to him. I'll catch him rubbing it sometimes, especially when he doesn't think I'm looking. It's crazy."

"That's interesting," Elizabeth said.

"Sometimes it's like he shows up for no reason. Just to talk or whatever. Other times it's when something's either happening or about to. Not something life changing, just something he thinks is important. Like a lesson. He told me that early on."

"Told you what?"

"That his job was to get me to pay attention. He said that everything means something, no matter how small it is. 'The familiar is just the extraordinary that's happened over and over,' he told me once. He also told me I'd need the box."

Elizabeth and I both looked at the wooden container on the table.

"This box?" she said.

"He told me to go up in the attic and find it. My grandparents kept everything over the years, but I'd never seen a box. He told me exactly where to look, and there it was." I kept my eyes on the box. It was the only friend I had left. "The Old Man told me to always keep this handy. He said I'd need it in the end."

"Need it for what?"

"He didn't say. The Old Man's never been one to offer much in the way of specifics."

Elizabeth kept her eyes on the box and began rubbing my hand again. I knew what she was thinking, what she wanted to say. Counselors were much like lawyers in their reluctance to ask a question to which they didn't know the answer. She studied my eyes and then decided yes, she would anyway.

"What's in the box, Andy?"

Everything I've shown you from then until now, every little thing, comes down to this.

This was the moment when I had to make a choice between keeping the secret of the Old Man in the shadows where it had always been or daring to drag it into the light.

I let go of her hand. Elizabeth didn't draw it back but kept it where I could find it. Without a word I reached over with my good hand and grasped one end of the box. Elizabeth took hold of the other end. Together we lifted and set it between us. I felt the top of the box and moved my hand around its edges. Close to opening it, but not quite. No one had ever seen the inside of my box, not even the Old Man, but that wasn't what weighed on me. It was the fact that if I were to open my box, I would open me. "The Old Man said I'd need this in the end. Guess this might be the end."

"Every end is just a new beginning," she said. I didn't believe it and didn't say so.

Elizabeth's hand went to the latch. With a soft click she pushed it up and out of the way. The box creaked and popped, reluctant to give up its secrets, and then it surrendered to her just as I had.

She slid both hands to the sides of the box and peered inside. I could see her eyes darting over the contents, trying to find a plausible explanation for the madness inside.

A baseball cap sat top down on the left side of the box. Never worn—the price tag was still on the underside of the brim. Sitting inside the cap was a small bundle of dead pine needles, each about three inches long and wrapped inside a letter to Santa Claus. I suspected that if Elizabeth opened the letter and picked up the needles, they would disintegrate in her hand. A small wooden cross, two inches long, rested beside the bundle. Its wood was dark and thick, its edges sharp. Laying on top of the cross was half of a fingernail

painted in the brightest red I had ever seen, red like fire, like
the color of an October sun yawning its good night over the
mountains. Or red like anger, as the case may be. A lime-
green golf tee sat near the brim of the hat, its bottom caked
with dirt I'd never trodden upon. They were all gifts in their
own right, whether they were given or taken, but the tee especially was one. I just didn't know that yet. Covering the
tee was a folded and worn business card with a smiley face
on the front that always managed to make me cringe rather
than imitate. BE HAPPY!! GOD LOVES YOU!! had been written below the smiley face, though I still wondered if the one had
any bearing on the other.

Beside the hat on the other side of the box was the sort of
slingshot you used to see in the movies, right down to the rubber hose and the Y-shaped end of a tree branch. The hose had
grown brittle over the years, a victim of the constant taking out
and putting back in. It had been shot once (and oh my, what
a shot it had been) and then stolen, though I'd justified that
since with the fact that I couldn't steal what was already mine.
A paintbrush rested atop the slingshot—I could still see white
paint near the bottom of the bristles. A small stack of five paper napkins had been folded and tucked into the corner. They
had never been used, as evidenced by the crisp Dairy Queen
logo on the fronts of them. They were held in place by an un-
delivered envelope to a stranger I had seen once but never
again, though I was still looking for him. If Elizabeth had cho-
sen to pick it up, she could have felt the letter inside. ALEX
was written in pencil on the front. I never got his last name.
I didn't see the piece of bubble gum but knew it was in there
somewhere, probably stuck to the bottom or along one of the
sides. I could still smell the watermelon, like an air freshener
of a long-ago autumn day.

And there, right on top of it all, right there to remind me
of what I could never possibly forget, was the pewter angel—
Eric's key chain. It stared at me with wings outstretched and
trumpet blowing, shouting to the world not that a king had

been born but that a boy had been killed, that Eric was gone and there wasn't anything that would bring him back.

Elizabeth peered around my hand and into the box. Her hands didn't move toward it, but her eyes touched everything inside. "I don't understand," she said. "What is all this?"

"I don't know," I said. "Memories, I guess. Signposts of some of the people I've met and some of the things he's shown me. That's what the Old Man would say."

"What would you say?" she asked.

"It's junk, really. I used to think it all meant something, but there's nothing of value in there."

"He said you'd need these one day?"

I nodded.

"Why?"

"I don't know. Don't make much sense to me, really."

Elizabeth kept her eyes on the contents, moving from one object to the other. I saw her mouth grow into a hidden smile, saw it tighten into thoughtfulness. Saw it draw in like she were about to cry. She nodded and smiled, then looked over to me. "Makes sense to me," she said.

"It does?"

"What do we take out of this world, Andy?"

"Nothing," I said.

"No, you're wrong. We take one thing with us—the narrative of our lives. You're not flesh and bone as much as you are a story, a first chapter and a last and everything in between. In the end, Andy, your story is all you have. And that's why it needs to be told."

"Looks like my story ends with a question mark," I said.

"Oh, I doubt that. You haven't told me what brought you here, but there was a reason behind it. Maybe the reason is in that box."

"I know why this happened. It doesn't have anything to do with that box. It doesn't have anything to do with anything. I know you have to help me, Elizabeth, but I promise I just don't see what you can do."

"I don't have to help," she said. "I want to. But you have to let me."

I looked at Elizabeth's face and then down into the box. The fingers of the good hand I had left slipped over the objects inside. I touched them and touched my memories— times when everything had been good and right and solid. Not like then.

"I'm willing to play along, but just so you'll let me leave."

"Good," Elizabeth said. She smiled again and patted my arm. "That's good, Andy."

"Where do we start?"

She reached into the box and rooted through its contents, finally settling on the slingshot. She carefully lifted it from the box without disturbing anything else and held it up to me.

"Let's start here," she said.

A chuckle managed to escape through my bandages.

"What?" Elizabeth asked.

"Nothing," I said. "Just remembering. He hadn't been around for very long then."

"The Old Man?"

I nodded. "I hadn't been with my grandparents very long, either. Like I said, they were great people. Mennonites. Nothing wrong with that, but boy, they were strict. No television, no radio. The phone was a necessity, but an evil one. I hated living like that at first, but it actually ended up doing a lot more good for me than harm."

"How so?"

I shrugged. "Oh, I don't know. Taught me to slow down, I guess. I couldn't listen to the radio, so I listened to myself. And I couldn't watch television, so I watched my grandparents. How they lived, what they did, what they believed. And the birds. I watched the birds. Grandma loved her birds. Grandpa put up a bunch of feeders and houses and baths to draw them, and Grandma tended to them. We'd walk through the yard in the evenings and she'd point out this tree and that, and where the birds were, and what they ate and where they went.

Our whole backyard sounded like a symphony. Robins, jays, mockingbirds, cardinals, you name it. But it was the purple martins she loved the most." I paused, remembering, and finished, "That's what got me into trouble."

Elizabeth leaned back in her chair and said, "Well you know I gotta hear about that."

She smiled again, smiled that beautiful smile, and I offered a pained one back.

And I began my story.

4

The Slingshot

We found the egg beneath the purple martin house beside the pear tree. It was small, barely the size of my pinky, yet it seemed as though gallons of bright yellow yolk oozed from the hole that had been pecked into it. Grandma stooped down to study the egg, then held it up to show me.

"What happened?" I asked.

She looked up and shielded her eyes against the setting sun. The martin house was about three feet square and sat atop a metal pole that stretched nearly twenty feet in the air. Eight nesting holes were carved into the front. Two on the top row bulged with feathers and grass.

"The sparrows have come."

I arched my neck and, looking at her first, shielded my eyes against the sun just as she had. "I don't see any sparrows."

"They're not there now," she said, "but they're about. They're starting to take over the martin nests."

"They won't share?"

Grandma was silent for a moment then shook her head. "Sparrows don't share," she said. "They just take. Your grandpa will be home from the gas station soon. He'll know what to do."

She left it at that and we continued our walk, past the garden and then toward my grandfather's tool shed to check on the rosebushes. Grandma was normally talkative for a Mennonite woman, always ready for conversation or, if the situation warranted it and if secrecy was promised, some gossip.

But she didn't say much after finding the sparrows. The invasion of the martin house had rattled her into thought. As we walked I glanced back toward the martin house just in time to see a sparrow light from the pear tree to one of the nests.

Da Vinci had his workshop, and Grandpa had his tool shed. It was a dilapidated wooden building in the corner of the backyard that housed all manner of tools and materials from which he could create or repair nearly anything. And as Grandpa, like the maestro, was reluctant to work on one thing at a time, the shed was in a constant and beautiful state of disarray. Hand-drawn sketches and blueprints were scattered about on three wooden worktables, along with half a dozen projects in various stages of completion and every sort of tool imaginable. Creepy-crawlies hid in the dark corners of the shed behind long-forgotten garden tools and construction materials. Those corners were the only parts of my grandparents' ten acres of land I dared not venture.

I watched as Grandpa cleared one of the tables and pulled a worn notebook from the shelf above him. He stood motionless but for tapping his pencil on the paper and waited for inspiration. Just as I was about to speak, he nodded and muttered "Thank you" to the ceiling.

"Whatcha doing, Grandpa?" I asked.

"I'm taking care of the sparrows."

I pointed and said, "But they're out *there*."

"Yes."

He began to draw as I stood at the door waiting for something—anything—to happen. Nothing did. My grandfather wasn't what one would call a man of action. To him, things were best handled slowly and deliberately. I pulled a stool over to the table to get a better view. Scribbled on the paper was a three-dimensional box from different points of view. An array of numbers and arrows surrounded it in a language I couldn't understand. I couldn't help but to think of Wile E. Coyote and his unfulfilled quest for the Road Runner.

"Grandpa," I said, "we have to get rid of the sparrows *now*."

"I thought you liked the sparrows," he said.

"That was before I knew what they did. Grandma said they were mean. I don't want them hurting the martins."

"Me neither," he said. He took his eyes off the notebook and put them onto me. "But there is a proper way to deal with those who wish harm, and we must take care to do it correctly."

Typical Mennonite gobbledygook, I thought to myself. Always the spiritual and the holy. A home where the only God was my father's beer and where my mother's tearful prayers for help were never answered had proven there wasn't any God who could bring a measure of optimism to my world-weary heart. I was willing to give Him a chance in my new life, if only because it would be another way to put my old one behind me. But this was too much. I said nothing to display my disagreement. My eyes did it for me.

My grandfather looked at me through his thick glasses. A small whistle of air came through his nose and tickled his long, white beard. "You and I," he said, "we are here in the shed."

"Yes."

"Is there anyone watching us?"

I looked out the door and toward the house. Grandma was somewhere inside, but I didn't see her peering out any of the windows.

"No," I said. "Nobody's watching."

"You're wrong. God is watching." He tapped me on the head with his pencil and smiled. "And we have to make sure we don't disappoint Him."

He turned away from me and back to his notebook, leaving me to wonder why in the world I shouldn't disappoint God after He'd disappointed me. This was no time for thinking and planning, and it was *certainly* no time to be drawing pictures. I clenched a fist because there was nothing left to do.

The few minutes that passed seemed an eternity. Then he finally placed his pencil down and announced a satisfied "There."

"What are we gonna do?" I asked him. "Throw the notebook at the birdhouse?"

Grandpa's look told me that was not the plan. He stood from the table and began gathering chunks of wood from the back of the shed, then set to work measuring and sawing and hammering. I clenched another fist.

"Frustration," he called to me, "is a form of anger. And anger is best reserved for someone who is not trying to teach you something."

I put my fist down and let out a barely audible growl I was (mostly) sure he couldn't hear. Then I turned and peeked out the door and toward the birdhouse, where the sparrows continued to stand guard over their pilfered property. On the telephone line nearby sat two purple martins wondering what had happened. A vain attempt by one to fly to her nest was turned away with relative ease by the enemy's stronger numbers.

That was it. I had to do something.

Weapons of any sort were forbidden in my grandparents' household. That included the obvious, such as guns and knives, and the not so obvious, such as water pistols and bows and arrows. Which meant I had to improvise. Grandpa's attention had been diverted by his project, so I crept to the back of the shed and rummaged through the piles of debris. I found a discarded bit of an oak limb in the shape of a Y and a length of rubber hose, then shoved the contraband into my jeans and peeked out the door.

The Old Man stood under the martin house dressed as though he was about to participate in a B-movie safari. His brown walking boots looked just thick enough to be useless. A pair of khaki shorts began near his chest and fell nearly to his knees. The space between there and his shoes was bridged by long brown socks. A white collared shirt and safari hat completed the ensemble. He peered at the nest through a tiny pair of binoculars, then looked at me and shook his head.

"I'm gonna go get a drink, Grandpa," I said.

"I'll be done here soon." He walked to the back of the shed and returned with a section of chicken wire. I had no idea what its purpose was, and I wasn't about to inquire.

"Yessir," I managed, but I was already out the door.

I made my way across the yard to the Old Man, still eyeing the birdhouse through his binoculars. He turned to me as I approached and said, "Well, Andy, it seems we have a problem."

"Grandfolks say that the sparrows are bad," I told him.

"The sparrows are just being themselves," he said. "It's their nature, you see. They can't help it."

"They've kicked the martins out."

He studied the martin house through his binoculars to make sure. "Looks like it. What should we do?"

"Well Grandpa wants to *draw* them to death, I guess. And Grandma just seems to want to let him."

"I suppose those are options. How about you? What do you think?"

I reached into my pocket and pulled out the piece of wood and length of hose.

He wrinkled his brow then looked at the slingshot through the binoculars. "Sure that's a good idea?" he asked.

Him, too? I thought. *Really?*

"Somebody's gotta do *something*," I said. "And I guess I'm the only one man enough around here to do it."

"That so?" he asked. "You're the man, huh?"

"Yes," I said. Then I thought through it, both his question and my answer, just to make sure he wasn't tricking me into something. "Yes," I said again.

"I think you should wait and see what your grandpa's come up with. Just give him a chance. He's been around awhile, you know. He knows things."

It was a valid point, and I knew it. So I ignored his suggestion and said, "Why are you dressed so funny?"

The Old Man looked down at his clothes. "I like it. It's *kitsch*. That's German."

"Does it mean 'ridiculous'? 'Cause if it does, you nailed it."

He smiled at me and said, "I really think you should wait, Andy. God's watching, you know."

Had this not been so soon after the Old Man had first appeared in my bedroom, I would have probably taken his advice. As the years went on he proved himself to be dependable when it came to knowing the right thing, at least until the end. But at the time I saw him more as an imaginary friend than an angel. And everyone knows you can ignore an imaginary friend whenever you want.

I tied the length of hose around the Y section of the limb and picked up as round a rock I could find from the driveway. Said, "I got this." Then I drew back on the slingshot.

"Okay then," the Old Man said, "as you wish." He raised his binoculars and looked to the sparrows again. In an awkward English accent, he said, "Two degrees to the right, old chap. Pip-pip and cheerio."

I shook my head. "Quiet," I said. "I'm aimin'."

I took a breath and then let go, rocketing the piece of gravel skyward toward the invaders. Halfway there, I knew I had aimed wrong. Three quarters of the way there, I knew the rock would hit the martin house instead. And just as the rock hit, I knew the Old Man was right.

I should have waited.

The ensuing crack echoed in every direction, including through the open window of the kitchen and through the door of the tool shed. Both grandparents came running, right past my jungle-prepared angel. Grandma took one look at the slingshot in my hand and let out a pained gasp. Then she seized my earlobe and pulled. Hard. Violence had never been her way—it was anathema to her faith—but I thought at that moment if a little bit of it got into her discipline, that was just fine with her.

"Just what do you think you're doing, young man?" she demanded. Her free hand slapped against her leg and searched for something to whip me with, and her lips shook with questions she was too upset to ask. White fear and red rage mixed in her face and gave it a pinkish glow. I realized I was staring into the face of a monster created by my own sin.

Grandpa provided no protection, choosing instead to ask "What have you done?" over and over.

I turned to the Old Man for help, but he offered little. His attention was still focused on the martin house and the sparrows who had retaken their posts around it. "I say, that was a smashing shot," he said.

I rolled my eyes at him and turned toward my grandparents. "I was trying to kill the sparrows."

"You were trying to kill the sparrows?" Grandma asked. She continued to smack her leg, and I was afraid she would soon realize she didn't need anything more than her hand to whip me with. She looked from me to Grandpa and said, "You didn't tell him the proper way to do such things?"

It was Grandpa's turn to stammer. "Well . . . yes, Mama. I was just in the middle of it and—"

"You cannot do this," she said, cutting him off and turning to me. Her voice was softer now, back to normal. The momentary flash of rage had been replaced by her ever-present calm. "This is not the way, Andy. This hurts you"— she pointed to my heart—"more than them"—she pointed to the sparrows.

Grandma turned back to her husband. "I expect you will teach him now rather than get lost in your notebooks and plans?" she asked.

She turned and tromped toward the house. Neither of us moved until the door had closed.

"Well, Andy," Grandpa said, still eyeing the door, "I suppose we should have that talk."

"Yessir."

"Come," he said. "I need to show you something."

We left the Old Man there—"Everything will be jolly good,

old chap"—and walked back to the shed. A cage sat on the wooden table by the window. The base was made of the wood Grandpa had gathered, thicker than my index finger and thumb together. Chicken wire had been fastened around the perimeter with nails. Hooks joined the sides to the top, which had also been lined with chicken wire. To the right, about six inches from the base, stood a small platform that extended eight inches or so into the cage. A hinge was fastened beneath. There was a tiny, almost imperceptible space between the platform and another block of wood attached to the base. Nailed to the left side of that block was another with a six-inch hole cut into the center.

"What's that?" I asked him.

"This is how we get rid of the sparrows," he said. "Come."

He lifted the contraption, and together we walked to the picnic table near the martin house, where he set the trap. From his pockets Grandpa produced a handful of birdseed that he poured into a pile near the middle of the platform. Satisfied, he turned to me.

"Let's have a seat on the porch," he said.

I turned to the Old Man and shrugged. He mimicked me and added a smile.

Five minutes later a sparrow darted from the martin house to the cage. Its tiny head tilted from one side to the other. Satisfied there was no immediate danger, it hopped onto the platform and toward its dinner.

Halfway there the hinge tilted downward, leaving the sparrow with no choice but to go through the opening and into the cage. When it did the platform raised up, trapping the bird inside.

I looked at Grandpa, who gave a satisfied nod.

"Bloody brilliant," the Old Man said. Though he was only ten feet away, he'd said it while looking at us through his binoculars.

"Why are you talkin' so funny?" I asked him.

"I didn't say anything," said Grandpa.

The Old Man shrugged and smiled. "Just thought I might try it. No?"

I shook my head.

By the time dinner was over all four sparrows had managed to let their appetites get them into trouble, a lesson the Old Man admonished me to remember. Grandpa and I went out to inspect our catch. He placed a blanket over the cage and set it in the back of his truck, then the two of us rode out to the main road through town. The Old Man hitched a ride in the back, dressed now in his more usual garb of jeans and a T-shirt. He spent half the time stooped down talking to the birds through the cage and the other half standing in the bed with his arms outstretched. I thought he was trying to hug the wind.

The only time he seemed conscious I was there was when he thumped his finger on the back window of the truck. I turned, ready to say I was looking at the sparrows if asked, and looked at him. The Old Man pointed to the area of the seat between my grandfather and me. My slingshot sat there, a victim of the shallow pockets of a homemade pair of pants. He motioned for me to pick it up and put it in my own pocket. I shook my head no. He motioned again. I shook my head harder—*NO*. Then with his hands he mimicked a square and the motion of a lid being raised. The box, I thought. The Old Man wanted me to take it for the box. He gave me the OK sign with his thumb and forefinger, as if he knew Grandpa would forget about the slingshot altogether. Thankfully, he did. The slingshot was the first thing to ever go in my box.

"Where we goin', Grandpa?" I asked him.

"To a place where birds need to sing."

He kept driving. Past the town square, past his gas station, and on into the hills. We finally parked at the edge of an old service road that was guarded by an ancient iron gate. The woods beyond were still and silent and dark.

I looked at Grandpa and asked, "Happy Hollow?"

"Yes," he said. "Let's not linger."

We got out of the truck and he reached into the back for the cage. His hand passed through the Old Man's leg like it was molecules of air.

"Bad spot," the Old Man said. "Bad woods. There's darkness here, Andy. A shadow."

The Old Man and I watched as Grandpa opened the top of the cage and set the birds free.

"The sparrows will have a new home now," he said. "They won't pester our martins again. They will be happy, and we will be happy. The world is too dreary a place to be without the song of even a thieving bird, and perhaps their songs will bring life to these woods."

The Old Man smiled as he watched them fly away. Then he looked at me.

"I want you to remember this day, Andy," he said. "People fight too much in this world. You don't always need a sling-shot. It's always better to do what your grandfather did. Defeat your enemies through love."

"Defeat your enemies through love," I repeated.

"Yes," said Grandpa. He looked at me and gave an approving pat on my shoulder. "Yes, indeed. Well done, my boy. Very well done."

5

We'll Always Be Who We Are

Elizabeth sat with her leg draped over the chair and the scissors tucked into her hand. She said nothing at first (which wasn't surprising, given what I'd just said), but she kept her eyes in line with my own. That did surprise me. We cannot keep our secrets deep within ourselves. They will fester outward and manifest in some way, leaving us with a disfigurement that others may not see but is surely felt. I did not doubt that Elizabeth sensed my deformity, yet she did not look away.

"That's pretty incredible," she said. "All of it."

I suppose there wasn't much she could say that would have made me feel better. Even if she had said *That's the most factual story I've ever heard!* I wouldn't have believed her. The Old Man had never made me promise to tell no one about him. That secret was mine alone.

"Incredible like amazing," I asked, "or incredible like . . . not . . . credible?"

"Oh, I believe the Old Man is real, Andy," she said. She spun the scissors in her hand and then stopped. "Real to you, at the very least. The human mind is an amazing creation. It will go to great lengths to try and put order to the chaos life can bring."

"The human mind?" I asked. "So you think he *is* all in my head?"

"I didn't say that. I'm saying you went through a great trauma when you were too young to understand it. And between you and me, I don't discount the possibility that something else is going on here. The world isn't solid, Andy. There are aspects of existence we simply cannot comprehend. If God decided to give you an angel, then He did. I can accept that. Either way, you two seemed to have a pretty comfortable relationship from the start."

I chuckled and said, "It would appear. Like I said, back then he was more of an imaginary friend. I wasn't convinced it was anything more."

"Was he always so carefree?"

"Wouldn't you be? Being able to waltz around unseen and unheard by all but one person and knowing things no one else could know? That would make me feel pretty carefree. So yeah, he enjoyed himself. It was like he was experiencing life for the first time. Which I guess maybe he was."

"Maybe," Elizabeth said. She leaned back in her chair and propped her feet on the sides of my bed. At some point she had kicked off her shoes, and now ten red toenails played peek-a-boo with the bed sheets. It was a gesture of ease. Of comfort. And though I yet felt neither toward her, I appreciated the fact that she felt both in my presence. "But I get something else from that story. He wasn't just along for the ride. I don't get the sense he was hanging around under that birdhouse just to see you screw up. He was there for a purpose. He was trying to teach you something."

I said, "Or he was just trying to keep me from looking like an idiot."

"No. He let you fail, Andy. You know that, right? He tried to talk you out of not shooting that rock, but you didn't listen. He let you choose, even though from what I gather he knew that choice would be wrong. Just to show you that sometimes the reasons you have for your actions don't mean much, no matter how well-intentioned. In the end, it's what you *do* and not what you *meant* to do that matters."

"I never thought of it that way," I said.

She leaned forward and slapped me on the hand. "Well see, that's why I'm here."

Elizabeth offered me a wink as a small gesture of faith that
she had snuck into my room and convinced me to talk to her
for my own good. I wasn't completely ready to agree with her.
But a part of me knew it was just a matter of time before the
last bricks in the walls I'd built around myself fell before her,
and another part of me knew there wasn't much I could do
about it.

"So were you always so contrary to your grandparents'
wishes?"

"Oh, I guess I grew out of that," I told her. "As much as I
could, anyway."

Elizabeth lifted her eyebrows. "And what's that mean?"

"Nothing. I'm just the kind of person who thinks we all
might grow up and learn more, but we're still always gonna be
who we are."

"And who are you, Andy?"

"My father's son. Not that I'm a drunk or anything—I don't
drink at all. But there are times when I feel like if I took a
small slip down a dark hole, I'd come out him on the other
side. I guess we're all like that. We're all children. From the
moment we're born until the moment we die. We might learn
how to talk, but we never quite learn what to say. And we
learn how to walk, but we never stop stumbling."

"And the Old Man told you that?"

"Not really."

I motioned for the box that sat by my leg. Elizabeth reached
over and handed it to me. I picked through the contents with
my good hand, shuffling them around until I found it.

I held the paintbrush up to my nose and sniffed. The paint
had dried, of course, along with the scent. A dozen summers
had passed since it had last been used, and even then it had
been held under the water hose to clean afterward. But I
sniffed anyway.

"It was more Mary's telling," I said.

6

The Paintbrush

The good thing about being my own boss was that I got to pick when I went on vacation. It was always when the weather was warm—a week around late April, then another one around August. That's the way I always did it. The second week was for whatever traveling I wanted to do, whether it was all the way to the beach or just up in the mountains— sort of like my own yearly walkabout. But the first week was usually just to get the house in order, painting and mending and whatnot. I didn't mind giving Timmy Griffith the extra customers at his Texaco on the other side of town, especially since he did the same for me whenever he got the itch to do some fishing, which was hardly ever. But that's the way it is in Mattingly. Everybody looks out for everybody.

That's true with neighbors, too. Especially when it comes to kids.

My plan was to spend that week repainting the garage, a task that required much in the way of patience and preparation. You don't jump right into something like painting a garage. That's what most folks don't understand. You have to ease into it, study it, and try to talk yourself out of doing it. Which was why I was sitting on the porch staring at the little girl across the road rather than just getting down to the business at hand.

Mary Thompson and her parents had moved into the old Phillips place about three months prior. Nice folks, the Thompsons. Especially for city folk. Her father was Stephen—

"Stephen-with-a-P-H" is what I called him. The kind of guy who cut his grass in khaki pants and sipped mint juleps in the backyard every Sunday afternoon. You don't call men like that Steve.

Stephen-with-a-P-H did something with banking up in the city. He'd tried explaining to me exactly what that something was more than once, but he lost me in his fancy talk, and I ended up nodding like I'd heard that all before. His wife, Barbara, she...well, I didn't know what she did. But she was nice just the same and often brought me a little supper in the evenings.

The Thompsons did their level best to fit in, but it hadn't been easy. They were outsiders, you see. From Away. And while no one in town ever made them feel anything but welcomed, outsiders was what they would be for a good long while. The fact they had yet to visit one of the local churches, much less settled on one, didn't make things any better. There were whispers that the Thompsons weren't religious at all. Or even worse, that they were liberals.

I watched Mary play through the small metal diamonds of their chain-link fence. She was the quintessential preschooler in both action and reaction. I watched as she scooped sand from the sandbox into a bucket and then dumped the bucket over her head. Saw her do things on her jungle gym that would make an Olympic gymnast proud, only to then trip over nothing and run screaming to her mama. She destroyed flowers, tormented her cat, and even managed to get her daddy's riding mower started. All in the span of fifteen minutes. I was exhausted just watching her.

I'll tell you what, it was impressive. It was also enough to make me realize two things. One was that I was glad I wasn't her father. The other was that the Thompsons' fence was likely there to keep Mary from the world a whole lot more than the world from Mary.

Stephen knocked on the door that evening after dinner. The glass of wine in one hand and the can of Coke in the other, coupled with the fact that he couldn't seem to look me in the eye, told me it was either a problem to share or a favor to ask. Probably both. I offered him the rocking chair on the front porch and he accepted.

"I hear you're taking the week off," he said.

"Gonna paint the garage and hang out a little." I took the soda he offered and thanked him. "Might watch *The Price Is Right*. Always liked that show, but I'm never here to watch it."

"Uh-huh," he said, listening but mostly not. "So you're planning to stick close to home?"

"That's the plan," I said. "Why you ask?"

Stephen sighed and sipped his wine. Christian or not, liberal or not, most men don't take to asking for anything, especially from another man. "You know how we like to keep Mary in the backyard?"

"Because of the traffic," I said.

"Yes, exactly. The traffic. Not that I think there's any danger around here, mind you. But Mary's . . . adventurous."

I had to chuckle at that. Calling Mary adventurous was like calling Grace Kelly cute.

"She wants to start playing in the front yard now," he continued. "She says backyards are for little kids."

I took a sip of my Coke and wondered just how honest I was going to be with my neighbor from across the road. Like I said, Stephen was a good guy. But you never know how a parent will take words about his child, whether criticism or praise. I decided to play it safe and said, "Well, I'd say Mary's a little kid."

"She is at that, Andy. Kids are in such a hurry to grow up. But she's adamant. She really wants to do this."

"And what do you say?" I asked.

He took another sip of wine. "I don't know. It's not such a big deal, really. Right?"

"Sounds like it is to you," I told him.

"Having kids just magnifies your fear. Everything seems scary, even the little stuff. But she has responsibilities. She has to keep her room clean and help with the dishes. Why not this? Why not something fun?"

"So when'd you give Mary the good news?" I asked.

Stephen grinned and said, "Just a little bit ago. I made her promise she wouldn't go into the road, and she swore she wouldn't even think about it. Four times."

I said nothing. A man doesn't have to be a father to know that parenting is all about trying to make sure the good things about yourself were passed on and the bad things were not.

Stephen straightened his tie. "I was wondering if you'd just keep an eye on her this week. Barbara will be around, but she has so much to do and it's easy for her to get sidetracked. I'm not making it a priority or anything. I'm sure Mary will be fine."

I nodded and tapped my plain Coke against his fancy wine. The sound of plastic meeting glass made a tiny *whup*. "I'll be happy to, Stephen," I said.

He finished his glass and said his good-bye, thanking me again on the way across the road. The chair beside me began to creak back and forth as I watched him go.

"Guess I'll have to start keepin' an eye on that youngun," I said.

"Somebody's gotta," the Old Man answered.

Shortly after I began putting the first strokes of paint on the garage the next morning, Mary bounded out the front door across the street to usher her father off to work. Stephen opened the door of his SUV, tossed his briefcase inside, and then bent down to offer one final warning that was punctuated by a wagging finger.

Mary nodded and flung her arms around his neck, squeezing him so tight that I could hear him cough, and then made a cross-my-heart motion with a finger of her own. The two exchanged waves as Stephen pulled away. Mary watched him all the way to the corner, where he turned and disappeared into the world.

Barbara poked her head out the door and smiled at her daughter. "I'll be right inside," she said. She offered me a quick wave before vanishing.

Mary had reached the edge of the driveway before her mother had shut the door.

"Might as well try to tie down the wind," I muttered to myself. Then louder, to her: "Hey there, Miss Mary." I raised my paintbrush and waved, just to make sure she saw me seeing her.

"Hey, Mr. Andy!" she said. She offered one of those floppily spastic little-girl waves back.

"What'cha doing?"

"Nothin'," she said. "I can play in the front now."

"So I see. Reckon you'd better mind the road. Plenty of grass to play in. Grass is always better than pavement, sure enough."

"Sure enough," she agreed.

Mary eyed the pavement. Quick glances at first, as if the road was some celestial event and staring at it too long would burn her eyes. Then longer looks. She peeked back toward the living room window. All clear.

There were no cars. Mary looked down the road to the right, then to the left, then back toward the house again. Then she raised her right leg, leaned back, and gently touched the tip of her pink tennis shoe onto the dark asphalt.

It was her first taste of blatant defiance. And it looked to me like it tasted just fine.

Mary spun and raced back up the driveway to the safety of the house, where she scanned left and right again and then peeked at the front door. Nothing. I could see her quick breaths from across the road. Her smile, too.

She was safe. And more than that, she had gotten away with it.

I kept one eye on the paintbrush and the other on her for the next few hours. Both managed to stay between the lines. Mary never strayed down to the road, never even beyond the little dip in the front yard that led to it. When I took a break around lunchtime, she was playing hopscotch on the sidewalk by the door.

Twenty minutes later I had sat down to some leftover chicken from Timmy's Texaco and watching some poor old lady doing her utmost to win a new Chevy from Bob Barker. I was doing my part by hollering out the price when the Old Man sprinted out of the kitchen.

"Come on *come* on come *on!*" he shouted, tearing past me and disappearing through the living room wall.

I lurched out of my recliner and ran for the door, but I was too late. Halfway there I heard the sound of brakes meeting rubber meeting pavement, followed by a bellowing horn.

I flung the front door open, half expecting to see a pint-sized pancake in the middle of the road. Instead, Mary was jumping up and down by the edge of the grass and waving to the back of the blue Toyota Camry that had almost hit her. The driver had her hand to her chest and her mouth wide open, no doubt pondering both the brevity of life and the ramifications of vehicular manslaughter. Barbara raced out the front door, gobbled up her little girl in her arms, and whisked her inside.

That was the end of the great front yard experiment. From then on, it was the backyard or nothing. Mary protested. And whined and begged and promised to run away. But Stephen and Barbara would not yield. Under no circumstances would Mary be allowed outside the fence. Constant monitoring was initiated and boundaries were set, along with the threat of the severest punishment possible—whatever that meant—if said rules were broken.

It was the perfect plan. Foolproof.

Not, however, childproof. Because in the end a fence is just a fence, and Mary missed the front yard.

One hour after her father left for work the next day, there came another screech, another horn, and another wave. Which was followed by another jumping little girl, another frantic mother, and another hasty trip inside.

From that point on, Mary was confined indoors. Which was kind of good for me, since I could finally get my painting done. But it was bad for Mary, I suppose. It never feels good to have your wings clipped.

Mary was paroled that Friday evening just long enough to walk across the street with her father and see how the garage had turned out. The three of us sat beneath the evergreen on the side of my house and caught up on neighborhood news. Not surprisingly, our talk eventually came around to Mary's grand adventure. That was most all the news there had been.

"I just don't understand it," Stephen said. He patted his daughter on the head. "She knows better."

Mary looked up to her father and smiled, and Stephen nearly drowned in it. It's an amazing thing, what a child does to a parent. A beautiful thing. But as beautiful as it was, I had to look away. Children weren't something the Good Lord chose to bless me with, mostly because having one involved having a spouse.

I excused myself to clean the brushes and found the Old Man waiting next to the garden hose. He was dressed in overalls that looked like he'd taken off a rack and rolled them in the dirt before putting them on. A painter's cap sat cockeyed on his head. His feet were bare. The Old Man always said toes were made for feeling more than socks and shoes. That was my philosophy exactly.

"You should have some help with that," he said. "Messy job, cleaning paintbrushes."

"Ain't nothing I've never done before," I told him.

"Bet Mary'd pitch in."

I looked over my shoulder at my neighbors, still beneath my evergreen. Stephen appeared to have forgotten about the trouble his daughter had caused and was holding her like the blessing she was.

"Are you serious?" I whispered. "She's liable to start painting herself and then me. And then burn the house down and do a happy dance."

"Still," he said, "might not be a bad idea."

"But I don't *want* to."

"Okay, fine," he said, raising his hands in mock surrender. "I mean, it's not like I know what I'm doing or anything."

"You're seriously trying to guilt me?" I asked.

"Is it working?"

I didn't say anything. I did nod, though.

"Hey Mary," I called. "Wanna help me with these brushes?"

Mary was more than willing. And despite my misgivings, she was the picture of ladylike demeanor. She was polite and talkative, discussing the garden hose at her house and how her father used it to wash their car and how their car smelled like cherries inside and she didn't like cherries that much.

The Old Man knelt down beside us and nodded at Mary's profundity. He turned to look at me and said, "You should ask her."

I shook my head.

"Seriously, ask her. It's important."

Mary finished her soliloquy by saying that she liked cherries but only when they were in ice cream. I glanced over at Stephen to make sure we were out of earshot—in my experience, kids were honest to a fault except when a parent was around. He was still sitting in the grass, leaning back on his hands and staring across the road at his home, no doubt thinking that moving to the country was pretty much the best decision he'd ever made other than marrying Barbara.

"Mary," I asked, "you kinda got into a little trouble for going out into the road, didn't you?"

She shrugged. The Old Man smiled.

"Because your mom and dad were pretty scared," I added.

Another shrug.

"You really do know better, don't you?"

"Yeah," she said. She handed me a brush still caked with white. I ran it under the hose and then shook it, sending a white mist into the grass.

"Then why'd you do it?" I asked her.

Mary thought. Then she let out a small giggle and leaned toward me so her father wouldn't hear.

"I did it," she said, "because I wasn't supposed to."

It wasn't the answer I expected to hear, but it was an honest one. I looked from Mary to the Old Man.

"Profound, huh?" he said.

I nodded.

The Old Man bent lower and lifted up his cap to gaze into Mary's eyes. "Remember this face, Andy," he said to me. "Look at this little girl and burn her image in your mind, because she is you and you are her. Every day you both stand at the edge of should and should not, torn between what you know you're not supposed to do and the overwhelming desire to do it anyway. That's why the world's in such a mess. Why people do bad things. They just can't help it. Everyone's fighting their own darkness and waging their own war, and sooner or later it all spills out onto someone else. That's why you always have to forgive, Andy. Always. No matter what the harm might be. Because in the end people are born broken and spend their lives trying to put the pieces together. Your job is to help them find the pieces. You remember that, Andy. And you take that brush she just gave you and put it in your box so you will."

I nodded again.

"I guess I should try to be better anyway," Mary told me.

"I guess we all should," I said.

7

The World's a Hard Place, Andy

Outside my hospital room window the vague noises of civilization waned. Specks of headlights on the highway were fewer, the *thump-thumps* of teenagers and their stereos lessened. The world was nodding off without me. There was little wonder why I was so awake; I'd been sleeping off and on for three days. But I still longed for rest, though I suspected it was the sort of rest sleep couldn't provide.

Elizabeth smiled and said, "So do you think that's true, Andy?"

"What's true?" I asked.

Elizabeth's chin was in her hand, which was propped up by an elbow that rested on the top of my box. For a moment I almost asked her not to do that, to stop touching what was mine and give it a little respect (though I didn't know how much respect a box of junk deserved). Then I decided against it.

"Helping others pick up their pieces. Do you think that's your job?"

I shrugged and said, "I guess. I think that's everyone's job, don't you?"

She ignored my question and asked another: "Do you agree with the Old Man that everyone's basically bad?"

"Speaking from personal experience, yes. Like I told you, we're all children. Every single one of us."

"And does that make it easier to forgive someone?"

"I guess it should, though that's harder to do than believe. The Old Man said we're all fighting our own darkness and waging our own war. Not to say there shouldn't be judgment or consequences, because there should. But there should also come a forgiveness and a moving on."

"Is that so?" she asked. Her chin was out of her hand then, her head cocked a bit to the side.

"Yes."

Elizabeth's eyes moved from mine to the bandages on my face and head.

"In all cases?"

I didn't know if I had fallen into a cleverly disguised trap or an inevitable turn in our conversation, but I was leaning toward the former. I had forgotten Elizabeth was there for more than mere listening. She was supposed to be making me feel better, too. That was her job. Her . . . focus. That meant asking a few questions that were bound to hurt. Even though I knew all of that to be true, I don't mind saying that in that moment my heart cracked. Not because of what Elizabeth had said, but because it was all business.

"Nice try, counselor," I said.

"Just thought I'd throw that out there," she said. "Do you think Mary came to realize the choice to disobey was really hers?"

"I don't know," I said. "I don't know if a lot of people ever realize that. They'll blame God or the Devil or genes or parents for their screwups before they ever blame themselves."

"Because it's not their fault," she said.

"Exactly."

"But it is their fault, at least in your opinion."

"You can't hit all the curveballs life throws at you," I told her, "but that doesn't mean you can't at least foul a few off. There are a lot of things out there beyond our control. Lot of things that aren't, too. See? I know a little about the human condition myself."

"You are quite the nice surprise, Andy Sommerville," Elizabeth said.

Despite myself, I said, "I gotta say you are too, Elizabeth."

The two of us allowed that mutual admission to sink in. I almost said more and didn't but hoped she would. At the time I thought it was the freedom of openness that had captured me, that it wouldn't have mattered who had been sitting there beside me listening, I would have felt that same feeling of release and trust, that same euphoric sense of sharing. Maybe that's true. But looking back I think that was because it was Elizabeth rather than anyone else.

"And how's Mary now?" she asked.

"I'll see her in the gas station from time to time," I said. "She's sixteen now. Still a kid."

"I'm guessing she's allowed to play in the front yard now," Elizabeth said.

"She is," I said with a smile. "But she's still Mary. She'll learn like we all do. She'll grow and experience and fail and hurt. She'll gather regrets that will haunt her and joys that will sustain her. And when the time comes, she'll vow too that her children won't suffer through the same mistakes she's made. But I can see her one day telling her own child not to play in the road. And I can see a few minutes later another small shoe tiptoeing the edge of should and should not and then stepping into the world of the forbidden."

"Because we can't help it?" she asked.

"Because we can't help it."

Elizabeth's head cocked to the other side and allowed her ponytail to swish. "That worldview doesn't really sound like a recipe for happiness."

"Happiness?" I asked. "Please."

"Come on, Andy. You want to be happy, don't you? That's what everyone wants out of life. A lot of people would say it is the definition of true success—not your measure of wealth, but your measure of gladness. So let me ask you this: are you happy?"

"Not at the moment," I said, then regretted saying it. "You know, with my condition and all."

"How about before your condition?"

"I wasn't doing cartwheels or anything, but I was okay."

Elizabeth wasn't looking at me but through me—into me—trying to find what I wasn't ready to show her. I was familiar with that look. It was the Old Man's and my grandmother's look. A look that said *I know the truth, even if you don't want to tell me.*

"Stop it," I said.

"Stop what?"

"Stop analyzing me. Do you have any idea how tough it is being able to see things no one else can? Or thinking you see things no one else can? Whatever. It's like a wall between me and everyone else. It doesn't matter how much education you have or how many people you've talked to, you can't possibly understand how that feels. So no, I'm not Mr. Sunshine. But I guess you could say I'm as happy as I can be."

I'm not sure if that comment took her aback or not, but I was pretty sure it stung. I hadn't meant to do that. But the old adage of the truth hurting was an old adage because it was exactly right.

"That sounds awful, Andy."

"Awful?" I asked her. "No. It is what it is, Elizabeth. I've had a good life up to this point. Don't you sit there and pity me."

Elizabeth looked at me confused. I couldn't blame her. A man needs to feel a certain way around a woman. Pitied is not that way. And that was something a woman could never really understand.

"Sorry," she said. "What do you mean by 'up until this point'? You don't think you have a good life now?"

I held up my bandaged right hand and used my left to point at my head. "Oh, I have a *great* life right now," I said. "Who wouldn't want my life? Why, I'm sitting here in a hospital with burns all over me and my brains scrambled. My gas station's a mess, but nowhere near the mess my life is. I've lost"—I almost said Eric's name, but didn't—"a lot. Everything, really. So yeah, I can say I've had a good life up until this point, but I'm just not a whole heck of a lot sure from here on out, Elizabeth.

Besides, I think you need peace to have a good life, and it's hard to have peace when you're angry."

"The world's a hard place, Andy," she said. "People deserve as much real happiness in it as they can find."

"Be happy," I said, and loud enough to catch Kim's attention outside the door. She looked up at me and then down again, then shook her head. "Happy, happy, happy," I continued, "Sheesh, you sound like *her.*"

"Her who?" Elizabeth asked.

I motioned for the box, and Elizabeth switched it from her lap to mine. I opened it and rifled through the contents until I found the worn and folded card. The words were still bright and bold—BE HAPPY!! GOD LOVES YOU!! I held it up to Elizabeth.

"Her," I said.

8

The Happy-Face Card

I called her Willa to her face since that was what politeness demanded, but in whispered company and the privacy of my own thoughts, she was the Singing Christian. All it would take for you to understand would be getting caught standing in front of her in line at the market or beside her at the Laundromat. In a town known for its more colorful citizens, Willa was the electric lime among us—loud, bold, and impossible to miss. She was neither family nor close friend, yet she still managed to keep a place in my life that was just as familiar. And, at times, just as aggravating.

Grandpa died a year before I graduated from high school. His heart gave out on him one Friday afternoon while he was pumping gas for a stranger passing through on his way to Charlottesville. That left just Grandma and me to make ends meet. She'd never worked outside the home and was getting on up in age, so it was up to me to provide for the both of us. That wasn't too terribly hard. I'd been helping Grandpa at his gas station for years at that point, so I just dropped out of school and took over the business. Lots of people did that back then. Young men, especially. Times were tough, and education didn't mean as much then as it does now. You had to do what you had to do.

That's where I met Willa. Our paths crossed regularly, as did the paths of so many townspeople who drove in and out of the station. She visited me four times a week to gas up an oversized station wagon which mainly doubled as a billboard for God. Bible verses were plastered all over the sides and back window with those stickers people used to put their names on the mailbox. Willa and her husband ran a hospice for the elderly—a difficult, often heart-wrenching way to make ends meet. But if anyone could have done it and done it well, it was her.

She walked into the gas station early that day and interrupted a conversation I was having with the Old Man. He sat in one of the three booths by the door and finished his thought while studying her. He smiled at Willa like she was an old friend. That seemed about right to me. I figured all the angels knew about Willa.

"When the Roll Is Called Up Yonder" was the song of the day. The previous three visits that week had been to the tune of "The Old Rugged Cross," "What a Friend We Have in Jesus," and "How Great Thou Art." Sometimes she hummed and sometimes she vocalized, but neither was an under-the-breath kind of thing. You could hear Willa before you saw her, and she was pretty hard to miss as it was.

She stopped at the register and plopped down a purse that could near have doubled as a suitcase for most folks. "Hello, Arthur," she said. "How are you today?"

Yes—*Arthur*.

Willa did not know my name. Never did and never would. I'd tried at first to correct her in the most polite way possible— "My name's Andy, ma'am" or "You can just call me Andy"— but it never stuck. Over the years I had been Arthur, Anthony, Adam, and Albert. Also Darlin', Sweetie, Honey, and Child. But never Andy. Which was okay with me. I figured I'd been called worse.

"I'm good, Willa," I said. "How about yourself?"

"Saved and blessed, sweetie."

From his booth, the Old Man watched. Me now, not her. I met his eyes and then returned to hers and smiled. "What can I do for you today?" I asked her.

"I would like to pay for this." She pointed to the check on

the counter that had bounced so hard it had to be held in place by a layer of Scotch tape.

"Willa," I said, "that's not yours."

"Oh dear!" she answered. "Oh my, I know *that*. Passing off bad checks is an abomination to the Lord."

"Praise Him!" the Old Man shouted from the booth.

I cut him a look out of the corner of my eye and made a mental note to remind him yet again not to mess with me when I was with a customer, then brought my attention back to Willa. She was still pointing to the bad check. A lifetime of constant smiling had formed an oval of wrinkles around her mouth. Her hair, once brown but now the color of lightning, was neatly brushed and set just so except for the ever-present cowlick near the back of her head that reached heavenward. I had a nickname for that too—the God Antennae.

"So...," I began, hoping she would finish.

"Well, the Lord has laid it on my heart to help someone today, and I would like to help this person," she said, now tapping on the check. "Jesus died and paid for my sin, so I thought it'd be nice to help pay for this fella's here."

"That's a good idea, Bossman," the Old Man said.

I looked at the check again, nearly a month old and written for thirty dollars. I knew better than to take a check from a stranger, but it was all he had and he swore it was good. Yet another reason why I'd never be a successful businessman.

"You want to take care of someone else's thirty-dollar bad check."

"Yes, Arthur."

"To pay for his sin."

"Yes."

"But shouldn't this person pay it?" I asked, tapping the check myself. "I mean, to take responsibility and all?"

Willa lowered her chin and shook her head nice and slow, her signal that this had now become a Teachable Moment. Willa lived for her Teachable Moments almost as much as the Old Man did. I did my best to avoid them.

"They can't, Honey," she said. "I've seen that check at least a dozen times in the past few weeks, and it's still here. Don't you think he would've paid for it by now if he could?"

She had a point, and I told her so. I looked to the Old Man. He nodded and winked.

"Okay, Willa," I said. "You sure you wanna do this? I mean, I'm gonna have to add the service charge to this. That'll up it to fifty bucks."

Willa eyed me. In her opinion, I should know better than to deny a soldier of God her right to wage war on transgression, whether it was her battle or not.

She pulled out her checkbook and began writing, asking me twice how much the total would be.

"It's such a shame," she said as she wrote. "People do their best to get by in life. Don't you think so, Darlin'?"

"Yes, ma'am."

"I guess sometimes these things happen."

"Yes, ma'am."

"How are you, Arthur?" she said.

"I'm doing good, Willa."

"Are you happy, then?"

Her question caught me by surprise. Willa had never asked me that. She'd asked me plenty of other things, things that had sometimes applied to me and things that must have applied to whomever her mind had tricked her into thinking she was talking to at the time. Willa had thirty years on me at least, nearer to the Old Man than to me. And as much as I always wanted to hang on to this life as long as I could, having her walk into my store always tempted me into wishing my days would be cut short before I grew that senile.

"I expect," I said after some thought. "As happy as I can be, anyway."

"Oh, well that will not do!" she gasped. "That will not do at all. You can always be happy, you know."

"I can, huh?" I began pulling the tape off the check on the counter between us.

"Are you happy all the time, Arthur?"

"I can't say that I am, Willa."

(*Like right now*, I thought.)

She stopped writing and gave me a pitiful look.

"That's just the most horrible thing I've heard all day," she said. "I'm happy all the time, you know. It's God's will."

"It is?" I said it with a smile, but not a genuine one.

"Well of course it is," Willa said. "Lack of happiness is lack of faith."

The Old Man took that opportunity to clear his throat from across the room. He winked when I looked up at him. Outside Howard O'Malley (Old Howard O'Malley to us in town, Mr. O'Malley to the workers he supervised down at the factory in Stanley) pulled up to the gas pump opposite Willa's and began filling his Cadillac. Two more vehicles had entered the parking lot. Prudence dictated that I got rid of her as soon as possible before she had the chance to cause a human traffic jam in front of the cash register, but I just couldn't let her last sentence go.

"Lack of happiness is not lack of faith, Willa."

It was Willa's turn to look around, to Old Howard O'Malley pumping his gas, to the people getting out of their cars and making their way in, to the empty booths behind her. It was a strange sight to see; Willa had never cared about who had been around when she was in the grips of the Holy Spirit and a Teachable Moment.

"Son," she said, "my daddy died when I was twelve years old. The cancer took him, though it weren't for lack of prayin'. We all prayed, but me especially. I prayed for him night and day, I loved him so." She looked around again, satisfied that the people who were on their way in were now talking to each other. Then she turned back to me. "I was so *sad*. My daddy was leavin'. He was *dyin'*. Do you see?"

I nodded.

"But I prayed on like a good Christian should, and you know what? He died anyway."

"I'm sorry, Willa," I said. "I never knew that."

Tears welled in Willa's eyes, proof that sometimes the scars we carry can hurt us more than the cuts that made them. "It was his time, I suppose. But to this day I believe in my heart that God didn't answer my prayers because the faith wasn't in them. My sadness took up all the room. So I hope you pray for happiness. For your own sake, promise me you will."

"I will," I said. And I meant it at the time. Partly because she was so convincing, but mostly because the other customers were coming in and the line behind Willa was growing by the minute. I would have prayed for anything if it meant getting her out of the door. I would have prayed for an aneurysm.

"Good," she said. "And I'll pray for you, too." She reached into her purse and pulled out what I thought was a business card. It wasn't. Written on the front was BE HAPPY!! GOD LOVES YOU!! A smiley face was added for both emphasis and instruction. She handed it to me. "Here, I want you to keep this as a reminder."

"Well, thank you, Willa," I said. I took the card like it was a letter of parole and hoped that would be enough to free me from her, at least for the time being.

She patted me on the hand and turned to leave, picking up where she left off with her hymn. Twenty minutes and five conversations later, she finally pulled onto the main road and out of sight.

I dispatched the remaining customers with their smokes and soda and grabbed a towel to wipe down the counter. The Old Man remained in his seat. Neither of us spoke because both of us were occupied. Me with my stewing, him with his bracelet.

"Why don't you like her?" he finally said.

"Who her?" I asked him.

"Willa," he said. "You don't like her, do you?"

"Willa's a saint. Everybody thinks so."

"Hey," he said, and nothing else until I looked up to him. "It's me."

I tossed the towel over my shoulder and sighed. Yet another Teachable Moment from yet another wise soul.

"I hate that lady," I told him.

"That's pretty harsh," he said. "What's so bad about Willa? She seems like a happy soul."

I pointed at him and said, "That's just it. She's a *happy* soul. I've never seen that woman without a smile stapled to her face. Never heard her speak without that gooey sentimentality and that cheerful melody. She's the same way every single day. She's a robot welded together with merriment and mirth. She's the nicest, sweetest, most devout person I know, and every time I see her I want to rip her head off."

"I think that little speech she gave bothered you," he said.

"You're right."

"And I think it bothered you that you were bothered."

"What?" I asked him. I shook my head. "You make about as much sense as she does."

The Old Man leaned back in his booth and sighed. "If I had to settle on a word to describe your outlook on life, Andy, it would not be *happy*. Not that your days are filled with angst and dread, mind you. You don't pout or sulk or any of those childish things. You don't have *angst*. But you do have a certain sadness about you. I see it. And I know that even if you *say* you don't want to experience what she feels, a part of you wishes you could feel that happy. I also know a part of you wishes that once, just once, Willa would experience a bit of the winter that blows around in your heart. Because maybe then she could see the other side of life. Maybe then her views on God and happiness would change."

If I knew anything by then, it was that a body couldn't argue with the truth. That's why I didn't bother arguing with anything he'd just said. All I could do was stand there and look at him.

"You see in Willa all the traits every person should embody and you don't. She's smiling and singing and talking, and you're stoic and silent and listening. She displays her feelings for all the world to see, but you guard yours lest they be discovered. And most of all, she has the sort of faith that says all she needs to do is profess her love for God and man and everything will be roses. That's it, simple as that. Do that, and *whoosh!* Suddenly there's this heavenly force field that surrounds you and keeps the nasties away. You'll be safe and joyful, no longer left to be tossed about by life's thrashings, but securely tethered to the holy grail of glee. That's what you see, Andy. Isn't it? But is it what you *feel?* Is it what you *think?* Because I know better."

I stared at him and said nothing.

"You hurt, Andy," he said. He let that hang in the air for a bit and took his eyes off of me, resting them instead on the bracelet around his hand. He traced it with a finger and smiled. "You'll hurt for a long time, and more than you do now. I know you blame your father for that. I know the things he said to you about how you'll always be alone. But do you know what? You don't really hurt because of him. You hurt because of me."

We'd had our share of talks over the years, the Old Man and I. Moments when there were no lessons to be shared and no advice to be given and we simply sat like two normal people passing the time. But he had never spoken the way he spoke then. There was no sadness in his eyes, no regret. Just a statement of fact he could neither deny nor spare.

"What makes you say that?"

"You're a friend to many, Andy, but you don't have many friends. You get here most every day before dawn and close up every night after everyone's gotten home from work. Whatever free time you have you spend on your own. You go home to an empty house that is just that—a house. Not a home.

"That card Willa just gave you? I want you to do something with it. I want it to go in your box. Because it's important for one, and for another to prove a point. Remember when I told you to go into your grandpa's attic to find the box? I told you to keep it somewhere safe. Where's that box, Andy? Not at the house. It's right there on the shelf under the cash register. This is your home. This is where you feel most comfortable—where there's people, but where no one really lingers for long.

"This isn't the life you wanted for yourself, is it? You're comfortable enough, yes. But are you happy with where you are? I doubt it. You wanted a wife and children, didn't you? A *home*. But you'll never have them because of me. I'm too hard to explain and near impossible to accept. That's why Caroline left."

I threw the towel onto the counter and pointed to him. "Don't you mention her name. Don't you ever do that."

"It's true, Andy. You know it's true. You know having a wife means sharing everything with her, and I'm not something you can share. Not without coming across as a kook, anyway. Face it, Andy. I'm your secret. I'm your answered prayer, but I'm your curse, too. Just as much as I'm your blessing."

Only half of me was listening. The other half had drifted back ten years' worth of yesterdays to a time when life handed me a gift I thought God intended me to refuse. I shook the memories off, pulling myself out of the bright hues of the past and back to the black and white of the present.

"I prayed, you're here," I said. "How can an answered prayer be a curse? I don't think so."

"You must think so," he said. "Or else you'd be content with your life and not angry with the one Willa lives."

"I don't want Willa's life!" I laughed. "No way I could take care of all those folks."

"That's not what I mean. I mean her happiness."

I'd had enough. Enough of the Teachable Moments, enough about what I was doing wrong. Enough.

"Let me tell you something," I said, "and I'm only going to say this once. I loved Caroline. I'll love her forever. You're right, I couldn't tell her about you. But I couldn't keep you from her either. I let her go because I had to. I was willing to make that sacrifice."

"Why?"

"Because..." I trailed off, not sure how to say what I'd always known to be the truth. "Because you're my answered prayer. Because God sent you to me. And because I know that between Him and you, I'm pretty well covered. I'm in good hands. Don't matter how much two people love each other, sooner or later one will let the other down. Her and I would've been no different. I trust that won't happen with you and God."

The Old Man thought for a moment and nodded. Only after did I realize he never agreed with me. "Tell me this one thing, Andy. Do you really want that? Do you want what she has? Or should she be wanting what you have?"

With that he smiled and began to fade into the bench.

"I'm melting! I'm melting!" he shouted. Then he laughed and was gone, leaving his last question to linger like a shadow.

I took the towel from my shoulder and went back to wiping the counter. Should she have been wanting what I had? What did I have? My own private angel, yes. I'm sure that would have caused a considerable amount of envy even in Willa's sainted heart. But I didn't think that was what the Old Man meant. No, he meant the sadness I carried.

Was that true?

Life was a complicated thing full of mystery and wonder. There were some things that everyone, regardless of who they were or what they had, could count on. Happiness was not among them. Not the permanent kind, anyway. That came in the next life. Here in this life we were in the fire, and it was a fire that burned hot.

I could have tried to find Willa's happiness. If I wanted to and if I really thought it would be best, I could have forced my sadness down and covered it up with smiles and hymns. I could hope that sooner or later the happy life would become so ingrained that it would become the truth.

But the Old Man was right. Deep down in my secret places, I knew better.

I knew that life was not a sitcom. My troubles were fewer

and less painful than most, but rarely did they invoke laughter. My circumstances were seldom wrapped up in a half an hour. And I could not recall there ever being applause at the end.

To feel sadness did not mean I had no faith; it meant I had an abundance of it. It meant I could see things were not what they should be. What they were intended to be. That there had to be more. Better. It was not my fault and not my doubt that made me feel the way I did. I hurt for no other reason than because I was alive.

I reached for the card that still sat by the cash register—BE HAPPY!! GOD LOVES YOU!!—and then stooped down and placed it in my box. I had always allowed Willa her happiness, but from then on I vowed I would try to accept it. I would smile as she sang and prayed and laughed, which was a good deal of the time. I would tap my feet as she danced to the lusty melodies of life and I would join her when I could. But I would always hold dear to my own truth: that the real conquerors of life were the ones who knew not only when to laugh but when to cry.

9

No One's Here for Rest

Elizabeth sat immersed in her paper and scissors. I wasn't sure if she had heard me or not, if she had even heard that story or not. My eyes had kept to either the wall in front of me or Willa's card as I'd remembered her aloud. It was hard enough to share, harder if I had to look at the person with whom I was sharing. The few times I did glance at her, Elizabeth hadn't been looking back. She'd just been cutting. But now she glanced up to me. "It takes some people a very long time to learn that lesson, Andy," she said. "And sadly, many never do. They go to such lengths to avoid the pain in their lives that the lengths themselves become a pain that's worse. You should count yourself fortunate."

"What are you doing?" I asked her.

"What?"

"The scissors and paper," I said. "What's that all about?"

"Oh, sorry," she said. She rested her project on her lap and gave me her full attention. "Nothing personal, just a habit I picked up a while back. There was a little girl in here named Constance. Very sick, the poor thing. She'd spend hours with scrap sheets of paper and a pair of scissors, cutting out these wonderful little shapes of animals and hearts and snowflakes. It was amazing. She said it helped her to remember and forget at the same time."

"I don't understand what that means," I said.

Elizabeth picked up her paper and scissors again and said, "I didn't either, but she asked me to try it one day. Can't say it has the same effect on me, but it is soothing. Sort of allows me to put a picture to what I'm talking about."

"Or listening to," I said. "This little talk's been pretty one-sided so far. I know next to nothing about you."

"That's because the point is *you*, Andy," she said. "That's why I'm here, and that's my job."

"I get that," I said. "Pretty hard for a guy like me to keep opening up to a total stranger, though. Even one who's..."

"Yes?" she asked.

I cleared my throat and said, "Easy to talk to." It wasn't a lie. It also wasn't exactly what I almost said.

"Well, thank you. But in my defense it's a by-product of my work. I've spent a lot of time listening to a lot of people. I was made for it."

"So these people," I said, "you fix them up on the inside and just send them on their way? Do you ever see any of them again?"

"Oh, sure I do," she said. "I like to keep in touch."

"What happened to the little girl? The one with the scissors and paper?"

Elizabeth slowly turned the paper upward—"She died"—and cut out a small arc.

There wasn't a hardness to her words. Not much at all in the way of feeling. Elizabeth was stating a fact and nothing more. She might as well have said it was dark outside.

"That sounds a bit cold," I said.

"That she died? Why?"

"I don't know. Just sounded like it wasn't a big deal. It must have affected you."

"Of course it affected me," she said, though not enough to stop with the scissors. "Everyone I see here affects me, and I love every single person I meet."

I weighed the pros and cons of my next question and decided more bad than good could come out of it. Then I asked her anyway.

"Do I affect you, Elizabeth?"

She looked at me with those eyes and said, "Very much so, Andy."

I didn't push my luck further but hoped she heard what I'd left unasked. I wasn't fool enough to think a person could feel anything close to affection toward someone they'd just met, especially when you were wrapped up like a boogeyman in a Scooby Doo cartoon. But as Elizabeth snipped her sheet of paper and looked at me, I knew I was beginning to feel something. I didn't know what it was or what it could lead to, and I didn't care. Feeling it was enough.

"So you're okay with not being happy?" Elizabeth asked.

"Most times," I said. "Happiness is an overrated emotion at best."

She nodded. "I think you're right, actually. No one's here for happiness. Or rest. It's all about work, Andy. Everyone has their job to do. That's the important thing."

"What sort of job?"

"God wants people to dry tears and mend hearts. That's pretty much an impossible task until you've shed your own tears and had your own heart broken."

"I suppose you're right," I said.

"What about love? Is that overrated, too?"

"By no means," I said. My smile said more. "Of course, that's just me. I'm sure other people would have a different opinion."

"Anyone I know?"

I looked down and pulled the sealed envelope from the box. "One comes to mind."

Elizabeth studied the name that had been scrawled on the outside.

"I was wondering when you were going to get around to that one. Who's Alex?"

"Never got his last name. Doesn't matter, though. Because I think we're all Alex, at least at some point."

10

The Envelope

I dug into my pocket for two quarters and popped them into the giant binoculars at the boardwalk's edge. The lens clicked open. I panned to the right just before the setting sun and made out the cargo ship's port of call: Panama. A lone figure was leaning on the starboard rail, savoring one final look at the city. It was a sweetly ironic moment. A part of me longed to be him, free of the land and its trappings, and I imagined a part of him longed to be me, free of a life spent in motion. Such was man in his deepest self, always searching yet rarely finding his place in the world.

The man and the boat and the sun went black as the telescope's shutter snapped shut. Fifty cents bought only so much reverie. I felt my pockets again and found nothing, so I turned and instead focused my attention inland. What began less than an hour previous as a slow trickle of afternoon pedestrians was now a mini rush hour. Joggers and walkers and Rollerbladers paraded past me in varying degrees of speed and strain, all in search of that elusive prize of thinner thighs and flatter stomachs.

"Maybe you should get a little exercise, too," the Old Man said.

I turned back around to see him leaning on the guardrail and staring out at the cargo ship easing its way over the horizon. His linen suit flapped in the warm breeze. He bent the rim of his fedora down to shield his eyes from the sun.

"Me?" I asked. "I'm in great shape. I exercise all the time. You look snazzy."

"Walking out from behind the counter at the gas station to pour yourself another cup of coffee is not exercise," he answered. "And thank you."

"Like you should talk," I answered. I looked down to where his suit jacket wasn't buttoned. "You have a bigger gut than I do, and you're an angel. Thought you people were supposed to be beautiful."

He feigned insult. "You don't think I'm beautiful?"

"I wouldn't say you're exactly easy on the eyes. My opinion, anyway."

"True," he said. "Especially around here. Lots of beautiful people at the beach. Who, by the way, do not go out and about in a pair of cutoff jeans and a Dale Earnhardt T-shirt."

It was my turn to feign insult. "Fine, my clothes are ugly. But *you're* ugly, too. And I can change my clothes."

"Touché," he said. We both chuckled and switched vantage points, him now looking to the crowd and me out to sea. The sun was turning from yellow to orange to pink. In the distance a dolphin broke the surface, tumbling me into reverie again.

It seemed the Old Man was taking part in a little reverie of his own, because he spent the next few minutes stroking the bracelet on his arm. I'd asked him about it more times than I could remember, but he was as mysterious with that as he was with most anything else. The flow of information was always the same with us, and that was a current that never changed direction.

"What is it about the ocean that calls to the lovers in this world?" he finally asked.

I shrugged and said, "Never thought about it. Why?"

"Take a look over there," he said, nodding into the crowd.

I turned to see a couple near the pier, strolling hand in hand toward us. Their appearance stood in contrast with the exercisers who snaked their way around them. He was tall, with coal-colored hair and a deep tan that set off the tattoos on his right arm. She was a strikingly beautiful brunette with pouty lips and a smile that seemed brighter than the sun. With his beige khakis and white muscle shirt and her blue sundress and sandals, the two were a J Crew ad lost in a Nike commercial.

Their pace was slow and deliberately aimless. They did not scan the surf or the skies or even the pedestrians around them but kept them low and just a few feet forward to the boundary of their own private world. Each step was made in unison and coincided with some form of physical contact—a hand deftly moved behind her back, a gentle kiss on his cheek.

"Love is a beautiful thing, Andy," the Old Man said. He took his eyes off the couple and put them on me. "Isn't it?"

It was more than a simple question, and I knew it. Much more.

He was speaking of Caroline.

She and I had never gotten far enough to speak of love, but I always believed I had felt it for her. Not the love-thy-neighbor sort of love, but the sort that keeps you awake at night wondering what it would be like if you never had to wonder again. Yes, I thought, love was a beautiful thing. At least the little I knew of it was, before it scared me into breaking things off and breaking her heart. The Old Man was right as far as all of that went. I could never get close to anyone. Not with him in my life. But I knew what love looked like. Knew what it was and what it could do. I wasn't an expert at it, but that seemed immaterial. I could appreciate a picture without knowing how to paint one.

"Yeah," I answered. "It surely is."

The couple neared and I politely turned away. I heard her giggle at something he said and then mention how beautiful the sunset was. He maneuvered her away from the crowd to the railing beside me. She rested her head on his shoulder as she surveyed the scene.

"Be right back," the Old Man said, fading from sight.

"Okay."

"What's that?" the man asked me.

"I said 'good day,'" I answered, turning toward them.

"It is," he said.

The three of us exchanged hellos, and he asked to borrow my lighter. He pulled a cigarette from his back pocket, lit it with Sinatra-like panache, and then handed it to his lady for a puff. She exhaled a long stream of smoke and gave him another peck on the cheek as thanks.

I decided then it was time for me to move along. Though not intentional, the two made me feel like a passerby in their magical kingdom of love. Besides, all that kissing and touching was just a little too Cinemax for me.

But as I turned to walk away, something unexpected happened. The woman sighed. Not a contented, life-is-beautiful sigh. More of a this-is-going-to-be-hard sigh. I eased my way back to the railing. And just when I thought Snow White and Prince Charming had it and had it bad, she uttered the four words that invariably spell the death of romance and the sudden end of every fairy tale.

"Alex," she said, *"we have to talk."*

How many times had I heard that? For that matter, how many times had I *said* that? I wasn't sure, but I was sure enough to know that it didn't involve *we* at all. And very little talk.

We have to talk. Translation: "I have to talk. You have to listen. And this will not go well."

I considered the possibility there were other translations of which I was unaware. Maybe to some *We have to talk* meant "I'd like some ice cream" or "Let's turn in early." Maybe to some it even meant "We have to talk." But from the look on his face, Alex seemed most familiar with the standard interpretation.

Alex peeked at me from the corners of his eyes. I pretended to watch a pair of Navy F-18s flying out to sea. His weight shifted from one foot to the other as he tried to restart the frozen gears in his mind.

"We have to talk, Sweetie," his companion said again. Her voice sounded more confident this time. The subject had been broached, which meant the hard part was now over. For her, anyway.

"So let's talk," Alex said. He glanced again in my direction. I ignored it and kept watching the sky for jets. He whispered to her, "But why don't we go back to my place?"

"No," she told him, running a hand down his arm. "I think we should talk here."

Oh yes, I thought. *The public breakup. Get your business done out in the open with lots of people around. He'll be upset, but maybe he'll be too embarrassed to cause a scene.*

"Okay," Alex answered, though I think by then even he realized he had no choice in the matter.

"Alex, you know I care about you,"

[this guy's definitely getting the boot]

"and you know I'd never do anything to hurt you,"

[except rip your heart out and spike it like a football in front of this stranger]

"but I really think we need to spend"

[some time apart]

"some time apart."

She let go of his hand and took two steps backward. Alex shoved the hand into his pocket and proceeded to take the longest, deepest, saddest drag from a cigarette I had ever seen. He inched his head toward me. I knew what he was thinking. He was thinking that right then he would give just about anything if I would turn around and walk away.

But I didn't. Maybe I should have. My presence was probably only making things worse. But I knew that in just a few minutes that lady was going to walk back up the boardwalk without him, and both of them might need someone there to make sure nothing stupid happened.

"Lauren," Alex said, "I don't understand. Did I do something wrong?"

"No," she assured him. "It's me, baby."

It's me. Translation: "It's you."

Lauren rubbed Alex's arm to make her point, but her tactic was no longer welcomed. Alex was trying to maintain his composure and not doing very well at it. He inhaled the rest of his cigarette and tossed the butt into the sand.

"What are you doing?" he asked. He put his arm around her to both keep her there and remind her of how special she was. "We're great together. We have fun, right? I mean come on, we're *perfect*. I love you. You know I love you with all my heart. I tell you every day."

That's right, I thought, nodding. *Put it all out there. Now she'll have to think about what she's doing. Sure there have been mistakes, but those mistakes can be worked out. Hearts can be mended. We can start over. Move forward. Make it better. Right?*

Nope.

"I know you do, sweetheart," Lauren said. "I love you, too."

I was as confused as Alex at that one, and I wanted to say something. But he said it for me:

"Well if I love you and you love me, why are we having this conversation?"

Lauren sighed again. She had been for the most part subtle and kind through the whole ordeal, but now it was time for plain truth.

"I just can't do this," she said. "I need to *live*, Alex. College is starting soon and I'll be going away and I just...I *can't* get bogged down in a relationship now. It just won't work. If you really love me, you'll understand. If you *really* love me, you'll let me go."

With that she removed a ring from her finger and held it out to him.

Alex reached for it but caught her arm instead. "Please, Lauren," he moaned. "We'll be fine. We have to be."

She folded his other hand around the ring and turned to leave. Alex remained beside me, stunned by the suddenness of her rejection. Five minutes before, they were inseparable. Now they would likely never be together again. I knew the theory of the temporary good-bye. It was one that existed in movies and books, but not in real life.

Lauren stopped and turned to face him one last time. "Oh, Alex? Those tickets for the concert? I still want mine. Just give it to Jill, okay? And call me."

Call me. Translation: "Don't call me. Ever."

Alex said nothing. There was nothing to say. He had emptied his heart and bared his very soul, all to no avail. Our eyes remained on Lauren as she faded into the crowd. Shoulders slouched, he turned back to face the world without her.

We both stared out to sea. Without averting my gaze I again drew the lighter from my pocket and offered it to him. He accepted. No words passed between us.

Twenty minutes and two more smokes later, I was ready to leave. Alex would be okay, I thought. Maybe not right then or the day after, but eventually. But as I turned to go, he flicked his Marlboro into the sand by the small pile of others and said, "Dude? *This* is love? *This?!* If love's supposed to be this big wonderful thing, why does it make absolutely no sense at all?"

I slowly exhaled. Alex wasn't finished.

"Does love have to feel this bad? Huh? And if it does, why even *bother*? I mean I *love* her, man. She was a *ten*. Did you see her? Oh man, she was so hot."

He punched the guardrail and winced, perhaps hoping the physical pain would dull the emotional pain.

"We were meant to be," he said. "I swear we were. *Are.* Whatever. How can I find another woman like her?"

Alex paused and stared, waiting for me to say something. Something profound and wise that would put him at ease. I looked around for the Old Man but didn't see him. Evidently I was flying solo this time.

So I looked at him, opened my mouth . . . and closed it. All I could manage was a shrug.

Alex gawked at me. "Dude," he said, "you been standing here this long, and you got nothin' for me? Nothing?"

I shook my head. Then he began mocking me and accused most of my immediate family of unspeakable things.

And then he stormed out of sight.

I spent the rest of my vacation looking for him. Guilt had set in. I knew I should have said something, anything, but at the time my mouth felt like it was full more of cotton than words. The Old Man had given me the chance to be the angel for once, and I had failed. Miserably. I asked strangers and lifeguards, hotel attendants, even bartenders, none of whom confessed to any knowledge of an Alex or a Lauren. I tried describing them, but that didn't help. Apparently Virginia Beach was full of muscular men with tattoos and beautiful women who wore sundresses. The Old Man wasn't much help, either. He said he didn't know where Alex had gone and that it didn't matter. We're all on our own path, he said. Not sure what that meant.

He did say that a letter would be nice. Something written by me for Alex. The fact there was no way to get him the letter wasn't important, at least to the Old Man. He said the letter was more for myself, anyway. So I began to piece together what I could have said. *Should* have said, rather. I carried them around like fragments in my head, bits and pieces of observations and advice. I wrote, then rewrote, then rewrote again, until I had said what I felt was needed. I sealed it in an envelope, put his name on it, and left it in my box.

Even after all these years, Alex has never been that far removed from my thoughts. I still wonder what became of him, what he's doing. And yes, if he's in love. I like to think he is. I like to think that he's found his true Lauren, whoever that is. But just in case, I'm still waiting to find him one day. I have something I think he'd like to read.

11

The Letter

What's the letter say, Andy?"

Elizabeth was looking at me. The beginnings of a smile were on her lips, taunting me with the promise it would sprout then bloom and wrap me in its shade if I indulged her. This, I thought, was not a counseling sort of question. This was a personal one. Not just for my benefit, but hers.

I put the envelope back into the box, shut the lid, and pushed it away.

"I don't know," I said. "Heck, I wrote that thing years ago. Probably just a bunch of hooey anyway."

"Oh, I doubt that," she answered. "I can see more in you than you give yourself credit for, Andy Sommerville. You just need to show it to people."

"It's easier for me to do that with some people than others," I said. "I've learned to love the lonely."

"I don't think you have," she said. "Tell you what, then. We'll compromise. You don't have to read it if you don't want, but let me."

"Why are you so interested in this? I can't imagine how that letter has anything to do with what happened or getting me better."

"I didn't think you wanted to talk about what happened," Elizabeth said.

"I don't. I just don't see why you're so interested."

A childish and utterly beautiful thought passed behind my eyes just then. I sneaked a peek at Elizabeth's hand.

"I'm not married." She held up her left hand to prove it, and then added, "Except maybe to this hospital."

I blushed beneath my bandages.

"So you're saying your job is your Old Man?" I asked her. "That's the thing that keeps you from everything else?"

She smiled. "In a way, yes. I'll agree with that, though my job is something I enjoy. To me, there's nothing else I'd rather be doing. And my job is to help you. I care about you, Andy. I care about you a great deal. And you might not think that letter has much to do with why you're here, but I don't believe it."

The Old Man's words came back to me

(God sent her)

and I realized just how much I'd shared with Elizabeth in the past few hours. Nearly everything. Nearly. I knew then she sensed what I hadn't, biding her time until those final bricks were wedged away and there was nowhere left for me to hide. I didn't want to give her the letter. I didn't want her to hear the ramblings of an emotion, the grandest and holiest emotion, that I had pursued more than once but never truly allowed myself to feel.

"It's important, Andy," she said.

(God sent her)

I motioned toward the box.

"Have at it, then," I said.

She fetched the letter out and then settled back into her chair, placing her scissors and paper on the bed. I tried to see what sort of design, if any, she was cutting. There wasn't any. Just a hodgepodge of straight lines and gentle curves.

"Eyes to the front, please," she told me. And then she began to read aloud.

Dear Alex,

I hope that somehow, sometime, this letter reaches you. I know it probably won't. I guess in a way I'm writing this more for my own comfort than yours. But life can be funny, and sometimes even the most improbable things have a way of surprising us.

You walked away from me before I had the chance to tell you what I was thinking. I can't blame you. I imagine I was standing there looking about as bright as the inside of a cave. I promise I was trying to find the words, but something kept pulling them away whenever I got close.

I guess that was for the best, though. Maybe you didn't need any words. When people are hurting, the last thing they want is advice. I think what you needed was time—time to fall apart, gather yourself up, and move on. I'm sure you're not there yet, but I'm sure you will be.

Don't feel embarrassed because of the way you handled yourself. Such situations tend to bring out the worst in people. You did ask some serious questions, though, and you deserve some serious answers. I've seen my share of love, both the good kind and the bad, and even though I'm no philosopher or poet, I've been around the block enough to know where everything is.

Love is the most overused word in the English language, and maybe in any language. We can say we love anything—chocolate or a shirt or a pet or a picture. We love cars, houses, movies, and Saturdays. Is it any wonder, then, that when we say we love someone, the true meaning is lost?

The truth? No one can say what love is all about. It's beyond words and description. You might as well try to explain the color red to a blind person. You can hint and analogize all you want, but you'll never get it just right.

I think it has something to do with the fact that people can't seem to agree on what love is. I couldn't help but wonder that after you left. Are you sure it was love you felt for Lauren? I don't mean to belittle your feelings, but I have to be honest. You asked me if I knew how beautiful Lauren was. I did. You were right, she was beautiful. But that was really all you dwelled on. You never mentioned her kindness or her charm or her humor. I can't believe the only lovely features she possessed were those on the outside.

Maybe I'm overanalyzing. You just made it seem as though you weren't going to miss her nearly as much as you were going to miss her body. And that's exactly the point I'm trying to make.

You don't fall in love through the eyes, Alex. You fall in love through the heart.

The hurt that comes from losing someone we love can be unbearable. But the hurt that comes from closing ourselves off from the world is much worse. I know you're hurting right now. But pain isn't necessarily a bad thing. Numbness is.

We are meant to love and to share, and if we don't allow ourselves the opportunity to do so, we become less than we should. The more we're able to feel, the more we're able to do. And we can lose anything in this life—hope, desire, even faith—but it's only when we lose our love that we truly die.

So even though you feel like you're all alone in the world right now, you aren't. A broken heart is like the common cold—we all know there isn't a cure, we all know someone who's suffered through one, and we all know that despite whatever precautions we might take, sooner or later we're going to have to suffer through one, too. We are the only creatures who sometimes hurt the ones we love for no other reason than because we feel like it. That's why falling in love comes with a price. It means fully giving all of yourself, warts and scars and all. That's the only way it can be. And we give all of this to someone who is bound to one day at least dis-

appoint us and at worst make us wonder if we can ever love again.

Is it, then, worth all the risk? Every time.

Keep trying. She's out there.

Best,

Andy

"I think that's beautiful," she said.

"Guess it's not bad for someone who has no idea what he's talking about," I answered. "But then again, Alex wouldn't know that."

"I think you know exactly what you're talking about." Elizabeth made a subtle shift into Counselor Mode, but this one I managed to catch. "You've hurt, haven't you? A lot?"

"Everybody hurts, Elizabeth. Everybody who ever drew a breath has hurt. This world's made for it. You said so yourself."

"No," she said. "I said the world's not solid. That's different."

"I don't even know what that means. But to answer your question, yes. I've hurt a lot. Which makes me no different than anyone else."

"You hurt because of Caroline, don't you?" she said.

"I'd rather not talk about Caroline, if that's okay."

Elizabeth pretended not to hear me. "You mistook me for her, didn't you? You thought it was Caroline sitting here in this chair when you woke up."

I told myself to tread lightly. I needed to keep one small part of myself in the shadows. "In my defense," I said, "I was a little out of sorts."

"What was it? My eyes? My shape? Do we have the same hair?"

"All of the above." I left out the most striking similarity—they had the same heart, too.

"Is there anything of hers in your box?"

I shook my head no.

"And why's that?"

"Because when you think about someone most all the time, you don't need anything to remember her by."

"I don't think that's true," she said.

"Sure it is. I know plenty of married folks who don't wear their rings. Know plenty of proud fathers who don't cart around pictures of their kids, too."

"That's not what I'm talking about." Elizabeth put the letter down and picked up the envelope. Held it up for me to see. "I meant I don't think it's true that there isn't anything of hers in your box. I think this was hers. Or maybe almost was."

I tried to swallow but couldn't.

"Alex's name is on the envelope, Andy. But it was written over another name that you erased."

She dangled the envelope until I finally reached out and took it. I held it close. Even in the dim lights I could see the faint markings of the letters beneath Alex's name.

Caroline.

"You were writing that letter for him," she said. "But you were thinking about her the whole time, weren't you? Thinking about her so much that when you were finished and you addressed the front, you wrote her name instead of his."

I looked at her.

"What happened?" She didn't ask the question as much as whisper it. I had the feeling it was something she had to ask but would rather not, and I wanted to know why. Was it because Caroline had nothing to do with her job, or was it because Elizabeth didn't care to hear me talking about a woman who once meant more to me than any other?

"Caroline walked into my gas station ten years ago," I said. "She'd just moved to Mattingly. Her husband had up and left her and she was trying to start over. Poor gal. She was nice, real nice, but you could tell her heart was broken.

"I don't know what in the world made me ask her to dinner one night. The Old Man didn't tell me to. Just sort of came out. One second she was handing me a twenty for her gas, and the next we were sitting in the Dairy Queen eating sundaes. And it was great, you know? Just really...great. I'd never felt what I felt with her. She was funny and smart and so pretty. Dinner turned into a regular thing, and then we turned into a regular thing."

"Sounds like you two made a good pair," Elizabeth said.

"Good enough that folks around town started gossiping." I quieted for a moment. "I bet I started to tell her about the Old Man a thousand times. Ran it through my head about how to say it all. I even asked him. But he was always pretty quiet about Caroline. I don't think it was jealousy; I can't imagine angels being jealous. Guess he just knew it wouldn't end well. And it didn't. I took a lady who'd had her heart broken, helped put it back together, and then broke it again."

"Because of the Old Man?"

"Yeah," I said. "He'd stuck by me, you know? Guess I just thought I'd return the favor."

"So you embrace your hurt and shun your happiness. You don't seem like a masochist to me, Andy."

"We have a right to pursue happiness, Elizabeth. Not a right to find it. The first part's what living is all about, I guess. The second part is maybe an inevitable consequence. But we're all gonna hurt in our own way. I think that's a good thing."

Elizabeth looked down into the box. She'd made herself comfortable beside me, comfortable even to the point of intrusion a few times, but she still respected me enough not to touch anything inside without my asking. "You have anything in that box to prove that statement?" she asked.

I took the box and sat it on my lap. The pocket cross was still in the ball cap. I took it out and held it up to her. We watched as the wood caught the light.

12

The Pocket Cross

Y ou should come," Jackie said to me. "It's gonna be good. Hear me?"

I poked my head out from under the hood of her car and wiped the oil off my hands. "Oil's good, Jackie," I said. "Dirty, though. When's the last time Harry had this thing serviced? The seventies?"

"Oh, you know Harry," she said. "Love of my life, but to him preventative maintenance is keeping gas in the car. You didn't answer my question."

I slammed the hood shut and walked over to her window. "What question?" I asked.

"If you heard me or not. You should come."

It wasn't the first time Jackie had invited me to her church, and I was sure it wouldn't be the last. She wasn't trying to save my immortal soul (that had already been done, thanks to Reverend Barnhart down at the Mennonite church) or get me to switch teams and start playing for the Pentecostals. It was just Jackie's way. She invited everyone to church, whether they already went or not.

"Aww, I don't know, Jackie. I can go to my own church and hear singin'. That's twenty for the gas."

"I guess you can," she said. Jackie handed me two tens plus fifty cents for a tip. "But I expect you tend to your churchin' the same way you tend to your gas station, by which I mean you show up, say just enough to be polite, and otherwise mind yourself. You don't fool me, Andy Sommerville. And you understand that white folks can't sing right. Right?"

Anyone who might have been filling up their car at the opposite pump probably would have taken that to sound a tad racist. I didn't. Friends get away with saying things to one another that would maybe get them in trouble if said to someone else, and I was Jackie's friend.

I stuck the money in my shirt pocket and said, "Sure we can sing. We do it every Sunday."

"Didn't say that. I said you can't sing *right*. Now don't get me wrong, you can sing sure enough. Sing pretty, too. But there's a difference between singing and *singing*."

"There is?"

Jackie shook her head and wiped the sweat from her neck with a handkerchief she pulled from her bra. Thirty years of marriage and eight children had left her with bad knees and a worse back (which either had caused or been caused by a hefty frame she inherited from her mother, Thelma). Her ever-present Bible sat in the front seat beside her, creased and filled to the gills with a year's worth of church bulletins and prayer lists. To many people—even people in Mattingly—a Bible was something to get out on Sunday mornings and put away Sunday afternoon. Jackie's was a combination of purse, schedule keeper, and road map to lands inward. "You gotta be the whitest white boy in the world, you know that? Of course there's a difference."

"What's the difference?" I asked her.

Jackie reached through the window and patted my arm. "You come by the church Sunday night. You'll see."

"Come on, Jackie," I said. "You've been trying to get me out there for the last six years. I'd stick out like a sore thumb."

"Don't matter what color we are on the outside, honey. We all dirty on the inside. Right?"

"Gotta give you that one," I said. "You say hi to Harry and Mother Thelma."

"I'll look for you Sunday night," Jackie said. She gave me

a conspiratorial smile, rolled up her window, and pulled away.

I walked back into the gas station and rang up the sale. Jackie's tip of fifty cents went into the cigar box I kept on the shelf. The Old Man was sitting on top of the counter, staring out into the parking lot.

"So you're going, right?" he said. He clapped his hands together and then rubbed them, convinced that some unknown adventure was about to begin.

"Where'm I going?"

"To Jackie's church, of course."

I shut the cash register drawer and looked at him. "Nah," I said. "I got stuff to do."

"Stuff to do?" he asked. The ensuing snort doubled him over into a fit of laughter so intense it has no sound. When he finally settled himself, he said, "You have nothing to do."

The thing about having an angel around was there wasn't much you could keep private. The act of making up excuses to get out of something you really should probably get into is a time-honored human tradition. Unfortunately, it was one I could never use with the Old Man. He knew me better than I did.

"Look," I told him, "everybody gets along in Mattingly. We're all friendly. Don't matter who you are."

"Mostly," he said.

I cut him off before he could say more and ruin the point I was trying to make. "Okay, mostly. But as far as race goes, there's no problem around here at all. Black people can go wherever they want, and white folk can go wherever they want. But when it comes to worship, we kinda stick to our own. You know?"

"Yes," he said, nodding, "but no," he said, shaking his head.

"I know, it's confusing to me, too. But that's just the way it's always been."

"I think you should go," he said. "You know Jackie'll bug you forever if you don't."

He had a point.

"I'll think about it," I said.

"Don't think, just do it. Trust me."

The congregation of the Mattingly United Church of the Risen Christ met on the outer edges of town in a one-room building that was much smaller than the name. Lights were provided by a lone electrical line that ran like an IV from the pole in the middle of the graveyard to the left side of the church. There was no furnace, just an old woodstove that sat near a makeshift pulpit. The church seemed comfortable and welcoming, as was the young man who greeted me at the door.

"Evenin' to you," he said, as he handed me a bulletin. "Praise the Lord."

"Back at'cha," I said, which brought a chuckle and a solid thump to my back.

I took a seat about halfway on the left side and spent the next ten minutes standing up and sitting down with all the folks walking over to welcome me, including Harry, Jackie's husband, and Mother Thelma. A few *yes sir*s and *thank you ma'am*s later, and in walked Jackie with the rest of the choir.

Sixteen souls by my count, ranging in age from high school to retirement home. Evenly divided between men and women. Not much different than the choir at my own church, really. The only exception was that Jackie's choir held no sheet music.

"Nice to see you, Andy," she whispered as she passed. She continued on to the front, already swaying to music I couldn't hear.

The choir director floated behind the pulpit and led us in the opening prayer, a rousing and passionate entreaty that lasted about five minutes and resembled more a conversation with an old friend than the airing of pleas. His

"Amen!" signaled the end of one thing and the beginning of another.

The pianist began to play and the director turned to face the chorus, which had begun a uniform sway from right to left to right again. He then raised his hands as a signal for the choir's entrance.

Jackie smiled at me and winked a warning to get ready. I would have done so if I knew what I was supposed to get ready *for*.

More piano as the director's hands raised further, picking him up onto his tiptoes. Slowly, slowly . . . then . . . *down*.

"*PRAISE!!*" they sang.

The sound created a wind that whooshed from the front of the church and very nearly knocked me backward. I literally had to grab hold of the pew in front of me to balance myself. The church exploded into a song I had never before heard. Some in the congregation shot their hands into the air. Whether they were reaching for the words or for heaven itself I did not know, but at the moment I believed the one may well have been the other. Others clapped along with the melody. A few pointed their faces toward the ceiling. The Old Man stood in the middle of the choir in his own gown, dancing with hands raised. Our eyes met for a brief second. *Told ya*, he mouthed, then lifted his head to the ceiling and sang.

Tears welled in my eyes. I couldn't move. Couldn't clap, couldn't raise my hands, couldn't breathe. Jackie looked at me and smiled. Whitest white boy in the world indeed.

This wasn't singing. I knew that then. No, this was *singing*.

An hour later the choir finally showed me mercy and sang their last note. One last prayer by the choir director and the benediction by the pastor, and the service was over. I sat in my pew exhausted but smiling as Jackie and her family gathered around me.

"See what I mean?" she asked.

"Lesson learned," I told her. "That was incredible."

"Nothing incredible about it," Mother Thelma said. Her

eighty-seven-year-old bones still swayed with the last waves of music that still reverberated inside them. "Just different's all."

I smiled. "I see that. Still don't understand it, though."

"It's different because we're different, Brother Andy," Harry said. "Not much you can do about that. And I know I ain't supposed to say it, but it's true."

Forty-five years old and eight years Jackie's elder, Harry was an assistant pastor of the church and king of the family, though he'd be the first to say both came by his wife's permission. There were plenty of folks in town—black and white—who thought he'd make a fine mayor if he ever got the gumption to run for election.

"Look," Jackie said, "this here's my country. Not somewhere in Africa like where my ancestors come from. Here. Mattingly's our home. We got that in common. But my kin were slaves."

"I'm sorry," I said. "I just . . ."

Jackie shooed me away and said, "Now I know you ain't had a hand in that, but it needs saying. That's how we're different. We have the same faith, Andy, but we worship different."

Mother Thelma had been quiet and listening, nodding her approval at the words her daughter and son-in-law spoke. But now was her turn. "The faith you got from your grandparents was come by the easy way," she said. "That's nothing against them now, Andy. And that's not sayin' their faith is less than our own, because that ain't true. But the faith we were taught was born in the cotton fields and tobacco farms. It was hardened through the whippings and stretched when a mama had her child sold out from under her or a husband watched his wife get raped. They *hurt*, you see. That's why we can *sing*."

"I think I'd rather not hurt and not sing," I said.

The three of them smiled and offered a mix of laughter and hisses. Then Jackie's mother pulled a small wooden cross from her purse and showed it to me.

"See this here?" Thelma asked. "My great-grandmother carried this cross. She'd wrap it up in the folds of her dress while she cleaned this big plantation house in Carolina. My grandma said her mother didn't have it as bad as some. But it was still bad. Still lots of fearful times and humiliation. When things got bad, she'd take this cross out and rub it while she prayed."

She held the cross up to the lights. All of our eyes followed it. Including the Old Man's, who appeared beside me.

He bent close to my ear and whispered, "Rubbed it smooth, didn't she?" It was a curious act on his part. I'd never known the Old Man to whisper anything, and why would he? I was the only one who could hear him. But then I understood. His whisper was a shout with an exclamation point at the end. It was a warning to pay attention.

"See how it looks?" Mother Thelma asked. "Shiny and beautiful? Happiness didn't do that, sadness did. And it rubs our souls the same way."

"That's amazing," I said.

"Here then," she said, reaching into her purse. "I always keep some of these to give away. This one's for you."

Jackie's mother pulled out another small cross and placed it into my hand. It was rough, almost sharp around the edges. The grain glowed a bright brown.

"You hang on to this," she said. "Use it right. If you're lucky, maybe one day it'll look like the one I have."

"It won't look like hers," he whispered into my ear again. "Know why?"

I did. Coming to hear Jackie sing hadn't been the Old Man's way to steer me to something else to put into my box, but that had been a major factor. One I was unaware of until just then. I took the cross Mother Thelma offered and thanked her for it, knowing what a special gift it was. I'd been wished happiness before. And love and faith and good fortune. Never a dose of pain and hardship, though. But in that moment I knew she meant it as the blessing it should be. Jackie was right. We could all sing and we all should, but it was only the wounded who could sing truly. Only the maimed and the hurt and the broken. Because the best voices were those who had learned to praise God, and thank Him too in the midst of suffering.

13

The Difference between Singing and
SINGING

The smell of coffee wafted through the room, a sure sign today had turned into tomorrow. Elizabeth held the cross in her hand and smiled down at it, running her fingers down and across the holy lowercase *t*. She gave the cross a kiss and then placed it not in the box, but in my hand. As she did I heard more coughing and Kim quietly making her rounds in and out of the rooms surrounding me. The coughs ceased.

Kim saved me for last, knocking on the door and pushing it open all the way. She spied the box open on my lap. I closed it as quickly as I could without appearing to be hiding something. "How's it going in here?" she asked.

"As good as it can be," I said. I offered a wry smile in Elizabeth's direction. She returned it and settled back into her chair. "How's it going out there?"

"Oh, just another night in paradise. Nice and quiet so far, though."

"Didn't seem too quiet a little while ago." I turned the thumb and pinky of my good hand into a telephone and held it up to my ear. "Saw you on the phone. Didn't look like that was a very good conversation."

"Oh, yeah." Kim's dark cheeks turned a weak shade of pink before she added, "I'm really sorry if that disturbed you."

"It didn't, and I'm sorry for prodding."

Kim moved herself between Elizabeth and me to check my monitors and IV. "Owen and me, we're in sort of a rough patch."

"Happens from time to time," I said. "I'm sure you'll get through it."

"We'll see," she said. "You're looking just fine, Andy. I'm a little worried about your meds. I don't want to be giving you so much that you can't sleep. Holler if you start feeling strange or if you need me, okay? For anything."

"Yes'm."

Kim made her way back between us and left the door open a bit more than she found it. Elizabeth and I watched as she settled back behind her desk and looked at us.

"I don't think Kim's a fan of you," I said.

Elizabeth ignored me just as Kim had ignored her. "Your cross isn't smooth yet, Andy."

I looked down at the wooden *t* in my hand. "Well," I answered, "it's been in the box since that night. I like to think I'm a little smooth and shiny, though. Least on the inside."

I moved to place the cross back into the box, but Elizabeth stopped me. "No. I don't think you should put that back, Andy. I think now's the time to keep it out. I think you should do what Mother Thelma intended for you to do. I think you should carry it and work on those sharp edges. Let it be a reminder."

"Of what?"

"Of this time for you. Of what God is doing. He's helping you grow, Andy. He's molding you for something greater."

"Oh," I said. "He is, is He? Well isn't that special? Isn't that just truly...wonderful?" I paused to let those words sink into Elizabeth, to make sure she caught the sarcasm. The look on her face said she did. "I think I'd rather keep the smooth edges on my life than have them on this cross."

I moved the cross toward my box again, but again Elizabeth stopped me. "I know," she said. "I know this hurts. It doesn't seem right that God would allow people to suffer. If He's so loving, then He would do more to prevent the bad things in this world. People use that argument all the time to show He's really not there."

"But I know He's there," I said. "That's what makes it worse for me. People think believing in God makes everything better, but let me tell you something—sometimes it makes it worse. When suffering happens to someone who doesn't believe, they just chalk it up to the way life works. But when it happens to someone who does believe, they're left with the fact that either God doesn't care or that you don't matter."

"He does care," Elizabeth said. "And you do matter." She closed my hand around the cross. "God does not care as much about our comfort as He does about us. He doesn't want our happiness, Andy. You know yourself that happiness can be fleeting in this world. It's here one day and gone the next. It's like a cool breeze on a hot day. You can't grab it; you just have to enjoy it while it settles on you and then let it go on by. It's trust that God wants. Trust that He knows what's best, what's right. Trust is what allows Him to move through your life. It's what makes the impossible become the easy. Smooth edges around your life do not make smooth edges around your soul. In the end, it's the soul that matters. Your life doesn't last. Your soul does."

I opened my hand and looked at the cross inside—rough and unused, much like me. Maybe Elizabeth was right. Maybe I'd had it all wrong.

Maybe God was not casting me aside. Maybe He was lifting me up closer to Himself.

I closed my hand around the cross. "Okay," I said. "I'll keep it out. Still like to think I'm smooth and shiny, though. At least a little."

"I like to agree with you." She pointed to the angel box and said, "May I?"

I didn't see the harm; Elizabeth had already seen the contents. I slid the box over to her and watched as she went through the contents of the box, passing over the ones we'd already covered. Her fingers danced and weaved yet disturbed nothing. Elizabeth was careful, careful with my stories and my secret and me, and that care contained its own medicine.

I didn't know what was wrong that she deemed in need of
fixing, but I knew she was fixing it. Slowly, surely, she was
mending my broken places.

And then she found the key chain.

"This looks interesting," she said, holding it up for me to
see. The silver hoop hung around her finger and the chain
dangled beneath. She swayed the pewter angel at the end back
and forth. I felt as if she were trying to hypnotize me into
telling her the truth.

The chain. Eric's—

"I don't want to talk about that," I said.

Elizabeth's playful demeanor turned businesslike. She hid
the angel by wrapping her hand around it.

"What's wrong, Andy?" she asked me. "I'm sorry. I didn't
mean to upset you."

"Just put that back, okay? Please? That one . . . no. Just leave
that one alone. Don't touch it."

Outside the door, Kim started to rise from her chair. I waved
her off with my bandaged hand. She sat, though unwillingly.

Elizabeth nestled the key chain in a corner of the box and
said nothing else. I supposed the time would come when she
would press me to talk about it. I also supposed I wouldn't.
We had traveled a long way in a short time, and I had done so
as willingly as I could. But there were things we had to carry
alone in life, no matter who offered to help.

"More?" I asked her.

"Why not?"

"Because if you're looking at the clock it must be getting
late. Pretty sure hospital counselors don't work all night."

Elizabeth didn't look tired, not even weary. She appeared as
fresh and ready to go as she had been when she first told me
my hair would grow back (if I wanted it to).

"No, actually we don't. But I can't very well talk to you
while you're sleeping, can I? And that's what you've been
pretty much doing the past few days, according to the nurses.
I'm sure Kim won't mind as long as you're awake and we keep

things to a dull roar." She winked. "I get a little leeway around here."

I smiled. "You like the company, huh?"

"Yes," she said. "And I like your stories most of all, Andy. That's no snap judgment, by the way, which I'm sure you can appreciate."

"I can," I said. "Gotta watch those snap judgments. Those can get you in trouble."

A sly smile appeared on her beautiful face then, making it even more beautiful. "You sound like you know that from experience."

She set the box down on my lap and opened it.

"Which one?" she asked.

I reached in for the Santa letter and the bundle of pine needles inside, careful not to grip it so hard they would turn to dust. Their ends looked like tiny spears, more weapons than lessons.

"This one," I said. "Happened back right after September 11. It was Christmastime. Usually my favorite time of the year, even though until recently I didn't have anyone to buy gifts for. The Old Man, he's all about Christmas, too. Or was, I guess. He helped me stay up from the end of November to the end of December. That can be a tough time if you're..."

Elizabeth raised an eyebrow. "Lonely?" she asked.

"Yes. Lonely. Anyway, he made sure I always had a tree up. He even prods me into making peanut butter balls, even though he can't eat them. I usually just bring those down to the gas station and give them out. People like them. He makes me put lights up, too. Nothing extravagant, just a few strands around the evergreen by the garage and some candles in the window. And my letter to Santa. He's all about that."

"Wait," Elizabeth said. She leaned forward and held me by the knee. "He makes you write a letter to Santa?"

Too much, I thought to myself. *You'd better start paying attention to what you're spilling to this lady.*

"He said it's important for me to know what I want," I said.

"And I'm trusting that little admission falls under the protection of counselor/client privilege."

"Of course," she said. Elizabeth tried to swallow a chuckle and almost choked instead. "That sounds like fun, actually."

"It wasn't that year. That was a tough year for everybody. Things turned around, though."

"How so?"

"I found Rudolph," I said.

14

The Pine Needles

The big deal in Mattingly during Christmas revolved around the massive evergreen that stood guard in front of the rescue squad building. For as long as I could remember, a few firemen would gas up the ladder truck in the first few days of December and drive it the hundred yards or so from the fire department down the hill to the squad house, where they draped the big pine with thousands of multicolored lights. Aside from the summer parade season, this was the sole purpose of that particular piece of firefighting equipment; there wasn't a building in Mattingly anywhere near large enough to require a few hundred feet of ladder in an emergency. But to the townspeople, keeping the Christmas tree lit was well worth the eighty thousand dollars spent on the ladder.

The firemen took their time with this task and trimmed the tree with all the attention and care it deserved. They strung and restrung, carefully wrapping and tucking the strands of tiny lights around every limb. If they did it right—and they always did—the end result would be a delicate but perfect balance between *National Lampoon's Christmas Vacation* and something on the Home and Garden Network.

A notice would then be posted on the marquee beside the squad building that the tree would be lit on December 5 at five o'clock in the evening. It was always December 5 and always at five o'clock, though no one knew exactly why. It was as good a time as any, I suppose. Mattingly was always the sort of place where time never mattered much. The whole town was invited, and usually most of the town came. From the time my grandparents brought me to Mattingly until now, I never missed the lighting of that tree.

But I almost did that year. September 11 had happened just two months earlier, and the economy was going south. Everything just seemed...heavy. Like there was a thick blanket over the world that tried to smother everything instead of keep it warm. It was twenty days until Christmas. My decorations weren't up, my Christmas cards weren't written much less mailed, and I had yet to even write my letter to Santa. The Old Man was going nuts. He said I was an emotional corpse.

It was he who convinced me to go for the tree-lighting ceremony, further proving that his philosophy of When You Can't Convince Andy, Wear Him Down never failed. I grabbed my hat that night and got in the truck just to shut him up.

The crowd was a bit sparser that year. Like I said, everyone was feeling a little dead inside. I got there just after the tree had been lit and *hello*'d and *good evening*'d my way to the front to get a good look. Never, not once, had all that glowing majesty failed to inspire me. The tree had that effect on people. (Not even my Mennonite grandfather was immune. I remember him telling me on one long-ago December 5 that those lights were what guided Santa's sleigh to Mattingly.) Yet as I stood there feeling the heat from the bulbs, the very energy of the season, I felt nothing.

That's it, I thought. *I'm terminal.*

A few firemen were still milling about, dressed to the nines in their navy blue Mattingly Volunteer Fire Department coats. They were explaining to a group of serious-looking men how they managed to "get things just right" and pointing to a "very tricky place" high up in the tree. My eavesdropping was interrupted by the sounds of footsteps crunching the frozen grass to my left. I turned, and beside me was an older gentleman who had decided to get a close-up view of the tree himself. Late sixties, by the look of him. Dark khakis, darker button-up shirt, and a fedora. A pea coat was draped over his left arm, and in his right hand sat a half-eaten cheeseburger from the Dairy Queen around the corner.

I'd never seen him before. That was why he stood out. I knew most everyone in Mattingly, even the ones who weren't much worth knowing. But this man was new and therefore strange. I nodded and said hello. He wished me a good evening in a distinct German accent.

I turned my attention back to the tree and noticed a bare spot about a foot wide that had been passed over by the decorating committee. Instinct took over. I rearranged the surrounding strands of lights to cover the hole, then took a step back to admire my work.

The Old Man eased up behind me. "Not bad," he said. "But you'd better take your eyes off your own handiwork and pay attention. You can start with that fella beside you."

I turned and saw the German take a step forward, switch the burger from his right hand to his left, and slip something into the tree.

Now I know this is going to sound pretty ridiculous, but I have to say it anyway. You know what everyone was feeling back then. September 11 might be a distant memory now to most folks, and I think that's a shame, but it was fresh in my mind then. So I don't mind saying my first thought was that the man beside me in the snazzy clothes and the German accent was a terrorist. Never mind that this was Mattingly, Virginia, and not New York City or Washington, D.C. Never mind that this was a tree and not the Twin Towers. All I could think was that this was some sicko's jihad against Christmas. And it wasn't going to happen. Not on my watch.

I made sure my chest was adequately pushed outward and stepped toward him as he stepped back.

"Whatcha doin' there, buddy?" I said.

He looked at me, embarrassed that he'd been caught doing God knows what, and said, "Nothing."

It came out *Nothink*, and looking back I supposed I should

have taken that as a literal translation of my current mental state. But I didn't.

"Yeah?" I asked. "I saw you put something in the tree there."

He chuckled like he'd just been caught picking his nose. "Ah, I see."

"You think it's funny?"

A few of the firemen gave me a look. I waved them off.

"It was nothing," he said. "Really."

"Well then," I said. My chest was still out, and that was making it hard to breathe. I relaxed it just a bit. "If it was nothing I wouldn't think you'd mind sharing it. What'd you do?"

"I could tell you," he said through a smile, "but you would not understand."

Yeah, I thought, *there's a lot about you people I don't understand.*

I glanced over to the Old Man. His arms were folded in front of him and he was squinting. I couldn't tell if he was studying me or the German.

"Try me," I told the man.

"It is an old German tradition," he said. Then he bent his head toward me and whispered, "We put a pickle in the Christmas tree."

Oh, I thought. And then, *What?* Suddenly the unlikely possibility of a bomb in the tree was replaced by the very real possibility of a pickle. I felt the thought punch me in the gut. I let out a squeaky exhale.

"Did I do something wrong?" he asked.

"Yes," I said, and a little too loudly. I had to give another wave-off to the firemen. "Yes, you did something wrong. You just stuck the pickle from your burger into our *Christmas tree.*"

I could almost see the mental gears turning beneath the man's hat as he tried to build a bridge across the cultural gap between us. The only problem was that every brick he tried to put down I picked right up and tossed away. Not the nicest thing in the world, maybe. And not the right thing to do at all.

But I justified it by reminding myself that he'd just violated my Christmas tree.

"I am terribly sorry," he said, "but I did nothing wrong."

"What's your name, sir?" I asked him.

"Rudolph," he answered.

I looked backward to the Old Man. "Are you kidding me?" I whispered to him. He said nothing and lifted his hands in a "Why not?" gesture.

I turned back around. "You mean like the reindeer?" I asked him.

"Yes."

"You puttin' me on?"

"No."

"Well Rudolph, I don't know how y'all do things over in the Fatherland, but around here we don't stick pickles in our Christmas trees."

"You do not?" he asked.

He seemed genuinely surprised at that little tidbit, and that only served to make me angry. It wasn't enough that I was depressed at Christmastime, but to be dragged out by my best friend to witness the blatant vandalism of the town Christmas tree was too much to bear. To think that something so pure and right should be defaced by a *condiment* made me sick to my stomach.

I moved toward Rudolph until my nose was an inch from his. He didn't back away. To him, this was all a simple misunderstanding. To me, it was an affront.

"Rudolph," I said, "let me tell you something about this town. Around here we feel a certain responsibility to ensure things are thought of, approached, and cared for in the manner they deserve. Which means you take your hat off when the anthem is being sung, you respect the flag, and—now listen, because this one's important—you do *not* mess with our Christmas tree. We're serious about our Christmas tree, Rudolph. We *love* our Christmas tree, okay? We know what goes on it and where. And nowhere, nofreaking*where*, is there a place for a pickle. You got that?"

It was one of the most eloquent tirades I had ever offered, and Rudolph ignored it completely. I suppose that's the way it is with people. Everyone is more concerned with trying to convince than to understand. "You are okay?" he asked.

I stared at him and then the tree. "Where's the pickle, Rudolph?"

"In the tree."

"I *know* that. I want to know *where* in the tree."

Rudolph took a bite from his burger and then bent down to peer into the branches. "I don't know," he said. "Maybe you should look for it?"

My back arched. "*I* ain't gonna look for it, Rudolph. You got that? I don't want to play any games, either. Now take that pickle out of our tree or I swear on all that is holy and good I will . . ."

What? What would I do? I didn't know, so I left that part off.

"I do not see it," he said, still peering. He gave up and looked at me. There was apology in his eyes. Apology and hurt. I felt baby pains of guilt. "Why are you so angry at me for this?"

His question gave me pause, not because I didn't know the answer but because I heard the voice behind the words. Kind and grandfatherly, and with it was a sincerity that embarrassed me.

"Because," I said, no longer exactly sure, "It. Is. A. Christmas. Tree. Not *your* tree, either. The town's."

"Yes!" he said. He raised his burger as a toast and a show of satisfaction. "All the more reason!"

We stared at one another for a few seconds, him still trying to build that bridge and me now thinking that letting him do so would not necessarily be a bad thing.

"What is your name?" he asked.

"Andy."

"Well Andy, I cannot find the pickle. I try. But my mind . . ." Rudolph made a circular motion next to his ear with the cheeseburger. " . . . not what it used to be. I'm sorry to anger you. Perhaps if you find it, you can take it out?"

There lay before me two courses of action. I could hit him, which despite my proper upbringing and my Christian guilt I was still prepared to do. Or I could look for the stupid pickle. The latter would surely bring me some sort of moral and spiritual distress. The former would likely land me in jail; even as friendly as Jake and I were, he wouldn't have a choice but to lock me up. The decision between damaging my pride and being arrested was a difficult one, but after a few moments I agreed to his terms. I stepped to his left and reached into the limbs, combing over the general area where I had seen him hide it.

The tree was alive with lights—blues and greens and reds that melted into one another to form a pale yellow. I peered past them, thinking the pickle had to be near the outside of the limbs. I glanced back to Rudolph, who other than making a waving motion for me to go to the right maintained his stoic expression, and then to the Old Man, who merely offered, "You're on your own, Sport."

Five minutes passed. I was getting nowhere. I didn't understand why it had to be a pickle. Pickles were green. Christmas trees were green. The whole thing was ridiculous.

"Find it?" Rudolph asked.

"No."

"Perhaps I put it deeper in than I thought?"

I shook my head, sighed, and bent closer. The needles formed a weblike maze that protected the inner limbs from most any disturbance. A few tiny drops of water remained there, evidence of the morning frost. They fell like a miniature rainstorm when my hand brushed against them. I found a perfectly circular robin's nest that had been untouched from last summer. A closer inspection revealed the remains of several eggs and a small beehive. And as I began to look for more of the same, I actually forgot to look for Rudolph's pickle.

I began to forget about other things, too. Things like my sadness and frustration and the hole in my heart I feared God would never let anyone fill. For one small moment, I was alone with the present. The universe shrunk into the small inner world of that tree, and it was a world that was just as beautiful—perhaps more so—than the lights that hid it.

"Well?" Rudolph asked.

I stood up and faced him. "Can't find it."

"Ah. That is too bad."

I raised my hands in mock surrender and said, "Fine, I give up. What's the deal with the stupid pickle?"

Rudolph shrugged and said, "I do not know."

"What?" I asked. "Are you kidding me? We just went through all that and you don't know why you put pickles in your Christmas trees?"

"Do you know why you put lights on yours?"

He had me there. Other than the fact it just looked nice, I had no idea.

"I suppose sometimes the reasons we do things escape us," he said. "But that doesn't mean there isn't a reason. No?"

"No," I said. "I mean...yes."

"Well," he said, "I must be going. My child and her new husband are waiting. They just move here from the city. And I apologize again, Andy. I suppose looking at your beautiful tree just reminded me of times past. I was, as you say, caught in the moment."

I nodded. He turned to leave and then paused.

"Meddy Christmas," he said.

"Merry Christmas, Rudolph."

Rudolph walked into the darkness of the parking lot beyond. A sudden thought slammed into my head as I watched him leave.

"Sorry," the Old Man said. "Not an angel. Don't get greedy."

I rolled my eyes and said, "Oh, be quiet."

I sat in the recliner that night under the watchful eye of a full moon with pen and paper in hand. I had decided it was time for my letter to Santa. For a while I didn't think I wanted anything, if only because I felt nothing would make me better. But then I started thinking about what Rudolph had said. About how things that seem to have no reason to them still might. Somehow, someway, they still might. Mine was a good life, but there was plenty that had no reason in it. I had always wanted some sense of clarity, but maybe clarity was overrated. Maybe I didn't need a lot of the new; maybe I just needed more of the same. It was a wish, yes. One I desperately wanted fulfilled. But Christmas was all about wishes fulfilled, and so I wrote:

Dear Santa:

I've been taught since I was a boy that Christmas is a time of possibility. There is magic in the air, and miracles abound. For one month the world seems to move a bit closer to where it could be. To where it should be. There are gifts and joy and peace abounding.

There comes a time in life, as in Christmas, when we must grow up and decide which is more important, the presents or the Presence. I think I've reached that time. So it is with full clarity of mind that I ask for no gifts this year. I don't need things that can be purchased. They won't make me a better man. Instead, I ask only for the continuance of what God has given me every day.

I ask for friendship in those days of drear (of which I'm sure there will be many) as well as in those days of cheer (of which I'm sure there will be many more).

I ask for strength to see the world in all its cruelty and injustice and still believe that in the end good will triumph over evil, right will overcome wrong, and peace will reign forevermore.

I ask for the understanding that no matter how horribly I may act, there is not a day that begins without my solemn vow to make it a better one than the day before.

And lastly, I ask for the magic to believe that the spirit of Christmas can be found throughout the year, that the giving and sharing of our blessings and our lives draw us not only nearer to one another but nearer to God, and that miracles and angels abound every day.

Meddy Christmas.

15

The Muck and the Mire

Elizabeth was twirling the scissors around her thumb again, but that was only half of what she was doing. I was still trying to figure out the other half. I settled on *pondering* but then dismissed it for another, clearer word. I had the feeling Elizabeth didn't really need to ponder, that she knew enough about the world—both the inner and the outer—to not have to pause and turn things over in her mind. It wasn't that she didn't know what to say when she offered me those long pauses, it was more like she was sorting the words she wanted to tell me. Elizabeth guided the story rather than simply letting me tell it. I'd often heard that counselors had such tricks at their disposal. With all their training and expertise, it didn't take them long to size up their patients. Telling their patients what exactly was wrong and how to fix it wouldn't really solve anything; in the end, it was the patients themselves who had to discover that. The counselor's job was more Sherpa than doctor. Elizabeth was my guide, not my director.

"I know why they put pickles in their trees," she finally said.

"No way," I snorted.

"Andy Sommerville, do you honestly think all I know is how to shrink heads?" The feigned affront was playful and mocking, and in that she reminded me of the Old Man and how much I missed him despite what he'd done.

"Prove it," I said.

"It's more for the kids, really. Parents put pickles in their

Christmas trees for their children to find. It's sort of a contest. The first child to find the pickle gets an extra gift."

"Sounds a tad consumerist," I said. "I thought Americans were supposed to be the only ones who could be pegged as materialists."

"You're missing the point," she said. "It isn't consumerist at all. You wanted to know why it had to be a pickle. That's easy—because pickles are green. They blend in with the trees, so you really have to look hard to find them. You couldn't even find yours. That's the point."

"The point is to not find the pickle?"

"No, the point is to look so hard for it that you start to see something else. Like what happened to you when you were looking for Rudolph's. It isn't about the pickle, Andy, it's about the tree. The children learn to see beyond the decorations and the lights to the real beauty."

"So the real beauty...," I started. Elizabeth lowered her head into half a nod and urged me to put the rest of the pieces together. "...isn't the lights and the tinsel, the stuff put there by them..." Her head was lower now, as if to say *almost there*. "...but the tree itself, which was put there by God."

Nod completed. "Exactly," she said.

"Huh. That actually makes sense."

"It's the same with life, too. Sometimes there seems to be no reason for happiness. Times like now, with you. You need to remember that God always wants you to see the good in life, the *real*, because it's there. No matter how ugly things seem, there's always beauty underneath. You just have to look for the pickle."

My insides churned in a battle between believing those words or my own experience. It was always easy to tell someone else to look on the bright side of things. To say there was always a silver lining. But when you're in the muck and the mire yourself, those words grew sharp enough to cut.

"'The Old Man never told you what the pickle meant?" she asked.

"No, he never did. Maybe he knew you'd be here to explain it to me." The first part of that sentence saddened me, the last made me smile.

"Did Santa answer your letter?"

"Some of it, yes. The friendship and the sharing, not so much. Still had the Old Man, though, at least until now. I'm not *alone*, you see. I talk to people every day. But just because I do doesn't mean I'm not lonely. I think the loneliest people in the world are the ones constantly surrounded by others. Proximity has no bearing on isolation." I thought for a bit and then added, "Someone told me that once. He said, 'Andy, everyone in this town knows who you are, but most of them don't know what you are.' And you know what? He was right."

"Who said that?" she asked.

"Danny."

"Another customer?"

I nodded. "Was, anyway. He passed on a few years ago."

Elizabeth said "I'm sorry" in a way I knew she meant it.

"It was a long good-bye," I said. "Cancer took him. Some folks it takes all at once, others little by little. Danny went little by little. It was hard on him, but harder on his wife. If it weren't for David Walker, I don't think she would've made it through."

"And who is David Walker?"

"One of the farmers around Mattingly. And maybe the wisest man in town. Least he was on that night." I reached into the box for the stack of Dairy Queen napkins that had been thus far minding its own business in the lower right-hand corner. I held them up to her. "He's the one who gave me these."

16

Paper Napkins

The funeral home was typical—stately and bricked on the outside, muted tans and ivories on the inside, and flowers everywhere to remind all who entered that life continues on. The smaller rooms that ringed the main parlor were decorated with Victorian furniture and arranged for as much comfort and seriousness as possible. Most of these rooms were empty save for the few mourners who had broken off from the pack to either gather themselves or make sure their skirts and ties were straight. Smartly dressed parents made small talk with quiet whispers and faint smiles while trying to keep their children under control.

Most of the town was in attendance that night, some of whom I hadn't seen in a while. It is both tragic and reassuring that death seems to fold its wings around friends and draw them together in one place. Tragic because it sometimes takes such a thing to reunite people. Reassuring because we realize that though time and circumstance could separate us, we would always be there when it mattered.

In the large gathering room was the evidence of one man's mark upon the world. His children and grandchildren formed a parallel line to the casket in front of them. Each of them, even nine-year-old Jackson, offered the same stoic resignation as the clay shell of the man lying in repose behind them had offered in each of his seventy-seven years. The Layman family was holding their own in true Southern fashion. On the outside, anyway. They felt they had to be strong for the friends, acquaintances, and kin who had assembled to say good-bye for now.

His name was Daniel Alexander Layman—Danny to his friends, and I was proud to be one of them. Never could you have found a better, more decent man. You always hear that the world is going to hell and things are a lot worse than they've ever been before. I doubted that because I knew Danny. It was people like him who kept the darkness from snuffing out the light. When he died, Earth got a little dimmer and heaven grew a little brighter.

I picked my way through the crowd, pausing to say, "Good, and you?" to those who asked how I was doing and "He did, didn't he?" to those who remarked on what a good life Danny had lived. Then I made my way through the line of relatives and offered my condolences.

Helen was not among them. Was not even by the casket framed by roses, tulips, and sunflowers, Danny's favorite. I spied Jenny McCray, the manager of the funeral home, standing guard near the big archway that separated the gathering room from everything else. I said hello and then asked her where Danny's wife was.

"In the next room," she told me. "She's holding up. She's the first to say Danny's in a place where the cancer isn't. But I think that faith's a weak one."

"What makes you think that?"

"Oh Andy," she said, "you know me."

I did. Forty-four was a young age to be running a business that dealt in death, and being forty-four and a *woman* in such a profession was almost unheard of. Jenny turned all that on its ear. She had the business sense—savvy, if such a word would be appropriate—of your average middle-aged male funeral home owner, but with the softness of a lady's touch. Say what you want about the equality of the sexes, there were just some things women did better than men. Jenny was proof of that.

"A person can learn a lot about life by working with the

dead," she whispered. "Helen's deepest fears have just been realized. It's hard for some people to allow their hearts to intertwine with another's. There's so much to gain, but there's so much to lose, too. Helen gave all of herself to one man, and that man's gone now. Know what I mean?"

I could have said more. A *lot* more. I could have told Jenny right then and there that if anyone had written the book on deepest fears and the unequal balance of gaining and losing, it was me. But instead I just whispered back, "Yes."

Jenny was called away and we said our good-byes. I stood just outside the room and took a few moments to figure out what I would say once it was my turn to say my *sorry*s to Helen. I understood the fact that no one grieving ever really hears what's said to them at the time. Still, I thought Danny would want me to say something to her. Something to help. I owed him that.

The day we buried my grandpa, my grandmother sat me down in the front pew of the church before everyone arrived. That was a tough day for me. It had been years since they'd taken me in—raised me, really. But it still felt like death hovered around me. First my parents, now him. I think she knew I was feeling that way.

She took my hand and held it in hers, then she said, "Andy, the world's like a cocoon and we are the tiny caterpillar inside it. The caterpillar isn't meant to stay in there forever. God has better things in mind. So He lets the caterpillar grow inside that cocoon to the point where it just gets too big. It breaks free and finds it was a butterfly all along. So don't be sad for the cocoon—be happy for the butterfly."

That, I decided, was what I would tell Helen. That was why I was there. Danny was in that other world now, that better place where the cancer wasn't, and he'd been ready to go for a while.

Helen sat as stately as I had ever seen her, on the edge of a plush red couch that stood in contrast with her black mourning dress. Her posture was ramrod, her gray hair in a perfect beehive. Aside from dabbing her eyes when they filled with liquid good-byes she was motionless, staring at some unknown spot in the carpet a few feet in front of her.

Two men were with her. The Old Man stood behind Helen with his hand on her right shoulder, gently patting it as she tried to swallow her sobs. I watched as his fingers melted into her and then reappeared again. Helen could feel nothing, but still that shoulder seemed a bit higher than the other. I wondered if some part of her could feel his comfort even if she didn't realize it. Was that the way it worked for everyone else? Were our senses dull to the presence of the holy Others around us, but our spirits not?

The Old Man looked to me and held up his other hand, not as a wave but to tell me to wait a bit. A younger man sat to her left. His black suit and tie matched Helen's dress. Very dignified. He clutched a worn leather Bible and spoke softly to the silent widow.

Pastor Charlie.

Danny and Helen had spoken much of their pastor, who had taken over the Presbyterian church in town after Nolan Kalling had retired a year earlier. Their congregation had grown since then, and for good reason. I'd heard Pastor Charlie speak at a revival once, and he was a sight to behold. Doctor of Divinity from Dallas Theological Seminary, plus master's degrees in counseling and philosophy from the University of Virginia. He was without a doubt the smartest person who called Mattingly home.

Pastor Charlie was earning his reputation that night. I took the Old Man's advice and stood close enough to hear but far enough away not to be seen. Pastor Charlie tried to comfort her by sharing bits of scripture and counsel. Helen would nod an inch or so at his words and keep staring at that spot in the carpet, which marked the boundary of all she could comprehend.

The Old Man remained as he always had, an active observer to the passive reality around himself. He would lean over into

Pastor Charlie's face as he offered his wisdom and then watch the words as they entered Helen's right ear, as if he were gauging how far they penetrated. He looked at me and offered a sad shake of his head. After a few more minutes of trying-but-not-quite-doing, Charlie excused himself to get some water. He whispered a last little bit of comfort into Helen's ear as he walked away.

Pastor Charlie wasn't the only one not quite connecting with Helen. A steady stream of visitors came by to speak with her, each with their own words of wisdom and sympathy. And Helen would nod and smile and stare with them, too. She looked like she was being forced to endure something even worse than the death of her husband.

The Old Man patted Helen on the shoulder one last time and walked over to me.

"How's it going over there?" I whispered.

"Not too good. Pastor Charlie's doing the best he can, but the words can't cut through the pain. You wanna have a go at it?"

I pulled at my tie and tried to breathe. "Thought I did," I said. "Don't think so now. If he can't say anything to make her feel at least a little better, no way I can."

"I don't follow you," he said.

"That guy's got more college in him than I have schoolin' altogether," I answered. "He's a preacher, for crying out loud. I can't compete with that."

"Guess you're right," the Old Man said.

I looked at him.

"Hey," he said, "I'm not here to make you feel better. I'm just saying you're right. He's different is all."

"Yeah," I said. "Or maybe I am."

"Tell you what. I'm gonna walk back over there and keep Helen company. You hang here for a little bit. We'll see how it goes."

I shrugged and said "Okay," but by then my mind had been made up. Helen would have to learn about the butterflies on her own.

The Old Man walked back across the room—through people rather than around—and resumed his post at Helen's back. Resigned to the situation, I sucked in the first part of a long sigh. And almost choked.

Something smelled.

Bad.

I turned toward the direction of the funk and found David Walker by the door. From the scent seeping from his clothes, he must have come straight from his fields.

He saw me and raised his chin in the universal sign of hello, then made his way over. "Hey Bo," he said to me.

David knew my name was not Bo, but we both knew David couldn't remember yesterday, much less anyone's name. So in the interest of politeness and to save time, David called everyone Bo. And everyone obliged because we all liked David very much, even if the porch light in his head was usually off.

"Hey David," I said.

He offered a hand that was stuffed full of napkins from the Dairy Queen down the road. We both stared at it, perplexed, until David realized he had extended the wrong arm. Then he offered the other, this one caked with dirt and sweat. I shook that one.

"How ya doin'?" I asked him.

"Fair," he said. "Shame about ol' Danny."

"It is."

"How's she holdin' up?" he asked. He looked in Helen's direction. She didn't see him, but the Old Man did. And smiled, both to him and to me.

"She seems okay," I said. "You know how tough Helen is. But she's hurting inside, I can tell you that. Pastor Charlie's been trying to help her through the night, but he just doesn't seem to be helping much. Guess there's hurtin' that words can't get through."

"Uh-huh." David looked at her for a few more seconds and then turned back to me. "Okay Bo, I'll see ya around. You have a good 'un."

"All right," I said, too late and to no one. David was already walking over to Helen. He removed the ragged John Deere cap from his wet head and bowed like he'd just been granted an audience with the Queen.

The Old Man bent over, studying David first, then Helen, then David again. Then he straightened and looked at me with an approving smile. Twenty minutes passed. Neither David nor Helen moved, and not a word passed between them.

Pastor Charlie returned to see his seat taken and decided to try comforting other members of the Layman family. After a dozen or so more people had failed at getting through to Helen—and after I decided I didn't have much to lose—I made my way over. The caterpillar/butterfly thing? I knew that wouldn't work. I chose the normal over the profound.

"Helen," I said, "I'm so sorry for your loss."

Helen did exactly as I thought she would—she nodded and smiled and stared. As did David. The Old Man, too.

I turned to go, pausing at the entranceway to say good-bye to Jenny. I saw David rise to leave out of the corner of my eye. As he did, Helen reached out and touched his arm. And then she did something she had not done the entire night.

Helen spoke.

"Thank you, David," she said. "Thank you."

"Yes'm," he whispered.

He walked off then, leaving Helen with the first real smile she'd had all night.

I met David in the parking lot as he was heading toward his rusted Chevy truck, whistling what was either an Alan Jackson song or the theme from *Magnum, P.I.*

"I'll see ya, David," I said.

"Yeah Bo," he answered, "I'll see ya." He took a few more steps, paused, and then added, "Hey Bo?"

"Yeah?"

"Can you take these things for me?" He handed me the balled-up Dairy Queen napkins he'd been carrying. "I don't got no use for them. I got them for..."

" . . . Helen," I said.

"Yeah, Helen. Just in case she needed them, you know? But I reckon she didn't need them after all, huh?"

"I guess not," I said, taking them.

He opened the driver's side door and hoisted himself up and in. It took four turns of the ignition to get the truck going.

"Have a good 'un," he yelled over the engine noise.

"Yeah, David. Have a good 'un."

I watched as he puttered out of the parking lot toward home and tried to comprehend what had just happened. When I reached my own truck at the end of the parking lot, I found the old man sitting on the tailgate staring at the stars. I took a seat next to him.

"I love the nights here," he said. "Everything just seems so . . . close."

"Close is good," I said.

"Close is *very* good," he answered, and then pointed toward the funeral home. "But that's another lesson for another time. Still trying to figure out what happened in there?"

I leaned back on my hands and nodded.

"The world can pretty much be divided into two kinds of people, Andy—the Pastor Charlies and the David Walkers. The Pastor Charlies are the gifted and the intelligent, the ones who seem to have been given a little bit extra from God. They stand in the pulpits and reign in the boardrooms. They make your laws and cure your sicknesses. They're different. Special. Needed by God and by man.

"And the David Walkers? They're the people who grow your food and pump your gas and teach your kids. A lot of them look with awe upon the Pastor Charlies of the world. They want the smarts or the looks or the power. They think that unless they somehow get those things, they'll be pretty useless to do anything of great importance for God or the world or themselves. But try as they might, most eventually come to the realization that a David Walker will always be a David Walker, and there isn't much anybody can do about it."

"Well, that just stinks, then," I said.

"You think? Really?"

I shrugged. "There are times when I wonder what I could've been if things had been different. If my folks hadn't died and I'd stayed in the city." I left off the part about him not being there, about what I could maybe have had then. But I didn't want him to hear that. It would come out wrong no matter how I said it.

"Andy, it wasn't Pastor Charlie who comforted Helen tonight. He might have impressed her with his insights and helped her with his wisdom before, but that didn't matter much when she needed it the most. Helen didn't need pontification, she needed company. That's what David gave her. And everyone is here on this earth for no other reason than that— to love and stay close. To work and pray and make things better for as many as they can in the best way they know. Folks don't need a Ph.D. to do that."

"Maybe I should try to be more like David and less like Charlie, then," I said.

"I think that is a capital idea," he answered. He patted my shoulder. I felt nothing but a quiet breeze. "You remember this night, what he did. You take that wad of napkins he gave you and put it in your box. On top, where you can see it plain. It'll mean more later than it does right now."

"Why's that?" I asked him.

"Because right now you have all you need. But the day's coming when you'll have to realize you need all you have."

I wanted to say more. Should have, maybe. But I didn't. The Old Man looked at me and smiled, and then he was gone.

17

Needed by God and Man

What do you think he meant by that?"

It was a counselor's question, no doubt. One designed to probe the inner workings of a patient's broken and confused mind in order to get to the truth within. But Elizabeth wasn't the one who asked it.

I did.

Despite the ease by which she drew me out from behind the false safety of my own self (and despite the pitter-patter she made me feel in places no woman had since Caroline), Elizabeth had until that point been no different than anyone else in my life. I had given to her as I had given to everyone, just more. That remained the extent of things. I saw no risk in the giving of myself to others, whether that giving took the shape of time or attention. But I never took. It was only in the act of taking that we were bonded to another. Whatever we took we then had a responsibility to carry, however burdensome it might be. My question to Elizabeth was not merely an invitation for her opinion, it was a request for her wisdom. To take from it. The meaning behind those eight words was lost on neither of us.

"I don't know, Andy," she said. "That seems like a strange thing to say. Having what you need and needing what you have seems like two ways of saying one thought. Did you ask him later on what he meant by that?"

"I tried. He'd never say. But I think he was talking about now."

"You mean your accident?"

I was afraid to say more.

"Do you think that's two ways of saying one thought?" I asked her.

"Do you?"

"I did. Not sure now."

I rubbed my eyes and offered a sigh that was heavier than I'd intended. The only clock in the room was behind me, which seemed to be the worst place in the world for it. Then I realized that time had little relevance for the sick and the dying. I knew it was late. Maybe in more ways than one.

"Are you tired?" Elizabeth asked.

"More weary, but I'm fine. I like the company."

"Me, too."

Elizabeth's hands wandered to the box itself rather than the contents. She ran her fingers along its edges, pondering what it all meant. How could she know? Her with all the training and experience. How could she make sense of my life?

"I don't know," I said.

"You don't know what?"

"I don't know what all that stuff means. It's not like that box holds my life. I've had bigger moments that taught me more important things, at least by my reckoning. But those things in there, those were the times he said mattered. And I don't know why."

"We'll get there," she said. "You and I. Together."

Elizabeth took her hands from the box and wrapped them around mine.

"He told me God sent you," I said.

"What?"

"The Old Man. He said I should let you help me because God sent you to me. Do you believe that?"

"Do you?"

"I don't want to answer that, Elizabeth," I said. "I want you to."

Whether it was the weariness or the lights or neither, I could have sworn a tear was in her eye. "Yes, Andy. I believe that."

Outside, the nurses caught their second wind as the end of their shift drew closer. There was laughter and the smell of more coffee being made. But for a long time the only noise in my room was the beeping of my heart monitor. Those small valleys of quiet that had been peppered into our conversations were no longer evidence of the space between us. They had now instead blossomed into dialogues of another sort, the unspeakable words of two hearts that longed to say more but knew the time was not yet right. Elizabeth and I held one another in a gaze that was more knowing than longing, tethered to one another by the small grins on our faces.

"We should continue," Elizabeth finally said.

I nodded only because I had no choice. I'd have swum naked in that silence forever.

She rifled through the contents again, picking her prize. "Okay," she said. "I've been saving this one. I love it."

The baseball cap she held up had never been shaped or worn. Even the price tag dangled from the bill, obscuring a bit of her face. The white overlapping NY seemed perfect in the sea of the navy blue everywhere else.

"Are you a Yankee fan?" I asked.

"I'm a baseball fan," she answered.

"Well, that hat doesn't really have anything to do with baseball."

"It doesn't?"

"No. But I have to say it's a bit comical."

Elizabeth smiled.

18

The Cap

Leave me *alone*, you freaking *nut!*"

The words were loud enough on their own, but they were magnified even more as they bounced off the walls of the entrance. The few people making their way in or out, myself included, could only stare.

There were five of us at the moment, but I knew our small crowd wouldn't be small for long. Of all the instinctual abilities granted to humanity, few were more ingrained and absolute than the predisposition to gawk at an unfolding spectacle. We enjoyed peeking into the suffering of others, if only to convince ourselves that even though things in our lives might be bad, there was at least one other person in the world who had it worse. If only for a little while.

The person who had it worse than everyone else, at least in that place and in that moment, was a man. One of two principal actors in a drama that was growing increasingly passionate and voluminous. The other was a woman who seemed more than a little agitated. The two stood on opposite sides of the doorway no more than five feet apart. Her face held a motionless scowl that could turn holy water into vinegar. He countered with a confused, caught-in-the-Twilight-Zone stare.

Men do not usually enjoy the mall. It's the shopping and the crowds and the excessive spending. Not me, though. While I could probably think of few things I would rather do than shop, I actually enjoyed the mall. It was a great place to exercise that aforementioned human curiosity. I'd seen some strange sights there, sights like the one unfolding before me. Which, by the way, happened to be a bit stranger than usual. Because I was used to being the watch*er*, not the watch*ee*.

I was the confused man with the caught-in-the-Twilight-Zone stare.

I was the freaking nut.

My primary purpose for driving the thirty miles or so over the mountain to the city that day was not to people-watch. My intentions were much more functional—I needed a new hat. I wavered a bit in going, since it was to be a solo trip. I hadn't seen the Old Man in a while, but even then I didn't reckon he counted as real company. I figured I would need company for a trip like that. Charlottesville was a very cosmopolitan, very hip, and very liberal city. And I was a very country, very simple, and very conservative man. The two often clashed, sometimes with disastrous results. But in the end greed won out over better judgment, and I went anyway. I really wanted that hat.

I arrived early—except for a few employees and the dedicated troupe of elderly walkers, I pretty much had the place to myself. The smell of fancy coffee lured me upwind to the food court. I studied the menu. Between the fancy words and the fancier prices, I decided I'd better not.

"When in Rome," the Old Man said.

I turned around and there he was, the very picture of a fancy men's magazine cover. Pinstriped suit and fedora, silk tie and pocket square. Both just right.

"Where you been?" I asked him.

"I got a lot on my plate, Andy," he said. "There's always something going on in the spirit world, stuff behind the scenes. And don't ask me, because I can't say. Besides, I don't want to be getting too familiar. Might make the magic go away."

I didn't know what any of that meant, but I figured standing in line at the fancy coffee place was neither the time nor the place. I stole a glance to make sure no one was looking at me and said, "You look nice."

"Like I said, when in Rome."

I bought my fancy coffee—mochalottasomething, which the man with the twelve earrings behind the counter said was a best seller—and guided the Old Man toward the sports store. We walked and I sipped, and in the process I decided the only difference between the five-dollar coffee in Charlottesville and the fifty-cent coffee I served at the gas station was a prettier cup. Lesson learned. I bought my hat and made my way back up the mall, Old Man in tow. All was well.

He said something from behind as I reached the three big sets of doors leading to the parking lot. When I turned to answer I saw a blur of a woman rounding the corner. Huffing and puffing and mumbling to herself. Her orange sweatshirt proudly announced her attendance at the University of Virginia. Three giant Gap bags, a pink-striped Victoria's Secret box, a cup of coffee, a big pretzel, and a purse were all haphazardly arranged in her arms. Her lower lip stuck out and she let out a puff of air to shift a strand of brown hair that had fallen over her right eye. She steamrolled toward me while trying to look at the expensive watch on her left wrist.

"Watch out behind ya," I told him. "Don't think you can get run over, but this lady might be able to anyways."

We exited the mall and I stepped to my right, holding the door open with my left hand.

She charged ahead, still trying to check the time and still not quite doing it, then glanced up just long enough to gauge her distance to the door. Which, thanks to me, was already open.

I noticed the flash of confusion on her face. She kept racing forward. I looked at her. She looked at me. I smiled. She didn't.

And then she stopped. And by that I mean in an instant—moving and then *NOT*, like the Road Runner did in those old cartoons. It was so fast that the inertia kept her hair and bags going forward until she jerked them back.

"Excuse me," she said.

I kept smiling, thinking she had somehow misread the situation. "I got it," I said, holding up my free hand. "Come on out."

"Excuse me," she repeated. The tone in her voice suggested I was the one who had misread the situation.

So I said "I got the door" again nice and slow, because sometimes that's how you have to talk to college kids. "Come on."

Her face contorted into a look that was half indignation and half surprise. She blurted out a *humph* that served as both a warning and a way to get that testy bit of brown hair away from her eyes once more. She fumbled with her bags to free a finger, which she pointed at me. I had the feeling it wasn't the finger she really wanted to use.

"Don't you hold that door for *me*," she said, eyes bulging. "I am perfectly capable of opening the door without the assistance of anyone else. Particularly someone like *you*."

First thought: *Someone like me?*

Second thought: *I should've stayed home.*

"I'm sure you can, ma'am," I said. "But I just thought—"

"—I don't care what you *thought*! What is this, big strong guy rescues puny helpless woman? I don't need your help, big strong guy. I just need you to *get out of my way*."

"But ma'am, I didn't mean any—"

And that was when I was cut off by her "freaking nut" comment. Plus a few others I don't really care to repeat.

The woman's rant had escalated in decibels and language enough to become quite the attention magnet. Most everyone entering or exiting the doors paused to watch. She looked like an idiot, I thought. Then I considered the fact that standing there holding the door open probably didn't make me look like Einstein much myself. And I couldn't blame the spectators for spectating. I would have stopped and watched, too.

I looked over to where the Old Man stood. As his attention was currently on the small piece of lint he was trying to pick from his sleeve, I doubted I could count on any assistance from him. The thought did occur to me that maybe I really had done something wrong. That was followed by another thought that I had done no such thing. My grandparents raised me to be a gentleman. A gentleman loved his God and his country, said "sir" and "ma'am," and took his cap off during the national anthem. And a gentleman held the door for people when they were walking through with an armful of stuff.

"LET GO OF THAT DOOR LET IT GO NOW," she screamed. And stomped her foot for effect.

I rubbed my beard and thought. The rational side of me said this was no big deal, that if the lady wanted to go through the door on her own, I should let her. But the irrational side demanded I stand my ground, partly out of a deep ethical conviction that it was the right thing, and partly because I had decided that no yuppie college girl was going to tell me what to do.

I tried the Old Man again. The piece of lint was now gone. He looked at me and pulled a coin out of his pocket, positioned it with his hand, and flipped it.

The coin was still on its upward motion when he said, "Do you need to call it?"

I shook my head. The coin disappeared into the air. I turned back to the lady.

"I ain't gonna do it," I said.

Her face flushed to the point where I was worried she might spontaneously combust. I glanced toward the crowd, which had now swelled to at least a dozen nosy souls. More vocal, too. There were now mixed chuckles and catcalls. More than one person wondered aloud what the big deal was anyway. One voice pronounced the whole situation as stupid. But it was not, and that was the one point upon which the lady and I agreed.

I decided to try a diplomatic approach.

"Ma'am," I said, "I'm not trying to play a big macho thing here. I just thought that with the pretzel and purse and the unmentionables there, you might appreciate a little help."

"I don't need your help," she said, though she had to re-position the weight in her arms to say it. "I don't *want* your help. Do you understand me? I am not a helpless child. I am a *woman*. And I am perfectly capable of living my own life with-out you or anyone else sticking their nose into it."

And on she went. And on and on. That lady screamed at me like Hitler behind a podium. And as was usually the case with people who yelled hysterically at me, I started to tune her out. Started thinking about who this woman was and what she was trying to say exactly and when she would stop. About where our society was headed and why people had to be so doggone prideful and mean.

" . . . and don't you *ever* think otherwise, do you understand me?" she said.

I had neither the desire nor the inclination to tell her that I did not understand because I hadn't heard a word she said. So I just stood there and watched her glare, waiting for another puny retort. So, too, did the crowd, all of whom were no doubt mentally hedging bets on what would happen next.

But by then I was convinced she would stand there and lec-ture me until the Rapture if she had to. I was tired. Tired of holding that door open and tired of being in the city. I just wanted to go back over the mountains to Mattingly where the normal folk lived.

I took a deep breath and said as humbly as I could, "Ma'am, I am truly sorry for offending you. I didn't mean it. You're right. You can handle this quite well on your own."

She started to say something else, but the door closed and cut her off. I looked to where the Old Man stood. No one was there.

There was disappointment on the faces of the men in the small crowd, either because they wanted to see me wait her out or because they wanted to see her slap me. The faces of the women were mixed. They knew all along there could re-ally be no winner.

I glanced back inside. The woman was still high above

me on her soapbox, mouthing words that were surely meant to undermine both my honor and gender. No one, though, seemed interested anymore. Satisfied that she had just won a monumental battle for women's rights, she adjusted herself, turned around, and pushed the door open with her hip.

And then she tripped. It was not the sort of slow-motion tumble you'd expect, either. This was quick, almost instantaneous, as if irony had sprouted arms and decided to clothesline her. Coffee and pretzel and purse and unmentionables scattered in all directions. She hit the concrete with a loud thud.

There was silence all around.

The woman sat momentarily confused in a heap of freshly stained Gap T-shirts and a rather attractive nightgown. I barely managed to keep a straight face.

"You should help her up," the Old Man said from beside me. "Jesus would help her up. It'd be a turn-the-other-cheek kind of thing."

I shook my head no at first, then sighed and took a step toward her. Laser beams shot from her eyes and bore into my head.

"However," the Old Man clarified, "you're not Jesus."

I agreed. And from the look of things none of the other folks still milling about were Jesus, either, because no one moved.

The woman jerked herself up and then shot back down. She gathered the merchandise that had spilled around her, shoving her purse into a shopping bag and her pretzel into the now-empty coffee cup. She rubbed her sweatshirt in a futile attempt to erase the coffee stain, which managed only to weave it more into the material. Then she darted away like an Olympic walker.

The crowd began to disperse, some heading to the parking lot and others into the mall. One man opened the door for his wife, who laughed as she walked through.

"Well," the Old Man said, "I guess we've done all the damage we can do here. What say we head home?"

"Oh, so *now* you're giving me advice. Where were you a little bit ago? You could've warned me she'd go nuts."

He shrugged as we made our way to my truck. "My job isn't to keep you out of trouble, Andy. It's to point out things you're going to need someday. Speaking of which, you'd better hang onto that hat. That was one of them. Besides, you did the right thing."

"I really don't think I'm gonna need *that*," I said. "Did you see her? She was mad just because I was a guy."

"Oh, I don't think so," he said. "Maybe. Then again, maybe she's had some rough dealings with men before. Or maybe she's just a college kid who wants to prove she can survive on her own. She might have done the same thing if there was a woman holding that door instead of you. You're seldom privy to the stories behind the actions, Andy."

"Seemed to me that she was just naturally mean."

"Remember when Cain killed Abel and then God asked him where his brother was? Cain said, 'I don't know. Am I my brother's keeper?' That's the first question the Bible ever records a human asking. I think there's something to that."

I unlocked the door and climbed in. The Old Man was already in the passenger seat.

"So are we?" I asked. "I mean, we're all about the individual. We're free to pretty much do whatever we want so long as we don't break any laws. Our lives are our own. So how much responsibility do we have toward one another? A lot? None? As I recall, God never answered that question."

"Sure He did." He cleared his throat and raised a finger. "'As I have loved you, so you must love one another.'"

"Oh come *on*," I said. "I have to *love* that woman? Because if I do, you can forget it. And I am mostly sure that whatever feelings she has for me can definitely not be characterized as loving."

"But you did love her," he said. "You tried to help. The sort of love you're supposed to have for others is love that's a verb, not a noun. It's a love that *does* something rather than *is* something. Remember that. That'll come in handy, too. And there's one more thing."

"What's that?" I asked him.

"Sometimes love isn't just caring for others. Sometimes it's allowing yourself to be cared for, too."

19

My Brother's Keeper

Knock knock," Kim said from the doorway.

Elizabeth and I both looked up and smiled.

"Hey there, Kimmie. You still here at this hour?"

"Seven to seven, Big Guy. It's the life of an underappreciated nurse. Just checking to make sure you're feeling okay."

"Oh," I said, "I'm just enjoying the benefits of your fine staff."

Kim looked toward Elizabeth and smiled. "Good," she said.

"Anything we can do for you?" I asked her.

"You mean other than getting some sleep? Because you should try. I know you've pretty much been in and out for a few days, but your body still needs to heal itself. Best way to do that is with rest."

"Yes'm," I said. "But there's healing on the outside, and there's healing on the *inside*. Right now I'm concentrating on the latter."

I cut a glance at Elizabeth, who didn't even bother to cover her face and hide her smile.

"Well, I know better than to try and convince Andy Sommerville of anything he's not interested in being convinced of," Kim said. "Any pain or discomfort?" she asked.

"My face is itching a little," I told her.

"Thought it might be. I talked to the doctor on call a few hours ago. He said if it got too bad I could change the bandages for you. Maybe we should plan on that in a little while?"

"Sounds perfect. How about you?" I asked. "Any pain or

discomfort? You know, from the . . ." I made another finger tele-phone and held it to my ear.

Kim stole a look at her shoes and pursed her lips, signs I took as reminding herself that a good nurse never involves her patients in her own personal problems. But that was a minor technicality in my particular case. The truth was that if there were a gas station counter and not a hospital bed between us, Kim would be spilling her guts like any other customer. Because Andy Sommerville was the guy people talked to about themselves, if for no other reason than the fact that they knew he didn't have anyone else to tell what he'd been told.

She measured her words, realizing that while talking with me was fine, talking *to* me was another thing altogether in those circumstances. We were not on opposite sides of the cash register on a sleepy morning in Mattingly; we were in a hospital, and she was charged with my care. Kim wanted to talk but couldn't, so she compromised by trying to say a lot with a little.

"Boys have always been after me," she said. "I'd be a fool if I said I didn't like that. But sometimes I think God made me to just be by myself, you know? Not everyone has to chase someone else's idea of a fairy tale. I mean, you've never been married, right, Andy? And you're just as happy as you can be."

Elizabeth snickered into her fist but low enough for only me to hear it. I tried not looking at her. I did, anyway. The snicker had little to do with it.

"There's a lot Owen can offer, I guess," Kim said. "Least, that's what Mom says. But I don't want to be getting something and having to trade off a part of me in the process. Does that make sense?"

"It does," I said.

That was all the validation Kim needed, because she stopped looking at her toes and her mouth relaxed into a smile. She nodded and said, "Alrighty then, I'll let you get back to your healin'."

"Purely professional, I swear," I said, cutting another look at Elizabeth. The two of us chuckled as Kim left.

"That was nice of you," Elizabeth said. "Listening to her like that. It's quite a gift."

"Guess you're just rubbing off. Kimmie's taken care of me. The least I can do is try and do a little of that for her."

"That's been a difficult lesson for you to learn, hasn't it? Allowing yourself to be cared for?" She leaned forward to reveal what didn't turn out to be a shocking secret. "I know you're feeling more than an itchy face."

"Lots of people here are worse off than I am," I said. "I can handle it." As if to reiterate that point, the sound of Mr. Alexander's coughs came from the hallway. They settled into a long and pitiful moan.

"Can you?" she asked.

"I think a healthy sense of self-reliance is a good thing for a person to have."

"For you though, right? Because you're more than willing to offer help to someone else. Everything you've told me so far has told me that. You've just *shown* me that. You're not closed off from the world, Andy. You're just not a part of it."

"All I wanted to do was be a friend to Kim, who is a nice lady." I realized at that point that I still held the baseball cap in my hand. "And as for her," I said, holding the hat up and then setting it down into the box, "I just wanted to hold the door for someone who needed it. Where's the crime in that?"

"There isn't any," she said. "But I think you missed something there. Who knows, maybe she *was* just a mean lady. But maybe the Old Man was right. Maybe she was just struggling with something, whether it was something that was happening then or something that happened before. People's stories make them do unloving things sometimes."

"I was brought up to believe a man should stand on his own two feet," I said.

"But you don't. You *don't*, Andy. You might not need friends and you might not need a wife, but you need the Old Man."

"*Needed*," I corrected.

Elizabeth *mea culpa*'d by showing me the palms of her

hands, then lowered them to turn the ball cap upside down and fill the inside with Santa's letter and Rudolph's pine needles, Mother Thelma's cross, and Willa's card. The other objects she placed inside were Ms. Massachusetts's fingernail and the golf tee, ones we'd yet to discuss. "Do you know what I've noticed in these stories you've told me?" she asked. "You like him. You really do. He's the closest thing to a family or a friend that you have. You open up to him but not to anyone else. Probably because you don't think there's anything to lose. But when you're done remembering and you're back here, all that goes away. What did he do to you, Andy?"

I stared out of the wide windows along the far wall. The city unfolded beyond them, sprawling out like spiderwebs. Tiny pinpricks of light pocked the night sky in a celestial dance toward morning. And there, hung in the black like a beacon of hope and taunting, sat the Big Dipper and the

(second star from the handle, Andy. That's where God's answered prayers come from)

memory of seeing that star wink just before my answer came.

"He wasn't there," I whispered.

Elizabeth was silent.

"I trusted him, and he let me down."

"How can an angel let you down?" she asked.

"What?"

"You told me he was an angel. An answered prayer. Angels cannot let people down, Andy. They're not people. So you have a choice to make. Either the Old Man really is an angel and his not being there was a part of some bigger plan, or he's just a collection of neurons in your brain that didn't fire when you thought they should."

"You tell me how it is that *this* had to happen to me." I pointed to my bandages and then held up my right hand to show her the pus oozing from beneath the tape and gauze. "You tell me what kind of bigger plan would involve *this*. And *worse*."

"What 'worse,' Andy?"

"He *killed* Eric."

"Who did?"

"The Old Man."

Elizabeth leaned closer to me.

"Who's Eric, Andy? Who is Eric and what happened to him?"

Tears welled in my eyes and my lips began to quiver. The memories came back, but not in the fractured and sporadic images you see in the movies. I remembered everything. Everything from the knife to the fire to the blood. Eric on the floor, reaching for me...

"I can't, Elizabeth," I said. "Please don't make me. Please don't."

Elizabeth wrapped me in her arms. Her long ponytail spilled over me to form a shelter from the truth she was determined to pry from my heart.

"Hush now," she told me.

"Please don't make me," I said again.

"Listen to me, Andy," she said, pulling me closer into her. "You feel like you're being buried. I know that. You feel like you've been abandoned by the person and the God you've clung to your entire life. But you haven't. You have to believe that. You have to believe that no matter how you feel and no matter how much you think otherwise, you are exactly where you need to be. You are not being buried, Andy Sommerville. You are being planted."

Her sleeve soaked the tears dripping from my eyes, and I collapsed into it under the weight of my own regrets. This was not how things were supposed to be. This was not how my life was supposed to unfold.

She let go and settled me back into my pillow so she could look into my eyes.

"There is something to what's in that box, Andy. I know it doesn't seem to be anything to you, but there is no randomness with God. Everything means something. It doesn't matter if it's as small as a pickle in a Christmas tree or as big as what put you in this hospital bed. I need you to believe that."

"I need to believe that too," I said.

"Good."

Elizabeth leaned back into her chair and took a deep breath.

"Why did this have to happen to me?" I said. "Was it because of my prayer? Was the Old Man right when he said he was as much a curse as a blessing?"

"No, of course not. I think he was just trying to say that you'll always carry a certain sadness. But it's a holy sadness. A *good* sadness. I really think so. You just have to learn to see things a little differently."

"Again," I added. "I've already learned to see things differently once."

"You have?"

I nodded and reached back into the hat and retrieved a sliver of fingernail, still glistening in a bright and gaudy red. "Don't worry," I said. "It's fake, and the owner is safe. I guess she's safe, anyway."

"I'll admit I've been wondering about that one," Elizabeth said. "The Old Man told you to keep someone's fingernail?"

"It's fake," I said, thinking that somehow made everything sensible. "Besides, that was the only thing left by the time it was all over with."

"By the time what was all over with?"

"Well, you know how I said folks get along fine in Mattingly? That's true enough, but that doesn't mean there isn't a little something lurking underneath in some people. One of those people is Michael Potter."

"Is he a friend of yours?" she asked.

"No, not really. Maybe. I don't know. Just a customer. Big guy—six and a half feet tall, maybe three hundred pounds. A monster, but nice. To me, anyway. He stops by Saturday mornings in his beat-up Caddy for gas and a fluid check. Every Saturday, never fails. Always tips me five bucks for my trouble."

"He does seem nice," Elizabeth said. "Is the fingernail his?"

I said "No," which I followed with another snort. "No way. That fingernail belongs to Ms. Massachusetts."

20

The Fingernail

Michael pulled up to his customary gas pump that Saturday morning around seven. I watched him from the counter and finished my coffee and the newspaper. It would be another minute—maybe two—before he actually managed to hoist himself out of his car. Michael was never one to do much of anything quickly, what with that infernal gravity always fighting him.

"Got a customer out there," the Old Man called from his booth. He hadn't been there all morning—hadn't been around much at all of late. The serious look in his eyes told me this was not a social call.

"Still got a bit before he gets himself situated," I said. I traded the bad news on the front page for the good news on the sports page.

"Maybe better get on out there anyways."

I did, though that action was preceded by a heavy sigh that was normally reserved for teenage boys who'd just been told by their fathers to go out and cut the grass. I had managed to put on my happy face by the time I reached the double doors though, and I said "Mornin', Michael" like I was surprised by his visit.

"Same to ya, Andy," he answered. He waved and popped the hood of his car in one motion. "Might need a little oil this morning."

I doubted that, since I'd seen Michael's Caddy down at Bobby Barnes's shop for an oil change not four days earlier. I set the nozzle and walked around to the hood anyway. Michael was already there, looking at the motor like he knew what he was seeing.

"How's the shoe business nowadays?" I asked him.

"Fair," he said. "Got a sale goin' on boots, if you're interested."

"Might be," I said.

For the last twenty-five years, Michael Potter had spent his weekdays in one of the shoe stores up in the Stanley mall. I could never remember which. He was good at his trade (if you could call selling shoes a trade), though I'd heard he'd recently been turned down for a promotion that was given to someone else.

I pulled the dipstick and didn't even bother to wipe it. The oil was a bright amber and stopped exactly at the full line.

"You're good, Mike."

He nodded, satisfied, and cupped his thumbs between his suspenders. It was always suspenders with Michael, bright red ones that clashed with the brown belt he liked to wear. I always thought it was the very definition of insecurity to have both a belt and a backup.

I'd just topped off his tank when the BMW pulled into the lot. Brand new, bright yellow, tinted windows. Very expensive. The car came to a halt directly in front of the doors, its engine kept running. Out climbed an attractive black woman who checked her watch as she walked through the doors. Michael watched as she made her way past the counter to the coffeepot. I watched as the Old Man walked around and joined her.

"Who's that?" he asked. He let go of one suspender to shield his eyes against the car's impeccable wax job. The gleam coming off the paint looked like a small sun.

"Must be a stranger passing through," I said. "Ain't nobody around here driving a car like that."

Michael eased around to get a look at the license plate. "Lookie there," he said.

I followed his eyes and craned my neck to make out the state amidst a slew of letters and numbers.

"Massachusetts?" I asked.

"Yankee." Michael bent his head and shook it. I swear he would've spit if he had thought about it. "I swear, when they gonna shut the gates and stop the Yankee flood? They all call us rubes, but they sure don't mind comin' on down here to retire and enjoy the simple life."

Ms. Massachusetts had finished fixing her cup and was making her way to the cash register. The Old Man followed close behind and settled back into his booth. Michael and I walked toward the doors. He slowed as he passed the front of the car and stole another look at the license plate. Just to be sure, I assumed.

"Massachusetts," he said again. "Probably a liberal feminist lesbian who belongs to the ACLU, too."

I grabbed the door and whispered, "Reckon we should be on our best behavior then, huh?"

Michael walked in and waited while I made my way around the counter to the register. The Old Man said nothing.

Ms. Massachusetts was drumming her fingers on the Marlboro placemat in front of her.

"Mornin', ma'am," I said.

The woman smiled and offered an exhale that was either impatience or stress. Or both.

"This is all I need," she said. She checked her watch once more.

"All right. I'll get with you as soon as I take care of this man here." I punched a few keys on the register and then turned to Michael: "Anything else, Mike?"

"No," he said, "I guess that'll—"

"Excuse me," the lady said.

"Fifteen bucks, Mike," I said to him, then I turned back to her: "Yes, ma'am?"

Her long fingernails had stopped their tapping. The blank look that had greeted me at first had now turned into half of a snarl, and it looked as though the other half would be following shortly.

"What are you doing?" she demanded.

"Well, I'm just waitin' on Mike here." I eyed Michael, but he was eyeing her. "Is there a problem?"

"Yes," she said. "Yes, there is a problem. I'm in a hurry and I have to be in Richmond in two hours." The strong voice she'd thus far exhibited cracked under a quivering bottom lip. "My niece is having surgery, and it's frightening surgery. I want to see her before she goes under."

"I'm real sorry about that, ma'am," I said. "Sure hope everything goes well with her."

Michael handed me a twenty. I took it without knowing I did.

"I was here first," she said. Louder again.

I looked at Michael's money in my hand. He was staring at her and then me. The look on his face was one of puzzlement.

"Sorry," I told her. "Just a second, promise."

The drawer popped open and I dug for Michael's change. Ms. Massachusetts let out a small sigh that was followed by a chuckle, then she shook her head. "Oh, okay," she said. "I get it now."

"What's that you get now?" I asked. I started to hand Michael his money.

"You think I'm just an ignorant porch monkey."

My hand froze halfway to Michael's. "Excuse me?"

The Old Man finally spoke then. "Andy?" he asked. "'Anger, if not restrained, is frequently more hurtful to us than the injury that provokes it.' Seneca said that."

I ignored him. The woman did not ignore me.

"I will not excuse you," she shot back. "I knew sooner or later I'd get a taste of some Southern hospitality around here. I just expected it to be from some corn-farming good ol' boy and not a redneck like you."

Michael opened his mouth to say something, but I cut him off with my hand. I slid his change across the counter and turned to face her.

"Lady," I said, "I'm real sorry about your circumstances, but you can't come in here actin' all high and mighty talking to me like that. You don't know me, or you'd know better. I don't know where you get off—"

"Where *I* get off?" she screamed. "What, I'm not worth your precious time? You expect me to sit here like some quiet little servant girl who should know her place? Well excuse me for speaking my mind, Massa!"

"What did you say, ma'am?" I asked. I looked to Michael for help, but his eyes were riveted on her. My heart was thumping, ready to jump out of my chest. I felt blood race from my head and gather somewhere in my gut, pooling there in a wave of nausea. This lady—this *stranger*—had just all but called me a racist. Me. Andy Sommerville. The guy who'd always treated everyone the same. The fact that she was black had nothing to do with it. The fact that she didn't know me but had just made that snap judgment did. My conversation with Ms. Massachusetts had reached its apogee and was now beginning to spiral downward. I had two choices. I could either swallow my pride and follow the philosophy of the customer always being right, or I could not.

My anger chose for me—not.

"All due respect, lady, but if you'd have kept your mouth shut, you'd be halfway to the interstate by now."

"Yeah," Michael said, "I don't know how you people—"

"—'you people'?" she said.

You people? I thought. I peered over to the Old Man and studied the sad look in his eyes.

Michael leaned every bit of his three hundred pounds onto the counter and glared at her. Their eyes met for a few seconds, then she humphed and turned back to me.

"I know what you were doing. You waited on him first because he's one of your own. That's what all you people do."

You people? I thought again.

"I what?"

"Did you refuse to wait on me first because I'm black?" she asked me.

"Did you ask me that because I'm white?" I asked her.

Ms. Massachusetts's eyes shriveled into her head. I wasn't sure if that reaction was because she thought I was being obnoxious or because I had actually made a good point. Whichever the case, she slammed her fist onto the counter and then stormed through the doors, leaving her coffee behind. Her BMW gunned its engine and she sped out of the parking lot, leaving a thin layer of rubber along Route 320.

Michael and I stood motionless. Even the Old Man seemed at a loss for words. I took her cup of coffee and poured it into the trash.

"What just happened?" I asked.

I didn't care which of the two answered, but it turned out to be Michael: "You just stood up to a genuine, honest-to-God New England liberal darkie," he said. He slapped a giant hand onto the counter. "You tore her up and spit her out!"

"What?" I asked him.

"She was prolly a God-hatin' Nazi, too."

"Huh?"

"I always knew there was somethin' sensible about you, Andy." Michael beamed like some kind of proud father. "We're alike, you and me. We both been around long enough to know them people need to be put back in their place."

" 'Them people'?"

"Yeah, you know. The niggers."

My jaw fell open. "The huh?"

"*They*," he said, pointing out toward the road, "ain't worth nothing but trouble. You can see it in them, the way they walk and talk and act. Like that old Johnny Johnson. That's why they gave him my promotion, you know that? Just b'cause he's *black*. They *told* me that, Andy. Now you know what I gotta do? I gotta smell feet until the day I retire. Do you know how bad people's feet smell, Andy?"

I didn't. And I supposed the question was rhetorical, because Michael didn't give me a chance to answer anyway.

"Folks'll only take so much of them before they realize

them people outgrew their usefulness about a hundred years ago."

I stood by the trash can utterly speechless. I could not believe what this man had just said.

I looked to the Old Man—"'All looks yellow to a jaundiced eye.' Alexander Pope," he said.

Michael gathered his keys and turned to leave. Halfway to the door, he turned back.

"Dang, Andy. In all this excitement I forgot your tip." He gave me back the five dollars I'd given him as change, then stopped. "You know what? You deserve a little extra today." He pulled out a ten as well and tossed both on the counter. "You have a good 'un, Andy."

Michael walked through the door with one last "That was great!" and sunk into his Cadillac. The old boat sputtered to life on the fourth turn of the key, and he puttered away in a cloud of exhaust.

I turned off the lights that evening around 7:30. Most of Mattingly was either settled in or gone out by then, and there wasn't much use in staying open. I locked both doors and the cash register and slipped the keys into my pocket. My fingers brushed against the two bills Michael had handed me earlier.

I had never really looked to see how much money Michael had given me in the past few months. Over the years I'd just thrown it all back into the register, but lately I'd been keeping them in a cigar box on the shelf. Which, I happened to notice, was now so full that the lid would no longer close all the way. It looked like a sick grin that accused me of being a party to Michael's prejudice.

I lifted the box to the counter and opened it. Crumpled and folded five-dollar bills spilled out, trying to escape. I corralled them back where they belonged

(where did they belong?)

and estimated the pile. There had to be nearly a hundred dollars there, all told.

The Old Man peered over my shoulder and said, "Better keep that." He didn't point to the money, though. He pointed to what looked like a fake piece of red plastic that had lodged itself under the placemat by the register. Ms. Massachusetts's fingernail.

"Keep it?" I asked.

"Most definitely."

I pulled it out and put it into the angel box beneath the register. I felt disgusted, though I wasn't sure if that was because I was keeping someone's fingernail or keeping her fingernail.

The Old Man pointed again. "Lotta money there."

"You got that right," I told him.

"What are you gonna do with it?" he asked, pushing himself up onto the counter beside me.

"I was gonna use it for a new fishing rod. They got some nice ones over at the Super Mart."

He studied the pile. "Looks like you're in luck, then. Plenty there for a new rod."

"Yeah," I said, "and then some. But I can't spend that money now."

The Old Man raised his eyebrows and asked, "Why's that?"

I looked at him and wondered if he really didn't know. "He's my friend. At least as good a friend as I have, anyway. We talk and joke and cuss. The man's a deacon at *church*, for crying out loud. I . . . liked him."

"That's past tense, Andy. You don't like him anymore?"

"Are you nuts? The man's a bigot. How can he in good conscience sit there in God's house and read from God's word and have faith in God's son? How could a man who says he abides by the religion of love be consumed by such hate? That ain't even possible."

The Old Man raised his eyebrows. "It isn't?"

"No, it isn't. That's like being two people. Like livin' a lie."

"You sit in a church pew every Sunday, Andy. You read God's word and have faith in God's son. But deep down you have your own prejudices too, don't you? I think most people do. That lady all but called you a racist. You know you're not and I know it, too, but you still treated her different. You know that, right?"

I didn't. Not until then. But the Old Man had a way of being a mirror to me in many ways, and everyone knows that a mirror doesn't lie. I looked in his eyes and they replayed for me everything I'd said and done in those former minutes. The way I didn't hear the pain in that woman's voice *(and if there was one thing I seemed attuned to in people, it had always been their pain)*, the way I'd shown favor to Mike. Not because he was white, but because he was from town. Because he was not from Away, as she had been.

"She was disrespecting me."

"She was hurting. People do all kinds of things when they're hurting. You're different than Michael, Andy. He's a bigot. You're not. But that doesn't necessarily mean you're better than he is. You both tend to see with your eyes, when you should see with your heart."

I looked at the pile of money, which now seemed stained with more than the dirt and use of so many countless hands. "What do you think I should do?"

The Old Man smiled and said, "Well now, there's a question I think only you can answer."

"Well lookie here," Jackie said. "Andy Sommerville? Harry, you'd better get ready 'cause the Lord's on his way."

I slid into the pew beside Harry and shook his hand. Jackie had to reach around him and pinch my cheek just to make sure her eyes were working right. They were.

"Nice to see you," she said.

"Nice to be seen," I answered.

The prayer was said and the songs were sung and the preacher began his sermon. It was a beautiful Sunday morning, the sort that made you happy to be alive. I thought of Michael in his church across town, all decked out in his Sunday best and murmuring *Amen* to the high points of his preacher's sermon. He was a broken man, confused and twisted by his own fears and biases. Not unlike us all, I supposed. And if that was the case, then maybe a church pew was the best place for him to be.

And for me as well.

It was a good sermon *(I murmured my own* amen *once or twice, which felt quite good but was an act not encouraged in my own church)*. Jackie was pleased. An offering was collected just before the benediction and placed on the altar in front of the pulpit.

If there were any questions about the bulging envelope full of five-dollar bills that found its way onto the plate, I never heard them. I felt it was a cowardly act in a way; neither Michael nor the woman with the broken fingernail ever knew of my feeble attempt at making things right.

But it still felt good in the doing.

21

Black and White

W ow," Elizabeth said.

"Yeah." I considered saying nothing more, but since this had become the closest thing to confession I'd ever gotten, I didn't. "Know what the bad thing is?"

"What's that?"

"I took some of the money and bought that fishin' pole anyway. Not the one I wanted, though. Got something cheaper."

"Why's that bad?" she asked. "It's what you honestly wanted, right? And it didn't hurt anyone."

"I guess," I said. "But it's still sitting there in the garage. Never been used."

"And how about Michael? You still see him?"

"Oh, yeah. Still every Saturday and still with the fiver for a tip. I still take it, too. I'll let them build up for a few months and take them back down to Jackie's church. But you know what? Despite it all, despite who he is, I can't help but like him still."

"Do you feel guilty about that?" she asked.

"Sometimes." I paused, not so I could think of what to say next, but how to say it. "He used to remind me of me in a way. We had a lot in common. Have, I mean. Little things that don't really matter but still hold people together, like a love of baseball. We like talking baseball. But now he reminds me of me in some bad ways, too."

"You mean the way you both put people in little boxes?" she asked. "He didn't like that woman because she was black. You didn't like her because she wasn't from town."

"I can get along with most everyone," I said, "whether they're from town or Away. At least, I thought I could. I saw that woman as a stranger rather than a person, and I missed out on a chance to help her. I don't know what I could've done. People's hurts can be a wall sometimes, and it's a wall you can't breach. If anyone knows that, it's me. But I could've done something, even if it was just getting her out the door quick so she could get to her niece. I missed that opportunity, all because I was seeing with my eyes and not my heart. I think that's why that fingernail is in my box. So I won't forget that."

Elizabeth said, "I'm sure you haven't, have you?" She glanced above my bed to the clock, then moved her hands toward the box and rattled it, taunting. "Is there anything else in here that helped you learn that lesson?"

I wiped my eyes and offered her a smile.

"Oh yeah," I said. "There was the day I found out firsthand how tough being an angel can be. Talk about a lesson in humility." I took the box and rummaged inside it. "I know it's in here somewhere," I told her, but I couldn't find it. I began emptying onto my lap the objects from the stories I'd already shared. There it was, stuck to the side. I pulled the piece of bubble gum free and held it up to her.

"Smell," I said.

She did and asked, "Watermelon?"

"Crazy, huh? All these years later, and it still smells."

22

Bubble Gum

It was not merely *a* bench, it was *my* bench, and someone else was sitting on it. Someone who I was certain did not appreciate my bench nearly as much as I did, and surely could not. And I didn't know what to do.

I went to the park that morning for no other reason than to enjoy a respite from the demands of everyday life. The air was cool and the sky a clear and deep blue. Autumn leaves had begun to fall from the oaks and maples, blanketing the almost hidden trail in a fresco of reds and yellows. A few remaining robins lingered before making their southward trip for winter. The walk was a fairly short one, no more than a few hundred yards, yet long enough to put an agreeable measure of distance between myself and the world. I slung the loaf of bread I brought along for the ducks over my shoulder and slowed within and without. The smile on my lips dimmed only slightly when I realized I was often at my best when I was alone.

As I neared the grove of pines that hid my bench, however, I began to think that perhaps I wasn't alone at all. Amid the idyllic sounds of crunches and quacks and chirps came the sound of humming. I stopped for a moment to listen, then crept forward to peek through the limbs.

That was when I saw her. On my bench.

Little girl, skinny and dark-skinned. Her feet swung like a pendulum beneath the rotting wood of the seat in an awkward cadence. She continued her indecipherable tune, pausing only for a breath to blow bubbles with her gum. I eased away and looked down toward the tennis courts. Up to the basketball court. The softball field. The jungle gym. Not only was there no one I could peg as a parent, there was no one, period.

My bench offered little in the way of aesthetics, but the discomfort was more than made up for by the view it offered. It had been placed in the perfect spot along the banks of the South River, where the water tired of flowing fast and shallow and decided slow and deep would be better. There in that spot stood the Old Man, casting a fly fishing line over the waters. He looked at me, then to her, and then waved.

I wondered why she wasn't in school and how she had managed to find my bench. And more than that, I wondered what I could do to get her away and gone.

Selfish? Yes. But honest. Because, as I said, that was My Bench. I had been coming to that park and sitting in that spot since before she had been born.

I considered my options, none of which were very good and all of which would paint me in an unflattering light if acted upon. I decided—reluctantly—that patience would be the more proper means to my desired end. I would bypass my bench, stroll down to the picnic pavilion, and wait her out.

It seemed a flawless plan, and I suppose it would have been if I hadn't stepped on a very small but very noisy twig when I turned to leave.

"Better watch that twig behind you," the Old Man shouted, and then laughed at his timing.

The girl wheeled around in midbubble, her legs frozen in an open scissor, and she greeted me with a strange look of shock and amazement. Then she smiled. A big, toothy, Christmas morning smile. I smiled back. She raised the fingers of the small hand that gripped the back of my bench and waved. I waved.

And then she screamed.

"I knew you'd come!" she said, her voice cracking with excitement. "I knew it I *knew* it!"

"Pardon me?" I asked.

She turned fully around and raised up on the back of my bench. Her smile grew wider. Mine didn't. The Old Man floated his line above the water and then settled it. I was wondering if the fish could even see him, much less whatever he'd conjured on the hook.

The girl spoke again, this time in a whisper: "I knew you'd come."

"How did you know I would come?" I asked her.

"Because," she said. Her tone suggested that one word was sufficient to make everything clear to all but the slowest people. When she realized I still hadn't caught on, she clarified, "That's how prayin' works."

"You just say when," the Old Man shouted again, "and I'll come on up there. Don't think the fish are bitin' today, anyways."

I ignored him and turned back to her. The girl was still bent over the back of the bench—my bench. Her tongue was busy working her gum into a bubble. Her eyes were bugged and on me.

"What do you mean?" I asked.

She took a deep breath and exhaled like a frustrated parent trying to explain the plainly obvious to a child.

"Last night I prayed that God would send an angel to me at the park, so I came here to wait." She paused and then leaned further over the back of the bench. "You *are* my angel, right?"

"Oh boy," came the voice from the river.

My first reaction was to laugh, and I almost did. I'd been called one or two things in my life, but never an angel. But then I saw the expression on her face turn from joy to disappointment. The bubble she'd been working on now lay flat against the bottom of her lip, and I felt as though I was the one responsible for bursting it. Something was obviously wrong with this child, and laughing at something she said wouldn't be very appropriate. Or helpful.

"Why aren't you in school?" I asked, evading her question.

"Daddy said I could stay home today."

I nodded and took a step closer. Just one. "I see. Does your daddy know you're here?"

"No."

"Don't you think he's worried about you?"

She slurped the bubble gum back into her mouth and started chewing again. "I told him I was going to my auntie's house," she answered.

"How long have you been sitting here?" I asked.

"All morning," she said.

"How long were you going to wait?"

"Until you came." Then, "You are my angel, right?"

I looked down to where the Old Man was fishing. "You have no idea what you're doing, Andy," he told me. "My job's a lot harder than you think it is. You got a long way to go before you can be like me."

He was right, at least partway. I really didn't have any idea what I was doing. But his job was hard? Really? Popping in every now and then to make a little comment about something? Please. If that was tough work, then angels had it easy. The Old Man had no idea how easy he had it, and there he was telling me I had a long way to go before I could be like him. Well, we'd just see about that.

So.

"I'm your angel," I said.

"Have it your way," the Old Man said. "I'm outta here."

He tipped his cap and wished me luck, then let go of his fishing pole. It jiggled and danced over the surface of the river and then gathered into itself. There was a gentle *poof!* of air that made me blink, and when I opened my eyes I saw that the pole had formed into a duck that quacked and then flew away. The little girl turned at the sound and watched, no doubt wondering from where in the world the duck had come. The Old Man applauded his feat of prestidigitation. I had never seen him do anything like that—didn't even think he could. But I offered him no awe. I had the feeling he'd done it not to brag, but to show me he could and to remind me I could not. I paid his warning no mind. I would not need magic tricks just to talk to a little girl.

The Old Man winked at me from the river and then began to melt into the water. Just before his head disappeared, he said, "Take the gum, Andy, but don't chew it. You'll need it later."

The girl turned back to me, trading one marvel for another. "I knew it!" she said. "I'm sorry I kinda doubted."

"That's okay," I said, turning back to her. "I get that all the time. Hard for folks to believe much anymore. My name's Andy."

"I'm Jordan," she said. She extended a bony arm toward me. I crossed the space between us and shook her hand, nice and official like. When she pumped her arms, the shiny beads on the ends of her cornrowed hair clicked. "But I guess you already knew my name, huh?"

"Sure I did," I answered. A tiny burn formed in my gut. I tried to push it down, along with the thought that surely one of the straightest roads to hell was paved with lies told to innocent children.

"Want some gum?" Jordan asked, holding out a half-chewed package.

"Sure. Thanks." I took her offering and put it in my pocket. "I'll chew it later. I have a feeling I'll need it."

Jordan scooted over and patted the seat of the bench like she was inviting me into my own home. I took it anyway and even offered a thank-you. We sat in silence for a few minutes, both unsure what was next. Then she pointed to the loaf of bread on my lap and said, "What's that for?"

"God wanted me to feed the ducks while I was here," I said, surprised at how well and how easily I could slip into a lie. Like an old pair of shoes.

"Where'd you get it? At the store?"

"No, I just brought it with me."

"You mean," she said, eyes bulging, "*Jesus* made that bread?"

I looked down at the bread. Fittingly, the big red letters spelled out WONDER.

"Absolutely," I answered.

Jordan whispered a heartfelt "Awesome." She began to swing her feet back and forth beneath the bench again. Her eyes were studying me. "Are you sure you're an angel?"

"You don't think I am?"

"No," she said, eyes wild again. The thought of making an angel mad hadn't occurred to her, but now it had. "I mean, yes. I mean, I don't know." A pause, then, "Do you know why I prayed for God to send you down here?"

Now my own legs began to swing beneath the bench, if only to give me something else to do rather than answer.

"Well...," I started, hoping I could finish, "God didn't get real detailed. He just told me I needed to come see you."

Jordan gave me a satisfied nod, blew another bubble, and asked, "Are angels smart?"

"Sure they are," I told her. Then, catching myself—"We, I mean. Sure *we* are."

"So if I asked you some questions, you would know stuff?"

I thought about that. I'd been raised in church, and still hardly ever missed a Sunday. Read my Bible every day. Prayed often. And I'd had my very own angel for a very long while. Sure I would know stuff.

"Shoot," I said.

Jordan's legs stopped swinging and she looked down, almost embarrassed by what she was going to say next. "I guess I just kind of want to know what heaven's like."

The question took me by surprise. Heaven? How could I possibly talk about something like that? I cast a glance toward the river where the Old Man had stood, but there was nothing but current.

I'd asked him quite a few times about heaven when he first came into my life. The wounds of my mother's death were still fresh, like open sores on my heart. I needed to know there was an After to life's Now, and I needed to know she was there, that she was happy. That she was waiting. When I would ask, the Old Man would always smile in a far-off kind of way, and there were tears in his eyes that spoke of a joy that could not be told. He'd said that she had found her joy and was indeed there waiting, but that it was not an anxious sort of wait. And he would say no more. Heaven, he said, was beyond words. Describing it would be like describing the color yellow to a blind person. You could try, but the more you explained the further away from the truth you would be. *Wait*, he would say to me. *Wait, and you will see.*

I knew *wait, and you will see* would not help me in this case, but what would? All I could think of was the streets-of-gold, mansion-in-the-sky description. I figured that wouldn't appeal to someone her age. How could blissful eternity be explained in terms a little child could appreciate?

"It's sorta like every day is Saturday," I said.

Jordan smiled and said, "Good."

I thought my task was over then. Yes! Simple enough. I could pat her on the leg and send her home and everything would be fine. But Jordan wasn't done. Not even close.

"Where are your wings?" she asked.

"In my pocket," I answered.

"Can I see them?"

"No."

"Are Adam and Eve sorry?"

"Yes, and God forgave them."

"How old is God?"

"Really, really old."

"Does He have dreams when He sleeps?"

"No."

"Why not?"

"Because God doesn't sleep."

"Why not?"

"Because He's busy watching over you."

"Why does He watch over me?"

"Because He loves you and wants to keep you safe."

"Then why did He let my mommy die?"

My mouth, open and ready to fire off another automatic answer, suddenly became very dry. I'd been staring out at the river all that time, but now my eyes cut to the right and the left, searching for the Old Man. He wasn't there. This was another lesson. One more Teachable Moment. But this one would be coming at Jordan's expense.

"What?" I asked.

Jordan looked up to me. Tears pooled in her little eyes. She tried to look at me but found she couldn't and settled for her shoes instead. "I said if God loves me and wants to keep me safe, then why did He let my mommy die?"

The breeze wafted over us, blowing through the pines and into the river and carrying with it a thin and familiar voice that whispered, "Told ya so." If Jordan heard it, she said nothing.

Jordan sniffled and reached into her pocket for a tissue. She swiped at the tears trickling down her cheeks as she waited for an answer. I had none. This was not a child's question. This was adult stuff. Serious stuff. Stuff I still asked myself. And God, too.

Why did the world have to be so bad? Why do the innocent have to suffer? Why must good people have nothing and bad people have everything and why did it have to be that way?

Because bad things happened in this life, and to everyone. That was the easy answer, the one I'd learned to adopt myself. The world was a hard place and no one lived happily ever after. And no matter how wise we became, we would always leave with more questions than answers.

But how could I tell Jordan that?

I knew this was one of those moments in Jordan's life where she found herself at a fork in the road. One path led to healing, the other to bitterness. Whatever I said next may well be the very words that pushed her down either the one or the other. So I did what I should have all along. I told her the truth.

"Jordan?" I said.

She sniffled and wiped her nose. Her eyes were still on the ground, but she had nudged herself toward me. Her head was now very close to landing on my shoulder. "What?"

"I'm not an angel."

I spat the words out as quickly as I could, but their fetid taste remained. More tears would come now. Maybe a tantrum. Which would be completely justified.

But there was only silence.

Finally, she said, "I thought maybe you weren't."

"You did?" I asked.

Jordan nodded and pointed to my hat—"Daddy says God hates the Yankees."

I chuckled and she managed a weak grin, and then her steadfast countenance crumbled in a fit of tears. I wrapped my arms around her. Jordan huddled into the crook of my shoulder. I rocked her as she sobbed.

We sat for a long while on my bench—*our* bench—and looked out over the river. The ducks arrived. We took turns tossing them bits of bread and laughed as they quacked and fought over each chunk.

I told Jordan that I'd lost my own mother when I was near her age. I didn't know why God would do a thing like that, but that He must have had a very good reason. He always does, I said, and one day we would both find out what that reason was. That was what faith was all about.

"In the meantime, your mom still loves you and she's in a good place. The best place."

When the bread was gone and the ducks were full, Jordan said it was time for her to be going. She thanked me, gave me another hug, and assured me she felt better. I knew she didn't. But I also knew one day she would. I watched her walk toward the bridge that led across the river toward the soccer field and the houses beyond.

"See ya," she said from the bridge.

"See ya."

And she was gone.

I remained behind and watched the river flow by. After a few minutes I heard a creak beside me on the seat. The Old Man was now dressed in his usual jeans and T-shirt.

"You okay?" he asked.

I wasn't, but I nodded anyway. "Guess I could've used you after all," I said.

He smiled and offered me a pat on the leg that I couldn't feel. "Nice to know I'm needed."

I stared out over the bridge again and said, "If you had been here, what would you have told me to say?"

"Exactly what you did," he said. And then, just to make sure I understood: "Exactly what you did. An important lesson. For the both of you."

I fished the piece of bubble gum Jordan had given me out of my pocket and held it up to him. "This why I was here today?"

"No," he said. "You were here to help a little girl." He pointed to the gum. "That's extra. Keep it safe, Andy. Okay?"

I nodded. I knew what he meant by that.

"You two have a lot in common," he said. "Not just the fact that you both lost parents at a young age, either."

"What else?" I asked him.

The Old Man leaned in closer. "You're both sitting in a big, dark room full of questions, Andy. Side by side. In front of you is a window, and streaming through that window is the light of truth, all the answers to all the questions either of you could ever ask. But over that window is a shade, and it's drawn tight. Sometimes that shade draws up a bit and sheds some light on the things that hurt you so, but it's just a bit. You and Jordan, you both want that shade out of the way. You want to see the whole view from that window, the whole truth. But you know what, Andy? If that shade were pulled up all at once and all the truth shone through in an instant, you would be blinded by the light."

I nodded. Not through acceptance, but—for the first time perhaps—a bit of understanding. My eyes fell to the spot where Jordan had sat just moments before. I could still feel the wetness of her tears on my shirt.

I hoped to see Jordan again. Perhaps along some street

paved in gold beside a crystal sea. She would introduce me to her mother, and I would thank her for bringing such a beautiful girl into the world. And then Jordan and I would sit on a bench and share all the answers we would then know.

And we would laugh.

23

Hungry Dragons

Elizabeth turned the piece of bubble gum over in her hands and said, "So I was right. What the Old Man does for you is tougher than it appears."

"Thought I really messed up with that little girl," I said. "And who knows, maybe I did. I never saw Jordan again. I asked the Old Man about her, but he either didn't know or wouldn't say. I'm thinking he didn't know. Thought angels knew everything."

"Maybe they just know what they need to get the job done," Elizabeth offered.

I would have raised an eyebrow at that if I'd had one. "Still seems strange that someone like you could be pegged as a believer."

She sat in her chair and regarded me, measuring her words before she dared to speak. I knew I'd asked Elizabeth before what she believed and what she didn't as far as matters of the spirit, but she had deflected my question and I had allowed it. It was a curiosity then and nothing more, the equivalent of asking her where she grew up and where she had gone to school. But as our time together grew, I was beginning to understand that rather than simply wanting to know, I had to know.

"I can't imagine anyone being a counselor and not believing in God," she said. "But faith's a funny thing. I've talked with people who have come in here with all the belief in the world and lose it, and I've had people come in with no belief at all

and find it. Hospitals are like that. They concentrate all of life's
big questions into one point and force you to confront them."

"Which is why you're here," I said.

"*Right* here," she answered.

I looked into the box. The only two items remaining were
a golf tee and the key chain Elizabeth had asked about earlier.
Whether I admitted it or not—whether I *hated* it or not—an
end was coming. I would have to tell Elizabeth everything, and
then she would leave. A tiredness gripped me. I remembered
a nature show the Old Man and I had watched once about a
group of Komodo dragons hunting an ox. The ox had been
bitten by one of them but managed to escape into the jungle.
Its wound grew and festered as the dragons followed, waiting for its strength to finally give way. That finally happened
three weeks later on the edge of a swamp. The ox sat motionless, watching as the dragons circled ever closer. In the end,
it couldn't even cry out in pain when the dragons began to
feast. I felt like that. Tired and surrounded by hungry dragons
I couldn't hope to beat away.

"So it's your professional opinion that everything that's happened to me, from then until right now, has all been done with
a higher purpose in mind?"

"Between us?" she asked. "Yes. That's not exactly what
proper counselors would say, I suppose. Maybe not what they
should say. But yes, Andy. There is something greater here. I
think life is drowning in purpose. I think everyone's life is. You
simply have had the blessing of a clearer vantage point."

"It doesn't seem clearer," I said.

"It will. You just need the courage to find it. That means
talking about what you'd rather not."

I looked into the box again, then to the pile of trinkets on
my lap—my life vomited out in front of me, lessons I was supposed to learn but obviously hadn't. All our lives we longed
for a purpose, a reason for more than simple existence, but for
our pains and sadness also. Worse than the death of the body
was the death of hope and faith. We all wanted to matter, and

the nagging feeling that our souls were mere accidents rather than part of something larger than ourselves was the root of all human despair. Yet just as frightening as the thought of not having a purpose was the thought of having a purpose you felt incapable of fulfilling.

"I'm tired, Elizabeth. My heart is tired."

"Then let me carry you a while," she said. "I know there are two things left in that box. Let's do the easiest one."

I took Jordan's piece of bubble gum from her hand and placed it on my lap, then reached into the box. I was careful not to touch Eric's key chain, which wasn't hard to do considering it was just that and the tee left.

24

The Golf Tee

All I wanted to do was go fishing, because that's what Sunday afternoons were for. The fact it was the first week of November didn't matter. The weather was warm, nearly sixty, and David Walker had given me an open-ended invitation to visit the lake that backed up to Happy Hollow on the back part of his farm. No one wanted to fish there much; country folk are notoriously superstitious, and to them legend may as well be fact. I never minded, though. The Hollow was just dark woods full of darker stories. I had my pole by the door, my tackle box full, and my hat on. In other words, I was ready.

The Old Man, however, was not.

I checked the bait again and then the pole, and then jangled my keys at him like he was a pet rather than a higher being.

He raised his hands from the couch and pushed them out and apart. "Just...*wait*," he said.

"Daylight's burnin', Old Man," I said. "We gotta get."

"Cowboys are gonna score," he said, pointing to the television. "Bet you twenty."

"You don't have twenty," I said. "I'm gonna leave you here if you don't hurry up. I'm pretty sure you can catch up later."

"You can't go yet," he said.

"Why?"

"Because company's coming."

"It's Sunday afternoon," I said. "You know folks don't go visiting until Sunday evening, and you *know* nobody ever comes to see me."

"Company's coming," he repeated. "It'll be interesting."

"And why's that?"

" 'Cause it's a dinosaur," he said, then raised his eyebrows up and down and uttered a mock growl.

I sighed. Not because he said a dinosaur was coming to see me, but because I really had to stay. Because a Lesson was about to be imparted. And even though I knew it would be a valuable lesson—if not at that moment, then surely at some point—I really just wanted to go fishing. But the Old Man had always been of the opinion that what all people had in common was their amount of little moments. Big moments varied from person to person, he said. Some had more, others less. But we all had the same amount of little ones, and the secret of life lay in them. Wise, yes. And profound, too. But as a result he never let me miss one of them, even when it meant I had to wait to catch dinner.

I sat down beside him on the sofa and watched as Dallas fumbled on the ten.

"You owe me twenty," I said. "Guess you folks don't know *everything*, huh?"

His mouth said nothing, but the sudden and passing look of confusion on his face did. I'd never seen him surprised by anything.

He recovered enough to say "Put it on my tab," then he interrupted me before I could ask another question—"Someone's coming."

"Yeah, I know. The dinosaur. T-Rex or Stegosaurus?"

"T-Rex."

I nodded. "Sounds about right."

I got up and walked into the kitchen for a bag of jerky. If I had to sit around the house all afternoon waiting on a dinosaur, I might as well grab a snack. I'd just taken a Coke out of the refrigerator when the doorbell rang.

"Dinosaur's here," the Old Man called.

"Didn't know they rang doorbells," I answered.

I walked back into my small living room and looked through the glass on the upper part of the door. Nothing.

"You messin' with me?" I asked him. The doorbell rang a second time and answered for him. I grabbed the knob and said, "Sure are growin' them things small nowadays."

I opened the door and looked down. The Old Man had been right. There was a dinosaur on my porch. A T-Rex, actually. Styrofoam teeth jutted out from his head and a piece of brown felt had been glued to his chest. His long tail stretched all the way to the steps. Impressive.

"Trick or treat!" it said.

I turned to look toward the sofa, which was now empty. The Old Man had fulfilled his mission of keeping me at the house. I guessed he didn't think sticking around was necessary.

"Trick or treat!" the boy said again. He held out an orange plastic bag and shook it for effect.

"It's not Halloween," I told him.

"I know."

"Halloween was last week."

"I *know*," he said, shaking his bag again.

This, I decided, was a new low. A blatant example of modern society's pollution of young people with the poisons of greed and selfishness. Not only did I probably give this kid a handful of candy last week, now he was back for more.

"Didn't you get enough the first time around?" I asked.

"Nuh-uh." (Shake.)

"Little greedy, ain't ya?"

He wrinkled his brow and tried to decide if I'd just complimented or insulted him. "...Yes?" he asked.

"What's your name?"

"My name's Logan the Dinosaur!" he yelled. "Now give me candy or I'll eat you!" He added a "Grrr!" on the end that sounded like a frightened mouse.

"Well, Logan the Dinosaur, I think you probably have enough candy at your house, don't you?"

"No. I don't have *any* candy." He said those words with an air of defensiveness that implied he'd had that asked of him quite a few times that day, thank you.

"What'd you do," I said, "eat it already?"

"Nope. I didn't get t'go." He shook his bag again. *"Please?"*

"You didn't get to go trick-or-treating last week?" I asked.

His shoulders slumped and his bag nearly dropped onto the porch. From what I saw, what would have spilled out wouldn't amount to much. "I got dressed and went to Granny's," he said, "and then I got sick. I yarked in my bag."

"You did what?"

"I yarked in my bag. You know…" He stuck a finger halfway into his mouth and made a heaving sound.

"Gotcha," I said.

Then it was my turn to wrinkle a brow. Logan answered my question before it was asked—"No, not *this* bag."

"Oh. Good."

"Mommy says I can have a do-over," he said, pointing a thumb over his shoulder. "She says we don't get much do-overs and that's why they're special. I think do-overs are the *best*."

I followed Logan's thumb toward the driveway. His mother stood at the end, resting an elbow on the mailbox. She offered a wave and a what-was-I-supposed-to-do? shrug. I waved back and smiled because I was beginning to understand.

"Well, I've never been one to stand in the way of a good do-over. But I'm outta candy. Gave it all away last week."

"That's okay," Logan said. "Most everybody's been out. They just gave me cooler stuff."

He opened his bag for proof—two baseball cards, a pencil, some glue, three golf tees, and a five-dollar bill were inside.

"Not a bad haul," I said. "Okay, little man, I tell you what. You hang here, and I'll see what I can find."

I left Logan at the door and let him peek while I rummaged through the living room trying to decide if I had anything at all that would appeal to a boy his age. Unfortunately, the pickings seemed slim. In the end I settled on a small spiral notebook, two AA batteries, another baseball card, and an arrowhead I had found near the creek by my house.

"There ya go," I said, emptying it all into his bag.

"Awesome," he whispered. "Thanks."

"No problem. Happy Halloween."

"You the man who runs the gas station?" he asked.

"That's me."

"My mom and dad go to the Texaco, 'cause we live near there. They say you're a nice guy, just kinda crazy."

"Well," I said, "I reckon I appreciate that."

"Here," he said, reaching into his bag. "You can have this one."

He pulled out one of the golf tees and held it up to me. "Happy Halloween, too," he said.

Logan the T-Rex bounded back down the driveway to his mother. We exchanged another wave and shrug, and I watched as he knocked on the door of the Thompsons' house across the street. Stephen-with-a-P-H was the lucky one who answered.

"My name's Logan the Dinosaur!" I heard. "Now give me candy or I'll eat you! *Grrr!*"

I stood and watched Stephen-with-a-P-H scratch his head and try to figure out what in the world was going on. Then my eyes drifted. Not to Logan the Dinosaur, but to the person standing at the end of yet another driveway—his mother.

Her son might have been the star of that show, but she was the wisdom behind it. What had happened to Logan the week before was beyond his control, a stroke of misfortune that culminated in a yark into his trick-or-treat bag. At some point she realized that might be a night he would always regret, and then at another point she realized it didn't have to be that way. She could take that regret and turn it into a triumph.

She could change the future.

"*Now* they scored," the Old Man said from the couch. I looked from him to the television. Sure enough, several football players dressed in white and silver were acting stupid in the end zone. "See? I just had my time line wrong."

"You still owe me twenty," I said.

"Nice little Halloween present you got there," he said.

"Nice kid," I told him. "Guess I'm supposed to hang on to this."

"Like your life depended on it." There was a seriousness in his words that bothered me. I felt as though he were speaking prophecy rather than some old adage.

"Logan was right," he said. "Do-overs really are the best. You've always believed them to be rare. Impossible, even. I get that. But see your eyes, Andy. I watched you as you stood there thinking maybe you had that all wrong. That maybe such a thing is possible."

"I don't need a do-over."

He began to fade, but not before he offered one word.

"Soon."

25

Do-overs

For a moment I thought Elizabeth expected there to be more to that story. Another ending, perhaps. A better one. Sometime during my retelling she had gone back to her scissors and paper. I watched as she snipped and brushed the droppings from her knee into a small trash bin that she retrieved from my bedside. The pile of discarded bits was an impressive one.

"You know," she said as she cut, "of all the stories you've told me tonight, I think that one counts the most."

"Really?" I asked. I had never considered there were some things in the box that meant more than others. Were there things that should be remembered and others that *must*?

"Yes," she said, "because it's time for your do-over, Andy."

Another sliver of paper fell into the trash.

"What are you talking about?" I asked. "I don't have anything to do over. I don't need no second chance. I haven't messed up the first one."

She kept cutting and said, "That's not what I'm saying. I'm not talking about setting things right, I'm talking about doing what you were meant to do."

"What I'm meant to do?" I asked. "I'm doing what I'm meant to do the best way I know how to do it. I run a gas station. It's not rocket science. And I didn't have a choice. Grandpa died, and Grandma needed the money coming in."

"People are made for more than they usually become, Andy. Not to say that's their fault. Life gets in the way sometimes, and it's easy for people to lose their perspective. They forget about the things that matter because the things that don't can seem so big and so necessary." Elizabeth paused long enough to make the universal sign of *crazy* by moving the scissors in a looping motion around her ear. "Gets their thinking all screwed up. I'm not talking about a job, I'm talking about a *purpose*. That's two different things. One gives you a living, and the other gives you a life."

"Then I don't know what my purpose is," I said.

Elizabeth put the scissors down.

"That's because we're not through yet," she said. "There's still one more thing in your box."

And there it was.

Of all the futility of man, none was as pointless as the fight against the inevitable. I'd hoped to stretch out the contents of my box as long as I could, until either I gave out or Elizabeth did, and I was set aside in favor of other pained souls in other darkened rooms. But then came the inevitable, the rush of the expected, fueled by one man who wanted to set an order to his life and one woman determined to help him.

I had run out of stories.

Elizabeth had been right. She had always been right. There must be a valor to live this life, a courage born of grace and a knowing that things are more than they appear to be. For the first time I saw the world divided not according to race or nation or sex, but according to the ones who were conscious enough to know they were sleeping and determined to kick themselves awake, and the ones who chose just to roll over and slumber more.

Elizabeth drew near.

"There was a soldier here once," she said. "He had gone off to war because he felt his country calling. To him, it was an almost holy act. For three years he fought in sand and mountains, through city streets and tiny villages, trekking in lands that had been battlefields since time immemorial. He saw friends fall. He saw his enemy fall. He bled and he sweat and he cried, and then he came home. Three months later I sat in his room here at the hospital. He'd tried to kill himself."

"Why?"

"Because he thought the fight ended when the guns fell silent. It doesn't. Not for anyone. Because the real war is never five thousand miles away from anyone, Andy. The real war is in the heart. It's in the soul. This world's a mess because people are a mess."

"And I'm a mess?"

"Aren't you?"

I didn't answer. I didn't have to.

"Well then," she said, squeezing my hand, "let's find that out together. Small steps, Andy. We're almost done. I promise you that. Just a little farther now."

I looked down into the box. The angel key chain was the only thing left. It sparkled and stared at me, both taunting and begging for my attention.

"Andy, everything, every little thing, comes down to this."

I looked up at her. "That's what he told me," I said. "When he was here, that's what he said."

"The Old Man?"

I nodded.

"You might not believe him after everything that's happened, Andy. You might not trust him. I understand that. But do you trust me?"

"I more than trust you, Elizabeth."

Those words seemed less to me then than they would be later. At the time I spoke those words to say I trusted her with more than my secrets, I had trusted her with my past and my present as well. But later I knew the truth of what I was trying to say. In those words I had come as close as I ever had to telling a woman that I loved her.

"Tell me, Andy," she said.

I picked up the key chain and dangled it between us. It shimmered in the dim light and washed me in anger and pain. The truth? I had no courage. There was nothing more I wanted than to put it back into the box, latch the top, and never look at it again. But the truth was also this—sometimes courage arises within the hearts of men, and sometimes it arises in the fear of disappointing those whom we love. I could not disappoint the woman beside me.

The Old Man had been right to say Elizabeth had been sent by God. She, not he, had become my angel.

From wherever that courage came, I found it. And with that finding came not the last step of my journey, but surely the most important.

"His name was Eric," I told her.

26

The Key Chain

They walked into the gas station that first morning, and all I remember thinking is *Sweet fancy Moses, what is this?* If you would have seen the two of them, you'd have thought the same.

The older one—but not much older, I supposed—wore a faded pair of corduroy pants and a long-sleeved T-shirt that looked three sizes too big. An unkempt mane of brown hair and a poor attempt at a beard rounded out the look. His companion was only slightly more presentable; at least he'd bothered to tuck in his shirt. But his pants were so big they were sliding down his rear end, his hair was even longer, and his beard was even more spotty. They both looked like refugees from some hippie utopia who had somehow found themselves stranded in the land of reality.

How in the world the two of them had found Mattingly was beyond me. I assumed they were just passing through, troubadours along the road of life. Such sights weren't common in our town, but they happened from time to time. As they made their way up and down the aisles eyeing the chips and the drinks, I went ahead and began bagging some beef jerky and bottled water for when they asked for a handout.

I was surprised when both of them came up to the counter with not only a few groceries, but the money to pay for them. I made a halfhearted attempt at shoving the two plastic bags full of food and drink onto the shelf beside my angel box and smiled at them.

"Mornin', sir," the oldest one said. The other one said nothing but offered a smile and a nod.

"How y'all doin'?" I answered. "That'll do?"

"Yes sir," the oldest said.

I rang up the soda, the chips, and the smokes, trying all the while not to judge the two of them but doing so anyway. They were clean, at least. Messy but washed.

"Seven-forty," I told him with a smile. I took his ten dollars and handed back the change.

I repeated the process with his friend, whom I suspected was likely a brother. Both shared the same nose and cheekbones, and, aside from the slight difference in height, the same build. My questions of how he was and if that was all he needed went unanswered but not ignored. He offered another smile and another nod when I thanked him for his business.

The two of them walked toward the doors to leave, but not before the silent one stopped to pick a scrap of paper off the floor and put it in the trash.

"You have a great day now, sir," the other said.

"Y'all, too," I answered.

I watched through the window as they made their way around the corner. The younger one spoke (which told me he was shy rather than mute). The older one gave him a punch in the shoulder and a laugh. They pulled out in a battered Jeep and headed toward the interstate.

"Nice kids," the Old Man said from next to me.

"Seemed so," I told him. "What's up?"

"Nothing yet." The Old Man's eyes followed the Jeep. When the trees and the curve in the road swallowed it, he still watched.

They were back the next day, then the day after that, and then every day after that. Different clothes each time, thank the

Lord, though one outfit was just as ratty as the next. But after the first few days, I did what I should have been doing all along—I forgot about the clothes and concentrated on the people in them.

There is a certain familiarity that develops over time between the public and those whose job it is to serve them. I knew most of my customers better than their doctors and preachers and even their spouses did. Not because they confided to me the intimate details of their lives (though some did), but because you notice the little things that most others overlook.

The way that familiarity happened with those two boys went pretty much the same way it had with everyone else. It wasn't one giant leap from stranger to friend, it was a succession of small steps taken one day after the next. It was the same time on the same days, the same *Mornin' sir/How ya'll doin'*, the same soda and chips and smokes. It was familiarity that grew into expectation that grew into comfort.

One day the older boy gathered his soda, chips, and smokes and said, "My name's Eric."

"Good to know you, Eric," I said. "I'm Andy."

He shook my hand when I extended it. The grip was tight and confident. I was impressed.

"Pleasure's mine," he said. Then he cocked his head to the side and motioned toward his sidekick. When he did, his hair swept across his face and made me grimace. "This here's my brother," he said. "We call him Jabber."

"Jabber?" I asked.

"Yeah," Eric said. "He never talks much."

I smiled. "Gotcha. Good to know you, Jabber."

It was the first time Jabber traded eye contact for words. He managed, "Hey, Mr. Andy."

"Where you two from?" I asked, " 'cause I know it ain't around here."

"We live over in Nelson," Eric said. I raised an eyebrow at that one. Nelson was clear on the other side of the mountain.

"Jabber and I go to the community college in Traversville. Your store's pretty much halfway between the two, so we figured it'd be a good enough place to stop by every morning and take stock of things."

"I'd imagine there are other stores between Nelson and Traversville," I told them.

"Yes sir," Eric said. "But Jabber here calls this our spot. If you don't mind, that is."

I looked to Eric's brother, who nodded and smiled. I warmed to them both immediately. It wasn't just their manners or their words or their dress. In a strange way, they reminded me of me.

"Don't mind at all," I said. "I appreciate that, Jabber."

Eric grabbed their bags from the counter and said, "We'd best be gettin', Andy. My professor doesn't usually mind students showing up late, but Jabber's would tear him a new one. We'll see you tomorrow, though."

"I'll be here," I said.

When Eric and Jabber pulled out of the lot five minutes later, the Old Man was standing by the road watching them go.

It always amazed me how good-minded people would spend their money to get their futures told. Live long enough and you realize the future's not some big Unknown. Chances are tomorrow will be just like today, which is most times just a redo of yesterday. Life is like that, I think. It's not so much one thing after another as it is one thing over and over. Which is why Eric and I were both right. He and Jabber were back the next day, and I was right there waiting.

The two became a fixture of the early mornings, arriving just after the farmers had left with their coffee and the morning's copy of the *Gazette* and just before the first shift came through on their way to the factory. I began to expect them every morning, and they never disappointed. Eric and Jabber were there every Monday through Friday for almost a year.

And because of that, the familiarity that was shared between the brothers and me began to evolve into friendship. Then friendship became companionship. And then that companionship grew into a closeness that was expressed much more in feeling and much less in words. I had built a relationship with those two boys, though what sort of relationship it was I could not say. Still can't, really. There were unspoken boundaries we did not cross—the boys never asked about family or my life away from the gas station, and I never asked about theirs. I knew they went to school—even summer classes, which told me they were either the most dedicated students in the world or just two boys who needed somewhere to escape to—and that they were from Away. That was enough, at least at the time.

Once Eric mentioned something about their mother that was not flattering—it involved alcohol, as most unflattering things did—but I would not pry. One look at the Jeep they drove told me the father wasn't in the picture. The oil hadn't been changed in forever, which was likely due to the fact Eric and Jabber didn't know such maintenance had to be performed. Didn't know to even check it. And the license plates had been expired for five years. Kept telling that boy to fix that. He never did.

· I suppose I stepped into the role of surrogate father without realizing it, and I suppose that's what kept them coming back. There was always something they needed reminding of, whether it was a test to study for or an appointment to keep. I gave them money for bills, and when they refused it—those boys always did—I hid it in the bag of groceries they'd get every day. Once I even drove out to Traversville to watch Eric give a presentation for a religion class. His mother was busy, he said, and by then I knew their father had died when they were both little. I did for them, did what no one else was bothering to do, and in return they did for me, too. Eric and Jabber would show up at the house in the evenings sometimes to give me a hand in the garden or pull a few weeds. Nothing major, but it sure helped me out. The three of us exchanged presents that Christmas. Even had them over on the weekends sometimes for pizza and a ball game. It was the best way I knew how to be a father.

The words we said to each other were the best attempt we could make at fondness.

"You ever eat anything else?" I asked Eric one morning as he placed his chips and soda on the counter.

"You ever use that tiny brain of yours for anything other than how to make change from a ten?" he answered.

"Just to take a shower. You know what a shower is, don't you, hippie?"

Jabber chuckled.

"Sure I do," Eric shot back. "You know what a razor is? Or is that mangy beard you're wearing just a favor to the world so we all don't have to see all your ugly hanging out?"

I rubbed my thick beard and smiled. "Oh sonny, don't be so jealous. You could grow a beard like this if you didn't look like such a girl."

"I'd like to cut that beard off and see what's underneath."

"I'd like to teach you how to respect your elders."

We both paused and looked to Jabber, who had by then adopted the role of referee for our verbal sparring matches. He looked at Eric, then to me, and offered me a thumbs-up for his verdict.

"You win, Mr. Andy," he said.

I raised a fist over my head and nodded.

"Whatever," Eric said. He gave his brother a punch in the arm. "I totally got him today."

"The 'hippie' thing was good," Jabber told him.

"Thought that one up last night," I told them.

Seems a little mean-spirited, I know. But such were the conversations between men who had a genuine affection for one another—a macho mixture of sarcasm and callousness that safely masked any hint of genuine care. The more we picked on one another, the more we teased and taunted, the more our true feelings showed through.

But there was much more than the simple "bebop and scattin'," as Eric would put it. Jabber eventually confessed to me a knack for math. He was planning to attend the university after community college and study to be an accountant. I raised an eyebrow at that little revelation. Jabber didn't look like a numbers guy. Maybe an artsy musician guy or a guy who would major in philosophy and minor in sloppy dressing, but not a numbers guy. I nonetheless urged him to follow through on that particular career course, if only because becoming an accountant would greatly increase his odds of having to get a haircut.

If Jabber's desire for the future was unexpected, Eric's was downright shocking. He told me one day between our mock argument of *You're filthy/You're stupid* and checking the tire treads on the Jeep that his goal was to become a missionary. He wasn't kidding, either. And to where didn't matter, he said, so long as he was out there somewhere doing what God wanted him to do.

"You gotta be kidding me," I said with half a laugh.

"Honest Injun," he said. "You think I want to be like you when I grow up and sit behind a cash register all day?"

"Hey," I said, "you *know* you wanna be like me."

"I wouldn't wish that on anyone," he said.

Jabber regarded the two of us in silence and then raised his brother's hand.

"Dang it," I said. "I'll get you tomorrow."

I smiled as they left. Though I would never have admitted so to Eric's face, I saw something in him that was, for lack of a better word, special. Jabber, too. Though both were on the other side of their teenage years, they seemed untouched by the prevailing sense of angst and cynicism that infected so much of the world. Those two boys had direction. And most of all, they knew what God had called them to do. It was a purpose for which they had not only been well equipped to handle, but which had given them a passion for living. I envied them, and Eric especially. I was more than thirty years his senior and still struggling with my own sense of place in life. Eric's future had been ordained by God Himself, and he couldn't wait to get there.

The Old Man stood outside the doors as they left, then made his way through the wall to where I stood.

"Where've you been?" I asked him.

He shrugged. "Been busy," he said. "What's up?"

"Not much. Business as usual."

The Old Man nodded and stared out the window. He seemed more gone than there, like he was talking to someone far away.

"There's a storm comin', Andy. Gonna be a bad one, too. No one's safe from the world. Just have to tell you that. But you'll find your shelter, and it's going to be okay. Better than okay."

I looked up at a cobalt sky, empty except for a hawk that passed overhead.

"You ain't much of a weatherman," I told him. "Paper says we're free and clear for the next week."

The Old Man said nothing.

A month passed. The Old Man was staring out the window again one morning as Eric and Jabber drove into the lot and parked in their usual spot along the side.

"What's it going to be today?" I asked him. "The hippie thing's a little played out, I think. Eric knows that's coming. Maybe I should start in on that hunk-of-junk Jeep he has."

The Old Man looked at the Jeep. "Could," he said. "Then again, you got that hunk-of-junk truck parked out back."

"You have a point there. Maybe I'll just play it by ear."

The two boys walked through the front door. Jabber gave

his customary nod and "Mornin', Mr. Andy." Eric waved and gave his customary snide comment: "Mornin', Genius. I see you managed to find your way to work this morning."

"And I see you're still trying to grow a beard," I answered. "I'm sure you'll have better luck at that once you hit puberty."

He laughed as they made their way to the drink cooler and then the snack aisle. I grabbed a pack of cigarettes and sat it on the counter, exactly where Eric and Jabber sat the rest of their daily rations.

I didn't bother to tell the boys their total. By that time I didn't have to. Heck, by then they could've walked around the counter and rang themselves up. Bag of chips, soda, pack of smokes—seven dollars and forty cents, every day of the year.

"Puberty, huh?" Eric said. "I have more testosterone right now than you ever have, old man."

I smiled at his choice of words, especially considering who was staring at him from the booth by the door.

Eric reached into his back pocket for his wallet and froze. A look of horror lighted across his face. He patted and felt nothing, and then patted and felt the pocket on the other side. The result was the same.

"Uh-oh," I said. My mouth began to stretch into a sinister smile.

"Dude," he said to Jabber, "you got any money?"

Jabber's eyes bulged in what was the best attempt at emotion I'd seen from him in nearly two years. He returned Eric's gaze. "Are you kiddin'?"

"My, my. Now how are my two favorite customers going to get their heads full of wisdom and knowledge without their junk food? And what about their smokes? Oh wow, their *smokes*. Two junkies going all day without their nicotine fix? Wow, I'm always glad I'm not you two, but today especially."

The seriousness of their predicament began to settle into their thick heads. Having to go without brunch was one thing. That would be uncomfortable, but not impossible. But having to go all day without a cigarette? That was inhuman. They even gave prisoners of war cigarettes.

"Dude," Eric said, "lend me ten bucks."

"You gotta be kidding me," I said, feigning insult.

"Come on, Andy. Please? I just forgot my wallet. It's sitting right on my dresser at home. We'll miss class if I have to go back home. I'll pay you back by the end of the week."

To be honest, I didn't know if I wanted to front Eric the money or not. Not because I thought he wouldn't pay me back. I knew he would. And not because it's considered bad business. I did that sort of thing on an everyday basis for friends. No, I waffled because this could well be something I could torment those two boys with for months. You couldn't put a price tag on good material.

The Old Man looked away from Eric and toward me. "Lend him the money, Andy," he said. "Be a sport."

I was about to whisper something sarcastic to the Old Man, but then I regarded him. His face held a sadness I had never before seen. There was no sparkle in his eyes, no grin on his lips. He had the look of someone who had to do what he felt he could not.

"Come on, Andy," Eric said. "You know I'm good for it."

I uttered an exasperated sigh. "Okay fine," I said. "Whatever it takes to get you two losers out of here before I start getting busy. This lack of responsibility is what's wrong with your generation. And here y'all will be running my country one day."

They smiled and reached for their groceries.

"Now just hang on a minute," I said, slapping their hands away. "I'll spring for the soda and the chips, but no smokes."

"Dude!" Eric said.

"God doesn't want you to smoke," I told him. "If anyone should know that, it's the future missionary."

"But you smoke, too," Jabber offered.

"True, but I'm just a stupid cashier at a gas station, remember? I don't know any better. Sorry guys, I just don't want to be an enabler."

"'It has been my experience that folks who have no vices have very few virtues'" Eric said. "Abraham Lincoln."

"'Show me a man I lend ten bucks to, and I'll show you a man I'll never see again,'" I answered. "Andy Sommerville. Though now that I think about it, maybe I should give you twenty just to make sure you stay away for good."

"Deal," Jabber said. Then he smiled.

"I'll spot you the twenty," I told them. "But I'm gonna need collateral."

"Want my shirt?" Eric said.

He stretched his T-shirt out and showed me—some sort of rock band, I supposed, with a giant peace symbol that was dripping in blood.

"For what," I asked, "so I can wash my truck with it? No way I want those hippie germs all over me. Let's see." I looked him over and found nothing of even the remotest value. Then I saw his keys sitting beside his soda. "Give me your key chain."

He held it up to me. It was a pewter angel, the sort you would find at any dollar store in the country. Most said something quasi-spiritual like NEVER DRIVE FASTER THAN YOUR ANGEL CAN FLY, but Eric's said nothing. Probably because of the trumpet in her mouth, positioned at the ready to shout either to or from the heavens.

"Fine," he said. "But I need to keep the keys. And you need to keep this safe. It means a lot to me."

"I have a place it'll be safe," I said.

"Show me."

I snorted. "No way. Don't you trust me?"

"Yes," he said, "but I still want you to show me."

I considered his request and knew what showing him would mean. I knew, too, that this small conversation had just turned into something very big. This wasn't just crossing a boundary but erasing it. But it felt right. They'd given me much. It was time I did the same.

I reached down and grabbed the box from the shelf, then placed it on the counter. "I'll keep it here," I said. "And it'll be safe. No one knows about this box, so no one touches it. You two boys are the only ones who've ever seen it, and that's the way it's gonna stay. Can't say why or how or even *if*, but everything that's important to my life is supposed to be in here. That key chain means a lot to you? This box is my world."

I'll admit a part of me expected them to laugh and taunt, but they didn't. The boys stared at it and said nothing.

"You got yourself a deal, Andy," Eric said. "I'll be back Monday with your money."

"Oh no," I said. "You'll come by tomorrow."

"But tomorrow's Saturday."

"Is it? Hadn't noticed."

"You're going to make us drive all the way out here on a Saturday to pay you back?"

"Why not?" I told him. "I figure I gotta punish you somehow for not being responsible enough to carry your wallet. Besides, I see you boys during the week, why not the weekend every once in a while?"

"Oh, fine," Eric said.

He and Jabber then gathered their supplies and started for the door. Just before it swung shut, Eric poked his head back in.

"I'll bring it to you in pennies," he said.

We both laughed.

I turned to the Old Man, who was still in his booth staring out the window.

"Idiots," I told him. "The both of them. But they have a way, don't they?"

"They do," he said.

The Old Man watched as they pulled away. The pained look on his face was becoming all too familiar. The only comfort he found was in rubbing the bracelet on his wrist.

"What the heck is wrong with you?" I asked.

"It's hard for folks to think in terms of eternity sometimes," he said. "All that's around them is either the now or the then. Makes some things seem bad, like God's not watching. He's always watching, Andy. You know that, right?"

"Whatever you say, Boss Man."

He turned to face me. "I'm serious, Andy. You know that, right?"

"Yes," I said. "I know that. Happy now?"

The Old Man looked out the window again. "Clouds are gathering. Storm's coming."

I followed his gaze. A thick layer of gray was descending over the valley.

I didn't think he was talking about the weather.

27

Eric

I became conscious of the fact I'd exhaled after that last sentence without bothering to reverse the process. My heartbeat thumped in my chest, pushing it to my throat and then into my eyes and making my skin stretch and burn. For a moment I considered the possibility of never breathing again. It would be a small price to pay for leaving Eric's story unfinished.

And yet I knew his story was one that could not be untold. That must not. Not for my sake alone, though Elizabeth would perhaps disagree. But for Eric's sake and for Jabber's.

Maybe, I thought, that was my purpose. Maybe I survived to carry Eric's memory to someone beyond his family and friends.

I took in a deep breath of hard, sterile air.

"You're doing good, Andy," Elizabeth said. She was close to me but not nearly close enough. The scissors and paper in her hand were now an afterthought, there only because she had forgotten them. "Let's take a break."

I nodded but said nothing. Starlight still shone through the open windows, but I could see the faint beginnings of daybreak creeping through the trees. I drew strength from that tinge of orange and yellow mixed in with the black. Light was coming to chase the shadows away. I'd seen enough darkness in those days after it all happened, enough to carry me through a dozen lifetimes. I was ready for light.

I reached out for Elizabeth's hand. She met me halfway and smiled into my eyes. "There's time," she told me. "Plenty of time." She raised the paper in her hands. "See? Almost done."

The paper was cut to pieces, barely held together by thin strands around the edges. It reminded me of the old-timers in town who sat in front of the hardware store or on their front porches and whittled pieces of wood. To my knowledge, the end result was never anything artistic or even useful. It was just a nub and a pile of shavings on the ground. And I'd always supposed that was the point. It was a way to keep the hands busy and free the mind up to ponder. That's what Elizabeth looked to be doing with her paper—whittling. Keeping things busy so she could slow them down and slow me down in the process. Still, the fragile mess she held in her hand puzzled me. I didn't know how something that had no real purpose could be almost done.

Elizabeth hinted at an answer when she added, "That means we're almost done, too."

"What will happen then?" I asked her. "Are you gonna pick up and move on to the next patient?"

It was a childish thing to say. Elizabeth would move on. That was her job. She had much invested in me, but no more than she had invested in anyone else. I knew that. But I also knew that Elizabeth had been in only a small amount of the untold hours of my life, and I didn't want her removed from a single hour more.

"I'll be close, Andy. Promise. This isn't the last you'll see of me." She winked and added, "You couldn't chase me away with a stick."

"I wouldn't dream of it," I said.

We both turned toward the noise at the door. Kim stood there wearing the frazzled look of a nurse struggling through the final hours of a graveyard shift.

"Sorry to bother you," she said. "Just checking on my favorite patient."

"Still here," I said, squeezing Elizabeth's hand as I did. I only thought after that it was perhaps something I shouldn't have done. But whether it was an infringement of the rules or not, Elizabeth's hand continued to fold over mine.

"Good," Kim said. "The doctor will be here in a little while to give you the once-over. I'll be back before then to get those bandages off."

I said "That's great news" because it was what I was expected to say.

"Holler if you need me, okay?"

"I will. Thanks."

Kim smiled and lingered for a bit, studying Elizabeth and me. She finally left when someone called her from the hallway.

"I didn't just get you in trouble, did I?" I asked.

"Nah," Elizabeth said. "Don't worry about that. I haven't broken any rules."

"Good." I squeezed her hand again and felt her return.

"Eric and Jabber seem like two great boys," she said, steering our conversation back to the business at hand.

"I saw in Eric the sort of person I always wanted to be. He was confident and outgoing. He held nothing back from anyone, and I admired him for that. I was always more like Jabber. Poor kid. He's great, really great. Just needs a little confidence. He needs someone to help him along and give him a little guidance."

"Like the Old Man does for you?" she asked.

"Yeah," I said, then I smiled. "Maybe Jabber should pray like I did. Then again, maybe not. Never know what you're gonna get and what it'll lead to."

"Guess God knew what He was doing when He gave him Eric as a brother, huh?"

"He got that part right," I said. And it was true. "He screwed up afterwards, though." That was also true.

"God doesn't screw up, Andy."

I nodded. "That's what folks are supposed to say just to make Him look good. 'God's got His reasons' and all that. You know what, though? I bet those folks are the ones who never had their mama taken from them when they were just a kid.

I bet those are the ones who've never had to see the bitter side of this life. They're insulated from the bad in the world by what they have or what they do. It's easy for them to hand out those little nuggets of wisdom. Other folks are just left to toss in the wind, Elizabeth. And it's a cold, hard wind. You ask Jabber if God screws up. You ask him."

"I'm asking you, Andy, not Jabber. You're the one I'm here for right now. Someone else will tend to him."

"Ain't nobody to tend *to* him, Elizabeth." The words came out in anger I didn't know I had. I took a deep breath. "All he had was Eric. His daddy's dead and gone, and his mama's only home long enough to bring her latest boyfriend with her. The only thing he had in this world—"

"Was Eric," she finished. "And now he's dead, isn't he, Andy? Eric's gone."

I clenched my hand tighter around hers. "He's not just gone, he was *taken*. By God."

"You told me the Old Man killed him."

"The Old Man didn't do anything to prevent it."

28

The Weight of the World

I had come up with no fewer than four lectures to give Eric that covered everything from his lack of financial responsibility to the waste of valuable space that was the younger generation. I practiced them on the Old Man, who'd hung around most of the night before. We laughed a lot that night; things seemed better. Whatever it was that had been bothering him had settled itself. He was the Old Man again, and I was glad to have him back.

"Angels aren't all-powerful, you know," he told me. We were out on the front porch enjoying the crickets and the frogs before I turned in. That part of the night, the quiet time, was when he often would settle into something serious. "Some of us struggle. And we all cry. Folks will say that the best way to tell an angel is the wings and the halo. That's bull. You can tell an angel by his tears."

"What's an angel got to cry about?" I asked. "Seems to me that y'all have it pretty easy, what with gallivanting all over the galaxy and whatnot."

He rocked in his chair—he liked doing that, but only when he knew no one was looking—and smiled. "You're not too bright for a human being, are you?"

I smiled back. "And you're not too comforting for an angel."

"Well, there's a time for comforting and there's a time for teaching. I guess you could say there's been a lot of teaching."

"Then maybe I'm brighter than you think," I said.

"No, Andy. I know better. But you're brighter than *you* think."

I waved him off and finished my glass of mint tea. "Let's head inside. What's it gonna be, ball game or cop show?"

"Don't matter," he said.

"Ball game it is."

I opened the screen door and he was already on the couch. We found the Yankees on ESPN and settled into our normal routine of talking at rather than to each other through the first few innings.

I'd just gotten up to grab another glass of tea when he said, "Thank you, Andy."

"For what?" I called from the kitchen.

"For saying that prayer," he said. "The one you said to the star when you were a kid."

I walked back to see Mariano Rivera jogging in from the bullpen. *Game over,* I thought. I sat back down on the sofa next to him and laughed.

"What are you thanking me for? Feels to me like this has been a one-person job. You show me stuff, and that's it. Can't see that you get much out of it."

"But I do, Andy. More than you know. This has been just as much for me as it has you."

"Oh yeah?" I asked. "What'd you do, screw up the first time around and get me as a second chance?"

"Something like that," he said. "I'd explain it, but I don't know how."

Rivera had gotten the first man to break his bat on a weak ground ball. I turned to comment to the Old Man that the Yankees closer was responsible for more dead trees than a Brazilian timber company, but he had that serious look in his eyes again. And what could have well been tears.

"You ain't looking for a hug or anything like that right now, are you?" I asked.

He snorted. "No, I don't want a hug. I just wanted you to know. You've come a long way."

"I suppose," I said. "I'm gettin' darn near as old and ugly as you."

"I guess."

And that was all he said.

Saturdays were never that busy at the gas station. I always had a few loafers in the morning—farmers hanging out between milkings, retirees. But by nine or so they were off to tend to their cows and yards, leaving me to putter around and wait for the occasional car to pull up to the gas pumps. The Old Man showed up just after dinner.

"About time you got here," I told him. "Don't worry, you haven't missed anything. Eric hasn't shown up yet. I swear, if he skips out I'm gonna—"

"—he won't skip out." He walked past me and took a seat in his usual booth. "He'll be here."

"I gotta be honest, I kind of hope he doesn't."

"Because him showing up will prove he's a good kid?"

"No. I already know that. But if he doesn't show, I'll have enough ammunition to use on him from now until I'm old and gone."

"You really do like him, don't you? Jabber too."

I wiped the counter and without looking up said, "I love both those boys. Guess the time's passed for me to have kids. Don't get me wrong, that's okay. Not blamin' you or anyone else. That's just the way it is."

"I think so, Andy," he told me. "I think you're exactly right."

"So anyway," I said, still wiping, "I reckon they're like the kids I never had."

The Old Man fumbled with his bracelet and said nothing. Which was disappointing, actually. I expected him to be happy that I would say such a thing.

"Are you in a mood again?" I asked him. "Is there some kind of angel shrink you need to go see?"

"Remember last night when I said you could always tell an

angel by his tears?"

"Yep."

"You asked me what an angel has to cry about. I never answered."

"Nope."

The Old Man let go of his bracelet and looked at me. "Angels feel the weight of the world, Andy. They see all the pain and all the suffering, just like everyone else. But they *feel* it, too. That's the worst part. God mourns this world. He loves it—all of it—and He loves every person who calls it home. But He mourns what's become of it, even though He knew from the beginning what would happen. There's a weariness to this world that touches everyone who walks upon it. Not just people, either. It's a fight as old as time itself. And no matter how hard you try, you can't keep the world away. Do you understand?"

I could. Even in Mattingly, the place where time slowed and then dragged and then stopped altogether, the weight of the world found us all. I could see it on the faces of the people who came and went from my gas station every day. I could see it on my own.

"Yes," I said. "I think I understand that."

"There is more to this life, Andy. Beyond it, yes. But within it, too. You're going to have to look beyond what you normally see. You won't understand it, so you'll have to trust."

"Trust what?" I said.

"God and me."

"Sure," I said. "I can do that."

He looked at me and said "Remember that" in a way that made me feel as though he knew I wouldn't.

"Would you please stop acting so weird?" I told him. "You're not only depressing me, you're messing with my mojo. I gotta be on my game for when Eric comes." I looked at the clock—twenty minutes until closing time. "If he comes. Almost time for us to head home."

I grabbed the push broom from behind the counter and began sweeping the store, which was for the most part the only tidying that ever needed to be done before closing.

"I have to go, Andy," the Old Man said.

"Just like you to skip out as soon as there's work to be done," I said, as I corralled a dust bunny by the trash cans. "You're not gonna hang around to see if Eric comes?"

"He's coming. But I need to go."

"Suit yourself," I said. I didn't look at him. Didn't feel like I needed to. Our good-byes were always temporary. "I'll see ya later."

I put the broom aside and turned my back to empty the trash. My hand grabbed the front of the can as I pulled it out from under the coffee counter and sank into a thick layer of tobacco spit. I decided for the thousandth time I needed to tell customers to stop using it as their own personal spittoon. I was going to ask the Old Man to remind me of that Monday morning, but then I heard the door open and close.

"You're using doors now?" I said, still bent over the can. "What's up with that?"

"What am I gonna use, you old codger? The window?"

I looked up to see Eric leaning against the counter. The booth was empty.

29

Settling Up

W ell lookie here," I said to Eric. "I'd just about written your sorry self off. Do you realize what you'd have been in for when I locked the door in another five minutes?"

"Do you realize that between gas and time, I figure that pack of smokes from yesterday is gonna set me back about thirty bucks?" he asked.

"The gas I can see," I said. "But I find it hard to believe your time is that valuable."

I grabbed the trash from the coffee station and the can by the door and brought both them and the broom to the counter.

"Here." Eric took a twenty from his pocket and waved it in my face. "Happy now?"

"No," I said. "Where's my interest?"

"Interest?" He pushed the mop of hair on his head back with a hand. "Are you kidding me?"

"What do you think I am, a charity? Ten percent interest, so you owe me twenty cents."

"I ain't got twenty cents," Eric said.

"Well then, we have a little problem, don't we?"

Eric offered a grin that was more dread than happiness.

"Here," I said. "You grab one bag and I'll grab the other. I'll call it even."

"Deal."

Eric took the bag from the can at the front door and followed me outside toward the garbage barrels on the edge of the parking lot. The sweet April air pushed into our clothes like a hug. Crickets chirped in the fields beyond the station. Stretching out in the distance were the polka-dotted lights of the town proper. My home. It was the hand of God that had brought me to Mattingly. I couldn't see that when my grandparents first brought me there, but I could see it right then. I could see it as clearly as Eric walking beside me, as clearly as the moon hanging over me. I looked from the lights down below to those up above for proof. The three-quarter moon smiled through a haze that dulled all but the brightest stars, yet the Big Dipper and my star held fast. There if I needed it. And for the first time I thought maybe I didn't and wouldn't, not any longer. The Old Man was right when he said there was much in this world to mourn. It was broken and sullied by the misplaced passions of history. But even so, if you tasted life long enough you would find it had a certain sweetness as well. I had my town and my life. I had my quietness. That's all any person needed. All anyone could want, really.

"So that's why Jabber didn't come," Eric said.

"Huh?" I asked. "Sorry, drifted off there. Why didn't he come?"

Eric shook his head and sighed, heaving his trash bag into an open barrel.

"I said Mom took off for the weekend and left us at home. She said she'd call tonight. Fat chance that'll happen, especially since she's probably drunk already. But Jabber said someone should be there just in case she did, and that's why he didn't come."

"Gotcha," I said. "You get those new plates for the Jeep yet?"

"She's gotta sign," he said. "She said she would, but she won't. You know her."

I did. Eric was right; his mother wouldn't sign.

I was trying to figure out a way for me to take care of it myself when the headlights swept over us. I turned to see an old Ford truck pull into the lot and up to the door. Two men were inside the single cab. I'd say they *got* out of the truck, but *fell* out would probably say it better. The driver wore ripped

jeans and a black T-shirt. He bumped his leg against the front
bumper and tripped, almost hitting the pavement. The passenger, smaller than his friend and dressed in shorts and a tank
top, laughed and pointed. He managed to hang onto the open
door with his free hand to prevent the same fate.

Saturday nights always brought out the more entertaining
customers, those who were on their way either to or from
some back road party. Most were passersby who didn't call
Mattingly home. The truck, I noticed, wasn't familiar to me.
And if I knew anything, it was what everyone in town drove.

"Jabber wanted to, though," Eric told me. "He knew you'd
have something smart to say to me, and he was dying to hear
it. He likes you, Andy. I know that's tough to see, but he does."

"And what about you?" I asked.

He smiled. "I could take you or leave you, but I guess you're
okay for a bumpkin."

"Well I'll just have to remember this moment," I said. "That's
the highest praise you've given me yet. Got a couple customers. Let's head back."

That's what I said—*Let's head back.* Why I used the plural
is beyond me. Like I said, I'd had my fair share of drunks in
the gas station, both men and children who thought they were
men. If I had known what would happen, I would have told
Eric to just go. I would have called his debt paid and told him
I'd see him Monday morning. Would have said good-bye right
there at the trash barrels and watched him drive away.

But I didn't. I said *Let's head back.* The both of us.

Because I didn't know. The Old Man wasn't there to tell me
otherwise.

Eric and I walked through the door.

The man in the shorts was next to a display of bug repellent
I'd set out for the hikers and fishermen. He was turning a can

end over end, mesmerized by the sight. A thin stream of drool
oozed from the corner of his open mouth and jiggled each
time he exhaled a chuckle.

His friend was roaming the aisles, up one and down the
other, shouting "Yo" over and over.

"You work here?" the man in front of me asked.

"Sure do. How ya doing?"

"Here he is, Taylor," the man called to his friend. "I found
'im."

"Yo," Taylor called from the drink coolers. "Where's your
beer, old-timer?"

"Don't sell any," I said.

I walked past the man in shorts and grabbed the broom to
put it away. Eric followed me, serious and quiet. I supposed
those two men were a reminder of his other life, the one away
from the comfort of my gas station. I could understand that. In
all my years I'd seldom taken a drink. Not because I never got
the urge, but because every time I'd thought of it I thought of
my mother being crushed by a beer truck.

"You don't sell no beer?" Taylor asked. "You hear that, Charlie? This guy here don't got no beer to sell."

"Man don't sell no beer's a stupid man," Charlie answered,
and then bent himself over laughing. He dropped his can of
bug spray to the floor and chased after it like a drunk puppy.

"There's a Texaco right down the road a ways," I said.
"Timmy'll sell you some beer."

Taylor looked at me. "You tryin' to get rid of us?"

"Nope, just trying to help you out and close up."

"You got a bathroom in here?"

"Back in the corner."

The big man lumbered toward the back and flung open the
door, cussing both me and my store. Charlie remained where
he was, clutching the can. I half expected him to open it and
try to take a drink. I hoped he did.

"Man don't sell no beer's a stupid man," he said again.

"Got ya the first time, buddy." I turned to Eric, who was

standing on the other side of me. "Why don't you get on out of here?"

"You sure, Andy?"

I waved him off. "Oh yeah. These guys will get outta here in a few minutes, and I'm heading home after that. I'll see you Monday."

Eric nodded but didn't move. His eyes were fixed on Charlie, who was now going through the display of lighters on the counter. He'd pick one up, light it, toss it aside. Then another, and another, until they were all a pile by the register.

"You're gonna buy those lighters or you're gonna clean them up," I told him.

Charlie ignored my threat and asked, "You sell smokes, or is that like the beer? You one o' them Armish or somethin'?"

"I sell smokes," I said. "But I'm closing up. Texaco's open for another hour. You can get your smokes there with your beer."

"Don't you get smart with me, Grandpa. You hear me?"

Charlie tripped and lunged his way around the corner to where Eric and I were standing. Eric shrank and then reached out for my shoulder, but by then I had moved. I met Charlie before Charlie met me and shoved my face in his.

"You're drunk," I said. "You're drunk and you're an idiot, and if you and your buddy don't get out of here, I'm gonna teach you the manners your mama never did. You hear me?"

Charlie's eyes blinked. He raised his hands in mock surrender and backpedaled to his pile of lighters on the counter. He began clumsily snapping them back into place on the display, growling at me.

I turned back to Eric. "I'll see you Monday, okay?"

Eric was still. "You shouldn't drink," he told Charlie.

"What'd you say to me?" Charlie asked him.

"You . . . shouldn't . . . drink."

"Eric," I said.

Charlie slurred, "You best mind your own business, sissy boy." The last part sounded like *issy boy*. He pointed two fingers in Eric's direction. The last lighter for him to put back was stuck between them.

The bathroom door jerked open and Taylor stumbled out. One leg of his jeans had been tucked into his boots, the other out. The front of his shirt poked out of his open fly. He saw Charlie pointing at Eric and quickened his pace.

"What's goin' on here?" he said.

"Sissy boy over there's tryin' to preach to me," Charlie said. "Says I shouldn't have no beer."

"That right, sissy boy?" Taylor said to Eric.

I gripped the push broom in my hand. I'd seen my share of Charlies in my life, cowards whose only courage was a fleeting one found in the bottom of a liquor bottle. Taylor, though, was different. He had the eyes of one beholden to neither judgment nor decency, pale and deep and empty.

Eric moved closer to me.

"You ain't got age enough to be shootin' off your mouth like that to us," Taylor said to him.

"But I do," I said. "Now I'm telling you boys for the last time. You get out of here. Now. Closing time."

I met Taylor's stare and refused to look away.

Charlie watched us, fingering the lighter in his hand.

"Eric," I said, "you get along. Like I said, closing time. You two fellas get outta here, too."

"Hey, Pops," Taylor smiled and said. "We ain't got no problems here. Me 'n' Charlie just out having a good time. We'll get along, won't we, Charlie?"

Charlie snorted. "Sure. Like 'at fella said, 'we should all just get along.'"

Eric made his way past me and said, "I'll see you soon, Andy."

"See ya," I said.

He walked past Taylor, who extended his left arm toward him.

"Come on, buddy," he told Eric. "We ain't got no beef, right?"

"Right," Eric said. But his head was down and his pace was quick, and those things said *no*.

Taylor pulled him in for a sloppy hug and wrapped his left arm around Eric's back. Eric gave way in an act of surrender, looking at me with a grin. I began to return it but then saw Taylor's hand slip behind his own back. He drew the hunting knife out and back, giving it space for momentum.

Then he pulled Eric into the blade.

There was a pop and then a sucking sound. Eric's eyes were still on me and suddenly grew wide. His mouth fell open as Taylor drew the knife out and back and into Eric again.

And then again.

I screamed, raising the push broom and then bringing it down onto Taylor's head. The broom shattered in half, the bristles flying off into the corner of the wall and handle still in my hands. Taylor yelped and fell to his knees, dropping Eric onto the floor. The knife was still in the boy's stomach up to the handle.

Charlie leapt at me. I saw his advance and caught him with the sharp end of the broken broom, cutting his face from his right eye to his jaw. He shrunk backward, arms raised and pleading for mercy. I turned toward Eric, who lay with his back to the floor. His eyes were open, pleading. A pool of blood formed around him like a grotesque fountain.

"Eric?" I gasped.

His mouth moved, but the air escaped as hisses through the holes in his torso.

Taylor had managed to pick himself up and was now trying to bend over Eric to retrieve the knife. I swung the broom handle like a bat and connected with the side of his head, sending him sprawling.

"Eric," I said. Tears streamed down my neck. I was trembling from the fear and rage. "Sweet Jesus, Eric."

"Hey, Grandpa," Charlie said.

I drew the handle back with my left hand, but it was too late. Charlie had sobered enough to realize that even if he didn't have a weapon, he could still make one. He had the can of bug spray in one hand and the lighter in the other. I looked up just in time to see the streak of fire headed toward me, as yellow as the sun and as hot as hell itself. I made a useless attempt to throw up my free hand. Flames surrounded my head, robbing me of air and all sense, and knocked me backward onto the floor. Charlie's boot stomped down hard on Eric's chest. The other one smashed against the wound in his stomach.

One of them, I'm not sure which, picked up the broomstick and smashed it into my head. The handle snapped along with my skull.

I heard the ring of the cash register opening and things being thrown and knocked over. In the fog around me there was the sound of a door and the engine of their truck revving.

I lay near Eric on the floor. My head throbbed and burned, and my singed throat screamed for air. The ceiling stared down at me and began to swim in ripples as my body surrendered to spasms. I raised a hand to still myself. The blood that covered it was not my own. I dropped it back to the floor.

Eric wheezed. I turned my head toward him. The fountain of blood coming from his chest and stomach had turned into a torrent. He was moving his legs and arms. My first thought was of him making a blood angel in the floor because there was no snow.

"Andy?" he whispered. "You good, Andy?"

I could say nothing. My body had pushed the Pause button on my lungs, and I was stuck on exhale.

Eric reached out with his hand and took mine. "You good, Andy?"

His face had lost all color and his lips were blue and trembling. His grip was loose, almost lifeless, yet even so it dug into my exposed flesh and sent shock waves of searing pain through me. I held on. Held on to him and me.

Eric opened his mouth to speak again, but the words he whispered were garbled with the blood that spurted from his mouth. His hand went slack.

And then he was gone.

If there was any comfort in that moment, any notion of rightness, it was that I would follow him soon. We'd meet Jesus together. Shadows formed in front of my eyes as the room grew dark around me. Tiny pinpricks of black filled the air. I remember wishing I were outside again, out there in the sweet April air and staring up at my wishing star, saying my final prayer to please let me go. Let me leave. Let me find Eric in that distant land so I can tell him all the things I never had. That he was good and that he was my friend and that I loved him as my own.

I looked past Eric to the Old Man's empty booth.

And waited for death.

30

The Plan

Alpenglow gathered at the tops of the Blue Ridge beyond the windows of the hospital room and readied to spill onto the valley. Robins and jays sang for their breakfast. In the distance diesel engines roared and then idled. Stillness gave way to awakening in a manner I supposed was designed to give me hope, but was instead twisted into a harsh reminder that the world did not pause when it crushed you—it simply moved on with no regard for your catching up.

Yet aside from the beeping monitors and Elizabeth cutting her paper, the room was silent, as if it had paused to listen. We were each too busy thinking or not thinking about the story of that night, the horrid tale of the last object in my box. She offered no sympathy and I offered no tears. Both were understood if not present, and neither would have done much good at the time.

The silence was broken by Kim knocking at the door.

"Good morning, Sunshine," she said.

Elizabeth looked up at her and smiled.

"Morning, Kim," I said.

"Don't want to bother," she said. "Just wanted to let you know I'm going to call Jake. I wish I could've put it off longer, Andy, but I just couldn't."

"Don't worry about that," I said. "I'll talk to him whenever he's ready."

"He'll be on his way soon. I figured I could go ahead and change your bandages before then. It'll make you feel better, and that might make talking to him more comfortable."

"I'd appreciate that."

"Okay. I'll let you get your wits about you for a little while, and then I'll be back. Anything you need in the meantime? Maybe some breakfast?"

I looked to Elizabeth, who shook her head.

"Nope, we're fine. Thanks, Kim. Heard more from Owen?"

"No," she said. "I expect he's waiting on me to tell him whether this is just a bump in the road or a wall we've run into."

She stood at the door, watching. Waiting, I supposed, for a little bit of my advice. I didn't know what to say other than "Look in your heart, Kimmie. There's your answer."

"Okay, then." Kim lingered for a moment at the door just in case. "Sure you're fine?" she asked. "You don't look so good."

"I'm as fine as I can be. Promise."

She nodded and said, "Okay, then. I'll see y'all in a little while."

Kim left Elizabeth to me and closed the door. My left hand began to feel as though a knife had been shoved into the palm. I looked down and realized it was Eric's key chain. I'd held it tighter and tighter through the entire story until it nearly pierced the skin. When I loosened the grip, my palm held the outline of an angel.

I decided I'd come far enough with my story to warrant finishing it.

"They stumbled into Timmy Griffith's Texaco station a little while later," I said. "Bruised and bleeding and wanting their beer. Timmy wasn't going to sell them anything either, not in their condition. Charlie had found his courage again by that time, and he got in Timmy's face and said they'd do to him what they did 'down at the Armish man's place.' Once Timmy realized they were serious, he beat them both with the axe handle he kept behind the counter. One of them, the scary one—Taylor—he got away somehow. Timmy locked Charlie in the cooler and called over to Peter Boyd's place just down the road.

"Pete had guys over every Saturday night to grill up some steaks and play poker. One of those guys was Timmy's brother-in-law Jake, the town sheriff who I guess I can't avoid anymore. Joey and Frankie were usually there, too. Those are the guys who brought me here in the ambulance. Joey and Frankie took off to check on me, and Jake took off for the Texaco before Timmy could kill those two boys. That's the way it is in Mattingly. We're good people, and we're all a family. Hurt someone in that family, and you're apt to find our own justice. I'm not saying that's right, I'm just saying that's the way it is."

Elizabeth put her folded sheet of paper in her lap and slipped the pair of scissors into her pocket. "So Jake is still looking for Taylor?" she asked.

I nodded. "Guess that's part of the reason why Jake needs to talk to me so bad."

"I'm so sorry, Andy," Elizabeth said. "I can't imagine how that feels."

"Jake'll get him," I said. "Jake's a good guy. He sort of fell into that job. Family thing, in a way. You say you can't imagine how I feel? I can't imagine how he feels. Mattingly's never seen anything like this."

"Did Charlie confess to Jake?"

"He didn't have to. Kimmie said Jake got all he needed from the video camera I have at the store. Got the whole, horrible thing." I smiled to myself as a thought occurred. "I expect he got a lot of what looked an awful lot like me talking to myself, too. But ol' Jake is a good guy. He won't think any less of me."

"Well, maybe you really won't have to be that involved at this point since they have the tape."

"Hope so," I said, though I didn't really think that was the case. "I'm glad he got that tape. It'll make things easier for everyone involved except for Taylor and Charlie. But I swear, Elizabeth, that's one movie I never want to see. If they sit me up there in that courtroom and make me watch that, it might be the end of me. It'll be bad enough having to play it over and over in my head for the rest of my days, the way those boys who come home from war keep seeing all that hell they had to go through. But I never want to see it with my eyes."

Elizabeth smiled and said, "You're stronger than you know, Andy Sommerville."

"Strong?" I asked. The words came out in a chuckle. "I'm not strong, Elizabeth. Maybe there was a time when I thought that might be true, but not anymore. I don't have anything left now. It's all been taken."

"The things that matter in life, Andy, the things that make you who you are, cannot be taken from you. You can only surrender them."

"Then I surrendered them," I said. "I surrendered them on the way here."

"Tell me."

"Can't say much, I guess. I remember being in the ambulance and not knowing what was going on. I saw Joey and Frankie, but I didn't know who they were. I couldn't talk and could barely breathe. And then I saw the Old Man stare down over me. He said he was there with me and that everything would be okay. *Okay.* Can you believe that? Eric was lying somewhere with a sheet over his head and I was on the way to the hospital with my face on fire, but it was going to be *okay*. I lost it. Just lost it right there."

"I can imagine you did," she said. "I think anyone would in that situation. That was a traumatic experience, Andy. No one would be in their right mind."

"Oh, I was in my right mind. I was in as right a mind as I've ever been. I had nothing left. And more than that, I realized I didn't have much to lose in the first place. I'd spent my whole life drifting, not really giving myself to anyone or anything. Never had a family, never made any real friends other than Eric and Jabber, just...there. Taking up space. I never had anything to give to anyone."

"That's not true."

I ignored her. "Some things that happen in life stick to the soul like a burr and scratch it raw. Do you know why?"

"Why?"

"Because something like that makes a person question everything they've always believed in, that's why. All that happening and then the Old Man telling me it was going to be all right was my burr. In that moment I saw the world for what it really was, Elizabeth. Saw it clear and true."

Elizabeth crossed her legs and folded her arms.

"You don't believe me?" I asked.

"I don't know," she said. "Why don't you tell me what the world really is, Andy? Then I'll tell you if you saw it clear and true or if you saw it muddy and twisted."

I glanced out the windows again toward the yellow slivers of light peeking over the tops of the mountains. It was going to be a beautiful day, I thought. Spring in Virginia was the closest thing to perfection you could find in this world. It sparkled in greens and yellows and newness. Yet I felt a strange separation from that beauty then. The clear air and the tall mountains seemed images rather than the things themselves.

I had read stories of people who had cheated death, of how their closeness to the boundary between this world and the next had inspired them to live more fully and well. I would not be counted among them. I remembered then another story, a legend that said Lazarus never smiled again after Jesus raised him from the dead. I would be counted with him. He would understand.

"The world is a place where the weeds will always choke the flowers," I told her. "It's lost. Gone to hell. It's a place where children die, where people twist what should be beautiful into something sick. They choose selfishness over kindness. It's a world where faith is laughed at.

"People spend their lives trying to put a wall between themselves and the way things are. They think it's a barrier nothing can get through. But it's a lie. All of it. They can build that wall all they want, build it with money or family or prayer or whatever, and it won't matter. The Old Man was right, you can't keep the world away. It's too hungry to let you go. It will swallow you."

"Is that what you think happened to you?" Elizabeth asked. "Did the world swallow you because your faith was found wanting?"

"I trusted God," I said. "I lived a good life. I did everything the Old Man said. What did it get me?"

I paused so Elizabeth could answer. She didn't.

"What did it get me, Elizabeth?"

"You tell me, Andy."

"It got me *this*," I said, pointing to my bandages, "and it got my friend killed. That was my reward."

"Your reward? Is that what you were after?"

"No," I said, then, "Yes," and finally, "I don't know. No. I don't want a reward, Elizabeth. I just want to believe that in the end good people can make a difference in this world, and I don't think I can do that anymore."

"Is that what you really think, Andy?"

"I wouldn't say it if I didn't mean it."

"People say a lot of things they don't mean," she said. "They say it from their anger and their hurt. Speech is all about emotion, but you have to use your everything to *say* something. So are you saying that with your everything, or are you saying that from the part of you that feels angry and hurt?"

"I'm saying it from the part of me that doesn't understand why this *happened*."

"You're not going to understand everything, Andy. That's why you need a faith that doesn't ignore or deny those questions, but accepts that sometimes the answer isn't the point."

"Not the *point*?" I said, and a little too loudly. Kim's eyes met mine from across the hall. She looked worried. "Of course it's the point."

"So if you knew the reasons why God allowed this to happen, your pain would be lessened?"

I considered her question and almost answered a very firm and very loud yes. It would have been lessened. The sting of much of the world's suffering came not from the hurt it brought, physical or otherwise. It came instead from the unanswered questions it birthed, those gaping holes that were tilled and turned upward into the light by life's circumstances.

"God left me three nights ago," I said. "He left me, the Old Man left me, and Eric left me. I should have died that night. If that drunk idiot would've been a little more sober, maybe he would have hit me better with that fire. Maybe Taylor would have stabbed me, too. Then it would be over. Finally over."

Elizabeth uncrossed her legs and shot toward me. "Don't you ever say that, Andy Sommerville," she said. "Do you hear me? Don't you ever say those words."

It was the closest thing to anger she'd shown me. It would have been enough to take me aback too, but it didn't. Because suddenly I was angrier.

"I'll say them because I mean them," I shouted. "I'll say them because it's the truth. I've done nothing in my life, Elizabeth. I *have* nothing. Nothing but this stupid stuff in this stupid box that means *nothing*. And yet here I sit while the one person I knew who was worth *something*, who could have made a difference in this God-forsaken dump of a world, is getting *buried*."

There is within every human heart an empty reservoir that is ours alone to fill with either the beauty or the ugliness of life. Until that moment I had always believed mine to be filled with the beauty, or at least what I could summon of it. But I was wrong. It was anger that was spilling into that secret hole in my heart, a rage against a God who was supposed to be love but was apathy instead. One who would allow my father to kill my mother, answer the prayer of a little boy with an angel that would only abandon him, and allow evil and darkness free reign over the world to murder a boy so pure and so good that his last breath of life was spent asking me if I was okay.

But if I was fool enough to believe I held peace rather than anger, it was more foolish to believe I could keep it penned. It spilled out then, all of it, and I was powerless to stop the surge.

My left hand shot out and pushed Elizabeth backward into

the chair. She hit with a thud and glared at me, stunned at what I'd suddenly become. I sat trembling, staring at her as she stared at me, both angry and ashamed at what that anger had done.

Sprawled out on the bed before me was the story of my life, trinkets and mementoes of days spent with neither purpose nor any definable meaning. Pieces of a puzzle, Elizabeth had said. She was the one who had suggested we should piece them together. I was the one to see that once hinged together, what they formed was both pictureless and wanting. Eric's death had only defined how much he could never give and how much the world had lost. My survival only defined the opposite.

I flung the pieces and the box that held them, crashing them against the floor and the far wall. I wept my agony, crying out to Elizabeth, to God, to anyone left who could listen.

"Help me," I said.

I reached out, certain Elizabeth would shrink away. Instead I found her hand already reaching for mine.

"I'm sorry, Elizabeth," I cried.. "I'm so sorry. Please forgive me. I just don't understand. Help me understand."

Elizabeth rose to collect my box and everything that went in it, gathering them with the care and attention of someone charged with guarding treasure. She sat the box where it had been in my lap and then placed my hand over it.

"Never doubt the course of your life, Andy," she said. "Never doubt that God has a plan. There is always a plan. Always. And for everyone. That means you, and that meant Eric."

I sniffed and shuddered again at the mention of Eric's name. "God took him too soon," I said.

"No," she soothed. "No, God did not take him too soon. God took him just at the right time."

"You can't *say* that," I said, my voice rising again.

"I can," Elizabeth answered. "I can because I know it must be that way. We all have a purpose in this life, Andy. A purpose only we can fulfill. I know that to you, Eric was taken too soon. But you have to believe he had done everything God wanted him to do. The Old Man was right, Andy—the world is a bad place. But you're wrong to assume there isn't anything that can be done about it."

"It won't *let* you do anything about it," I managed.

"You need to think of this world as a house with many rooms. Some are big and wide and hold many people. Others are small and cramped and hold just a few. But all of those rooms are dark inside.

"When people are born, God gives them a light and places them in one of those rooms. Some are put into the big rooms with many other people. They're the ones who live long and touch the lives of many. Others are like you and Eric. They're given the smaller rooms. They may not live long and they may not touch many, but the lives they change would have been otherwise lost.

"You have to see that, Andy. You have to understand. The size of the room God puts you in doesn't matter. All that matters is that you shine your light. Eric shined his. And this," she said, placing her hand onto the box, "this is your light."

"It's not," I said. "There's nothing special in there."

"Oh yes there is, Andy. There is evil in this world, and that evil thrives by hiding the light. And do you know how it hides that light?"

I shook my head. When I did, tears wet the bandages around my eyes.

"It hides the light by convincing people they are ordinary," she said.

Elizabeth sat in her chair and looked at me. The smile that spread across her face was so bright I almost had to shade my eyes.

"How do you know all of that?" I asked her.

"That's easy," Elizabeth said. She held up the shredded piece of paper in her hand. "Because I'm done, and because you have no idea who you are."

31

Ordinary Things

Elizabeth and I stared at one another, her with the Cheshire Cat grin and me with the confused look of a man too worn for riddles. I had never been so utterly emptied inside. Eric's death, my injuries, and a sleepless night spent rehashing the circumstances surrounding both had left me questioning many things, but not about who I was. What I was supposed to do and when I was supposed to do it and why it had to happen, yes. But not who I was. My identity was the very last thing I felt I owned, the one thing that still belonged to me and me alone. And though it was an individuality that disappointed me, it was at least something. When you've been stripped of nearly everything, that last little something mattered. It mattered much.

"That's not a very good answer to my question," I said. "I know I got my head bumped, Elizabeth, but I haven't forgotten who I am."

"I don't think you ever knew who you are, Andy," she said. "Not really."

"I'm not Andy Sommerville?"

"You're not the Andy Sommerville you were."

"Then who am I?"

Elizabeth smiled and said, "The person you're supposed to be."

The room was spinning, though I wasn't sure if it was from the medication Kim had been pumping into my arm all night or the way Elizabeth had begun to talk. Or both.

"Elizabeth," I said, "I've sat here all night talking to you, right?"

"Right."

"And despite both my better judgment and my introverted nature, I think I've been fairly open."

"You have."

"I've told you things I've never told another soul. I even told you what brought me here. I'd hate to have to go through all that only to find a bunch of psycho mumbo-jumbo at the end."

"Good," Elizabeth said, "because I don't have any."

"What do you have, then?"

"Truth, Andy. Your truth."

I turned around to look at the clock on the wall above me. "You got that in seven hours? I thought people had to go through years of counseling to get something like that."

"I have to work a little faster here," Elizabeth said. "Time is an issue, and we don't have much of that left."

Her words were nonchalant, but for me they carried a weight of finality I was not prepared to hear. Elizabeth would have to leave. Eventually. But I supposed that to me *eventually* always meant later, and later would always be a safe distance away.

"Is it almost time for you to go?" I asked her.

"Yes," she said. The smile was still there, but it had lessened. "Like I said earlier, I should have left a while ago. But I wanted to stay here with you. It's important."

"You won't be here when Jake comes to talk to me."

It was a statement rather than a question, but the pleading was still in my eyes. I wanted to be strong for Elizabeth. I wanted to show her the very best part of me. But in the end, I knew I couldn't. Whatever masks I'd worn to separate my true self from the world could not stand against the gentleness of her presence. It was a hardness borne of understanding and patience, one that exuded a strength that could not only move mountains but convince them they should be moved. Elizabeth could see me for no one else than the man I truly was. I should have feared that notion. I should have seen it and shrunk from its truth. But I knew she would be the one to see that the man behind the parts I played, the man who hurt and struggled, was the very man I should show to the world. That and that alone was the very best part of me.

"Please," I said.

Elizabeth straightened her shirt and cleared her throat. It was a vain attempt at something that could delay her next words just one more second, for her benefit and for mine.

"I'm leaving soon, Andy. We need to hurry and get this last little bit done, because it's the most important part. We're close."

"Will I see you again?" I asked.

"Oh my, yes," she said. She nodded her head so hard that her ponytail flopped in the air. "You can count on that, Mr. Sommerville. I'd have it no other way. And to prove that to you, I'd like to do something."

"What?"

"Eric's key chain was the last thing you put into your box. Doesn't seem right that the last thing should be something that causes you so much sadness. I know the Old Man isn't around to tell you, but would it be all right if I put something in there? Just to hold for me until we see each other again? It'll be my promise to you."

At that moment, I could think of nothing more I'd rather have. "Yes," I said. "Please."

Elizabeth reached behind her head and wiggled her hand. In the next moment brown hair spilled down over her shoulders like a frame around a masterpiece. She held her hair tie up to me. It glimmered in the rising sun that shone through the window, and I saw that it was not leather after all. It was more a kind of silk. She sat it in the box. "There," she said.

"Thank you."

She smiled like a little girl keeping a secret. "My pleasure."

"Then stay with me. At least until Jake leaves."

"I can't," she said.

"Why?" I asked. "And don't say it's procedure or anything like that. I've known Jake since he was a boy. He won't mind."

"It has nothing to do with Jake, Andy. It's for something else. I won't be here for the same reason the Old Man wasn't in the gas station that night."

I tried to swallow but couldn't. I coughed instead, which served to start me breathing again and to hide the water pooling in my eyes.

"What?" I asked. "What kind of thing is that to say to me? Don't say that, Elizabeth. Don't you compare yourself to him."

"Why? It's true."

"Why can't you be here?"

"Because you won't need me."

"Because...what?"

I began laughing then—the sort of laughter people use when they're trying to decide if what they'd just heard was something that should make them amused or angry. I was leaning toward angry. This, I thought, *this* was why I'd never opened myself up to anyone. Why I never trusted. Because the moment you did, you were left alone again.

Elizabeth's smile was gone, replaced by the stone-faced appearance of someone whose only reason for speaking was to convey truth. No minced words and no flowery suppositions. Fact, plain and simple.

"You're saying the reason the Old Man wasn't there that night was because I didn't need him? That's what you're telling me?"

"That's what I'm telling you," she said.

"Did you not hear anything I've said?"

Elizabeth smiled again. "I've heard every word, Andy."

This time I didn't bother to cough and hide my tears. This time I showed them. "How can you say that to me?" I said. "Of all the things you could tell me, why would you tell me that?"

"The Old Man told you two things before he left. He said you were going to have to look beyond what you normally see, even if you don't understand it. That you will have to trust.

And he said that everything he's shown you has come down to this."

I sniffled and said nothing.

"He was right, Andy. Right about everything."

"I don't give a *damn* if he was right," I said. "He left us there that night. He could have done something."

"No, he couldn't," she said. "He couldn't have done anything, and you couldn't have either, Andy. It was Eric's time, pure and simple. But it wasn't your time. Your time is just beginning, and I'm here to help you do that. I'm here to tell you what it means. But first I have to tell you who you're supposed to be."

"And who am I supposed to be?" I asked.

"Jabber's angel," Elizabeth answered. She held her hands out and up in a curious way, one that reminded me of the way Jordan raised hers that day at our bench so long ago. A way that was meant to show her statement was not nearly as ridiculous as I would think it to be, that instead it made all the sense in the world.

But it didn't. There were so many untruths in her answer that my mind couldn't process them all. And despite the still-fresh regrets I carried of losing my temper with her earlier, I couldn't help but feel that reservoir of black in my heart filling again. This was what I sat up all night waiting for? This was the wisdom the Old Man said I needed? I didn't even know what she meant.

"Only angels get to be angels. Besides, if there's anyone alive least fit to have a halo and some wings, it'd be me."

"Now, I don't think that's so."

"Which part?" I asked.

"Both."

Kim knocked at the door again. This time she didn't bother to wait for our invitation, she just kept going. Behind her was a small cart. Scissors, tape, and gauze were arranged on top in their typical hospital fashion—even and straight and sterile.

"Okay, Mr. Andy," she said. "Ready to feel some fresh air?"

I looked at Elizabeth and tapped a finger on my wrist. "We have time," she told me.

"Sure," I said to Kim. "I could use the break. Let's see how ugly I am."

"Andy!" Elizabeth said.

"Now don't be saying that," Kim echoed. "You're gonna be just as handsome as you ever were."

"What if I was never handsome?" I asked.

Kim answered, "Andy Sommerville, you could have the pick of any woman in this state if you wanted to."

I looked at Elizabeth looking at me.

"Think so?" I asked, to the both of them.

"Yes," they both answered.

Kim took a pair of surgical scissors in her hand and eased up to me.

"Now you hold still," she said. "I don't want to be lopping off an ear."

She snipped at my bandages with the same easy intent and grace that Elizabeth had shown with her paper and then put the scissors back down on the cart. She slowly began unwrapping.

"Sure ain't how an angel spends his mornings," I said to Elizabeth. "Least not that I recall."

"Hold still now," Kim said. "Almost there."

The last few layers of bandages sloughed off. My face and head felt lighter, so much so that I thought I would have to hold them in place or everything above my neck would float away.

"Now let me get these pads off."

Kim reached out with her fingernails and eased one pad off, then another, then the rest. The cool air washed over my naked skin and left me tingling.

I raised my hands to touch my face, but Kim slapped them away.

"Now don't go doing that," she said. Kim stood next to Elizabeth and the two regarded me. I suddenly felt naked again.

"Well?" I said.

"Pretty as a June bug."

"I'll second that," said Elizabeth.

"I gotta say, Andy," Kim said, "you look mighty fine minus that big ol' beard. Maybe if Owen and I don't work out, I'll make a run at you."

"You get paid to tell lies like that all day?" I teased.

"Ain't no lie, sweetie."

"Well, I appreciate that. I expect I'll be growing it back as soon as I'm able, though. When's Jake coming?"

Before Kim could answer we were interrupted by a barrage of pitched electronic beeps. The quiet of the hallway erupted in organized chaos. Metal clanged, voices shouted, walks morphed into runs. A mechanical voice called a code I could not decipher.

"Gotta go," Kim said, bolting for the door. "I'll be back, Andy. Stay still, okay?"

I turned to Elizabeth and said, "What's going on?"

"Heart attack," she said, rising from her seat. "Down the hall." She reached the door and looked to her left, past where a throng of nurses and orderlies were heading.

"Sorry," she said, turning back to me.

"Who is it?"

"Mr. Alexander," she said. "the man down the hall, and Kim's other priority. He's put up a good fight, but I think that fight's over. Poor man."

"He didn't have a counselor?" I asked.

"No," Elizabeth said. She returned to the chair beside me. "The higher-ups make that call based on a lot of different criteria."

"So I guess since I'm an angel, I get preferential treatment around here."

Elizabeth leaned forward and took my hand the same way she had through the night. Had I known it would be the last time I would feel her skin against mine, I would have held on and never let go. But we're seldom told beforehand which of our times will be the last in this life. That, I suppose, is reason enough to treat them all that way.

"Listen to me, Andy," she said. "You are special. More than you know. The story of your life hasn't been finished yet. You're getting there, but then again everyone else is getting there, too. These past days? They're not a period, they're a comma. They're a pause and the continuation of a thought greater than your own. And you already have every answer to every question you've ever asked."

"Then where are they?" I asked her.

Elizabeth pointed to the box on my lap. "Right there," she said.

The box sat closed on my lap, and for the first time I felt afraid to open it. It didn't repulse me as it had before I had thrown both it and its contents across the room, but neither did it bring me the sort of confused comfort it had always brought. My box was simply a thing, not unlike the bed I was in or the clock on the wall behind me or the morning sun outside. And perhaps, I thought, it was even less than a thing. At least the bed and the clock and the sun were useful.

"Stop it," Elizabeth said.

"Stop what?"

"Stop thinking whatever you're thinking. You have to trust what you don't understand, right? That's what the Old Man told you."

"First of all," I said, "I'm not even convinced he knew what he was talking about." I paused and then added, as gently as I could, "Or you, for that matter. And second of all, I'm not sure I want to listen to someone who wasn't around when I needed him most."

"And now you're not sure you want to listen to me either, right? Because I said I was leaving. Leaving just like everyone else has left. You wear your loneliness as a badge, Andy. You think you've suffered for your faith. I don't think that's true. I think it's just easier for you to see your isolation as God's will than it is to see it as your fear."

Her words crushed me with the weight of their truth, a weight that no amount of denial or reasoning could balance. It was true. All of it. It was a truth born the day my parents died and reinforced when my grandfather passed on years later. Then my grandmother. By then I had been made aware of this one great truth—nothing lasted in this world. People came and people went like tides, and every time they were snatched away a bit of my shore went with them. I could not bear that hurt. Would not. And for that, I had suffered far worse.

I left Elizabeth's question unanswered and instead pointed to the box. "My answers are in here?"

"Yes."

"All of them?"

"No," she said, "I don't think so. You'll never have all the answers, Andy. You know that. God only gives you the ones you need. The Old Man said you'd need what's in that box one day. He was right. And you were right when you said that day is today. But you're not supposed to sit there and stare at them. You're supposed to put them together to see what they become."

"Don't tell me that," I said. "There's no puzzle here, Elizabeth. I based my everything on the assumption that I had someone...something...concrete in my life. I thought I could put my weight on the Old Man when I needed to. But when I did, I fell through. I'm still falling."

"And you're afraid no one's going to catch you?"

"Maybe," I said.

"Or maybe this has left you feeling like you're not worth catching. You're a smart guy, Andy Sommerville. Seems to me you should have put most of this together by now."

"What's that mean?" I said.

"It means you're angry and you're hurt, and I can't blame you for that. But those are two things that can keep people from seeing the truths of their lives. I'm not belittling what happened to you, Andy. I'm just saying that sometimes you can focus so much on the noise that you miss what's being said."

"I need to know why Eric and I were left to die that night," I said. "And I need to know what I'm supposed to do now."

"Once you understand the what, the why won't matter. And you already know the what."

"I'm supposed to be Jabber's angel."

Elizabeth smiled and said, "Yes."

"Elizabeth, I want to understand what you're saying, I really do. But I just don't."

"You're thinking in parts, Andy. You think everything's separate, and it isn't. Everything is connected. You, the Old Man, your box, Eric, Jabber. Even me. We're all spokes on a wheel."

"And where's that wheel going?" I asked her.

"Somewhere wonderful," she said. "I promise. You just have to hang on a bit longer. The ride gets a little bumpy before it smoothes out."

I opened the box and peered inside. All of my—*souvenirs?* I thought, then, *Trinkets? Pieces?* I settled on *pieces*—pieces were inside. Her hair tie sat on top like a crown.

"There are no answers here, Elizabeth," I said. "They're just things. Ordinary things."

"I think the magic lies in the ordinary, Andy. For everyone, but especially for you. You kept those for a reason."

"I kept them because he told me to," I said.

"There was a reason."

"Then tell me. Tell me that reason. No more talk, and no more stories. No more questions. Just tell me, please. If this is a puzzle, then help me put it together."

Elizabeth pulled her hair behind her shoulders and took a deep breath. I had the image of someone who was about to jump into deep waters.

"Okay, Andy. I think you've earned some answers. Let's start with the Old Man."

32

Heisme

Elizabeth rose from her chair and began walking around the room. Slowly at first, folding her arms in front of her as she watched her feet take first one step and then another, to the window and the clear spring day, and then back to my bed. She seemed nervous, which made me wonder how difficult it was going to be to hear was she was about to say. It was enough to tempt me to change my mind. I could tell her I didn't really want to know after all, that perhaps she had been right all along and I didn't need the answers I thought I did. I was injured. A victim, no less than Eric. And when you are a victim, you lash out and say things you don't really mean.

Yet I couldn't bring myself to say such things, because I didn't believe them. Could not. Regardless of what Elizabeth's answers were, she was right. I deserved them. Any hell upon this earth can be endured if there is truth and light to be found on the other side of it, and I had to trust there was truth and light to be found on the other side of mine.

That didn't mean I didn't steal a look at the door and harbor a small, secret hope that Kim would come walking in to bandage me back up. At that moment, I would have even settled for Jake.

She rested her hands on the side of my bed, looked at me, and said, "The Old Man is your angel."

I waited for her to say more, but more did not come. I felt as though she were pausing to allow the obvious to sink in.

" . . . Yes," I said. "Please don't tell me you've been sitting there all night concentrating so much on your scissors and paper that you missed the particular seven hours or so I spent talking about him."

Elizabeth winked at me and smiled. "Yes, I heard that. I heard every word. Now it's your turn to hear. What I mean is the Old Man is not a figment of your imagination."

"That might get you into some trouble with all those God-denying colleagues of yours," I said.

She waved me off. "There are counselors and there are Counselors. I am of the latter."

I offered Elizabeth a sigh. "Well, I'm glad. I thought for a minute you were going to tell me he was all in my head."

"No," she said. "The Old Man is real, Andy. And he is an angel. But he's not a real angel."

Instinct instructed me to massage the back of my head again in preparation for the pain I was certain would soon return.

"I don't understand what you mean."

Elizabeth sat back in her chair beside me. Her smile was gone, and though the tenderness was there, it was now of another sort. One with the purpose of not helping me to understand, but to hear.

"Almost every religion in the world incorporates something akin to angels in its belief system," she said. "Not just Christianity and Judaism. Islam, too. Even Buddhists and Hindus. Most of them have differing opinions about what angels are and what they do. But I'm going to stick to the Bible, okay?"

I nodded.

"It's easy to get weighed down by the concept. The Bible mentions archangels and cherubim and seraphim and just your plain old ordinary angels, if there is such a thing. Some folks have taken it further and said there are actually nine different types. That's not really important to us. What's important is what the term *angel* originally meant. The Hebrew word is *malach*. It means 'messenger.' And it's related to the word *melacha*, which means 'task.'"

"I really don't see how this—"

"Wait," she said. "I'm getting there."

"Okay," I said.

"To the Old Testament Hebrews, angels weren't restricted to harps and halos. By their thinking, anyone could be an angel. You. Me. The neighbor down the street. Friends and strangers. Even people who aren't very angel-like. Anyone who helped you accomplish a task or convey some truth about God was an angel. Not a real one, maybe, with the glory or the trumpeting or the fiery swords. But a good image of one that was just as real. And in that respect, the Old Man is an angel."

"So you're saying . . . what? That he's a ghost? Some kind of spirit?"

"No," Elizabeth said. "But what he is and where he came from and how he came to you is . . . well, that might be the part that has to go unanswered for now. But I know this, Andy— God heard your prayer that night. He heard it and He answered it, and He sent you exactly who you needed."

"It doesn't matter to me whether he wore a halo or not," I said. "Doesn't matter if he was a real angel or sort of an angel. All that matters to me is that he always knew when stuff would happen, so I'm pretty sure he knew what he was skipping out on when he left me at the gas station that night. He didn't say a word to me, Elizabeth. He just left me and Eric there. The Old Man left Eric there to *die*, and he left me there to almost join him."

Elizabeth looked at me and pursed her lips. Then very slowly, very clearly said, "But you did join him, Andy."

I'll admit the first thing I thought was that I had misunderstood what Elizabeth had said, which wouldn't have been too difficult considering what she'd spent the last few minutes telling me. I'll also admit my second thought had something to do with a movie I once saw about a dead guy trying to help a kid who saw ghosts.

"You ain't saying I'm dead, are you?" I asked. "Because you and Kim can see me just fine."

"No, Andy. You're as alive as you can be. But in a way you

did die that night. Life isn't one unbroken line from beginning to end. There isn't one birth and one death, there are many of both. Things end so other things can begin. The Andy Sommerville who spent his life in the world but apart from it, who was intent on not getting too close to anyone? He died. You're not supposed to be him anymore. It's time to be the man God wants you to be, and you don't need the Old Man to do that. He's done his job. He's given you what you need. And as far as him leaving, I'm afraid nothing I could say would make your anger any less. I'm pretty good at what I do, but that's just something you'll have to work out for yourself. And you will. It won't be easy, but nothing worth anything is easy."

"And who is this man I'm supposed to be?" I asked her. "Because honestly, I don't feel like much of a man anymore. I don't feel like much of anything. All I want to do is go back to the way things were and erase the past three days."

"Life is lived forward, Andy. God put your eyes in front of you so you can see where you're going, not where you've been."

I stared out at the bright morning and said, almost to myself, "If the stars were out, I'd find mine. I told myself once that I didn't need to ask God for anything anymore, and that was stupid of me. I'll always need God, maybe more in my comfort than in my pain. I know you're trying to help me, Elizabeth. I know you're saying the things you think I need to hear. But I promise you the next time I look up into the night sky, I'm going to ask God to take it all away. To let me go back. And I'm going to pray just as hard as I did when I was a kid, and I'm going to watch and see if that star winks. You're telling me I have to be to Jabber what the Old Man was to me. I can't. Because the old me is the only me I know how to be. I'm not good for anything else. I'm not smart. I'm not wise. I'm just a man."

"You have all you need," she said. "You just don't know it yet."

"You keep telling me that," I said, "but I can't accept it. A part of me wants to believe that everything you're telling me is the truth, but another part of me thinks you're saying this just so I'll have a reason to keep going. Being there for Jabber would give me a purpose. And I want to do that, I really do. That poor boy has no one now. But you need to know that I can't be like the Old Man. I don't have all the answers. I'm stumbling through this life like everyone else."

"Listen to me, Andy," Elizabeth said. "God knows what He's doing. Knows better than you or me or anyone else. If this is what He wants you to do, and I think it is, then He's going to make sure you can do it. You didn't need answers the night when you were eleven and looked up at that star to pray. You didn't ask for an angel, Andy. You asked for someone who would *understand*. That's what Jabber needs now, and God's picked you for the job. Who better to send to a frightened young boy than someone who will understand?"

I offered her no answer.

Elizabeth reached into her pocket and brought out a small, square mirror. "Besides," she said, "you might not think you're an angel, but you look just like one."

She handed me the mirror for proof. I turned it over and closed my hand around it.

"No way," I said. "The last thing I need right now is to look at Charlie's handiwork."

"Part of this," Elizabeth said, "part of your healing, is accepting who you are. Trust me, it won't be easy. But it's the last step."

I looked from Elizabeth to the back of the mirror in my hand. I knew on the other side lay some sort of truth, the kind that comes with the facing of not What Could Be or What Should Be, but What Is. *The last step.* Elizabeth might have said those words, and yet I felt as though they'd been sung to me. It was a faint welcome just down the path of a long and raw journey. Not the end, perhaps, but at least an end. I considered then all the times over the years I'd told the hurting and the tired that when it comes to a journey, it was the going and not the getting there that made it worthwhile. What rubbish. What utter nonsense. No journey is worth taking unless there's a place to get to. Maybe Elizabeth was right, I thought. Maybe I was supposed to start over. And the best way to start over is to find out what you have to start with.

But if I was going to see *what* I had to start over with, I had to know *who* I had to start over with, too. If the Old Man had indeed left because his purpose had been completed, if life truly was a series of deaths and births, then I had to believe his leaving was so someone else could come. That someone was sitting beside me, and I had to tell her. Once and for all.

"Elizabeth," I said, "I just wanted to say that..."

I looked up to finish my sentence, looked for those beautiful eyes to drown myself in and those beautiful hands to rescue me from that drowning, but there were none. The chair was empty.

Elizabeth was gone.

"Elizabeth?" I said. "Hey. Where'd you go?"

I looked toward the bathroom. The door was open and the room was empty. Then to the hallway.

"Elizabeth?"

No answer. From outside the door, the hallway was now quiet and still.

Panic built in my chest. My heart thumped, my stomach sank. I let out a small whimper, like a lost child.

She didn't tell me good-bye, I thought. *She can't be gone, because she didn't tell me good-bye.*

"Elizabeth?" I called louder. "Where'd you go, Elizabeth? I'm ready to look now. I promise."

To prove my point and coax her back from wherever she had gone, I turned the mirror over. The polished surface cast an image I was not able to comprehend.

I was no longer me. My beard was gone, singed away by Charlie's makeshift flamethrower, which had also taken my hair and eyelashes. Left in their place were streaks of cracked red and pink skin that had aged me beyond my years.

But that was not the worst. Oh no, not the worst by far. That distinction was the sole property of what was staring back at me.

It was the Old Man's face.

In that moment my life shattered in a thousand pieces of glass, exploding out and around and into me, piercing skin and soul.

"Elizabeth?" I whispered.

I couldn't find her, couldn't see her. I reached out for the chair and took hold of air

("ELIZABETH HELP ME!")

but nothing was there. Truth blurred until I could not tell what was inside of my mind and what was out, what was real and what was not. Was I really there, in that room? Was Elizabeth? Or had that time and those people existed only in the darkness that Charlie had left me in?

Kim burst into the room, eyes wide and arms outstretched, ready to catch my fall. "Andy, what's wrong? What happened?"

"Elizabeth," I cried again.

Kim reached me and took me by the shoulders to keep me in my bed. The mirror Elizabeth had given me disappeared in our struggle. I reached for it but could not find it. "Andy, what's wrong with you?"

"He is me," I told her. The words came out slurred and panicked. Kim's grip recoiled slightly, then returned even stronger than it was before. "He is me, Kim. *Heisme.*"

She tried to ease me back into my bed. I pushed her away. "Someone help me here!" she called out into the hallway.

More nurses came. Orderlies. A man in a white coat.

"Heisme," I said again, and then, "Elizabeth. Where's *Elizabeth?*"

"Andy," Kim said, "I need you to listen to me, okay? You're okay. You've had a lot of medicine to ease your pain, okay?" And then she muttered, "Maybe too much."

"ELIZABETHHEISME!"

White Coat gave orders. Hallucinations, he called himself. Or me. Or to me. What?

Hallucinations.

Head trauma. Maybe too much.

Nurses and orderlies on me, holding me down.

I heard Kim tell White Coat: "He was alone all night talking to himself."

There was cold in my arm, cold like the ambulance.

You're gonna be okay, Andy Sommerville, the Old Man says. Said.

I murmured "Help me," though I felt sure I had cried that name into my mind rather than the air. Shadows enveloped me.

It was not Elizabeth who answered.

33

The Anvil

Walk to me *is what I am told, but not by sound. It is instead a knowing that feels surer than words could ever feel, one that pulls me forward in my darkness with no thought of danger or fear. What hellish shadows that grope for me are cast aside by a light that grows from a pinpoint to a star to a sun to something beyond my telling. It moves toward me as I move toward it, and the warmth I feel is the love I always handled but never embraced.*

The man's back is to me, his face hidden by long strands of black hair. I hear the clanging of the hammer in his hand as it is brought down upon an anvil, black and worn from countless ages of use. The mangled metal upon it glows red. Even from this distance, I feel its heat. He swings the hammer in a CLANG *I cannot fathom.*

Is this real? *I ask him.*

I know no unreal, *he says.*

What are you making?

All things new.

I do not face him. I cannot. And yet I know he smiles deeply and always has, even in his mourning.

What is taken away I will give back a hundredfold, *he says, and he brings the hammer up and*

CLANG

down again.

He moves. The light from the metal consumes me. I raise my hands to shield my face as he places something upon the anvil. A box. My box.

You need all you have, *says the man.* You have all you need.

From the shadows comes a form that shimmers from spirit to flesh. Strong and young and so, so alive. He carries in his hand a section of rubber hose attached to a Y-shaped piece of wood.

Grandpa?

My grandfather smiles and says, The peace you wish for the world begins inside yourself. *He hands the slingshot to the man.*

CLANG

Now a little girl from behind me. The bristles of the paintbrush she carries sweep against my arm. Who we are is not who we should be, *Mary says, and skips past me to the man. He stretches out his hand and takes the brush, placing it on the anvil.*

CLANG

Willa walks across the room in front of me, singing a verse that is not a hymn, but a Psalm—You have taken account of my wanderings; Put my tears in Your bottle. Are they not in Your book? *She gives the man the card she had given me.*

Alex is beside me, my letter finally in his hand. There is no greater pain than love, *he says,* and there is no greater joy.

The man takes the letter.

Jackie's mother walks past, a small wooden cross in her hand. Our troubles do not test our faith, our troubles make our faith.

Ms. Massachusetts hands the man the tip of her fingernail—We are separated only by our prejudices, *she says, and then she is gone.*

CLANG, CLANG, CLANG, CLANG

Pine needles from Rudolph, who says there are worlds I do not see and yet see me. Napkins from David Walker, who says the wheels of history are turned by the hands of the ordinary.

The woman from the mall gives the man a hat and tells me we all will stumble without one another.

There is Jordan, sweet Jordan, who hands over a piece of bubble gum and says, We are each other's angels, all of us, and our questions lift us upward.

There is Logan, still in his dinosaur costume and with a golf tee in his hand, who says that every day can be a day of birth to who we are and a day of death to who we were.

And there is one final person. Standing alone near me. He walks to me and smiles, then places his hands on my shoulders.

You're good, Andy, *Eric says. It is not a question now. Not a dying sort of wondering. It is truth and it is fact and it is good.*

Eric walks to the man and hands him the key chain. The man takes it in one hand. Resting the hammer on the anvil, the man reaches out with his other hand and rests it on Eric's shoulder. He gives Eric a squeeze and a pat, much as a proud father would give his son for a life well lived and a purpose fulfilled.

Eric takes his place among the rest as the man lifts the hammer one last time and

CLANG

molds it into the metal.

It is finished, *the man says.*

He turns his face, plain but kinglike, and invites me to him. He raises the work of his hands.

A mirror.

It gleams by an unseen light and catches the reflection of the Old Man. I touch my face and he touches his, and I know they are both one and the same.

He points beyond where we stand toward the darkness. Two paths appear before me: one narrow and steep, one wide and flat. The man says, Walk on.

I don't know the path, *I answer.*

The man smiles as a light now shines upon the wide path. A figure is bathed in white, arms outstretched. She faces me.

Elizabeth.

Gone are the glasses and the streak of gray in her brown hair. Gone is the rumpled denim shirt and the untied tennis shoes. She is not Elizabeth as she was, she is Elizabeth as she is.

The man says, The world is not solid, Andy. Keep to the deep places. See a new way.

He reaches to touch my face and my heart bursts, too big for my small body. I look into his eyes and think to myself that this is love and this is companionship and I have never been alone.

Never.

I walk toward Elizabeth.

She opens her arms to greet me.

The man smiles.

34

Jake

I awoke to a different kind of light sometime later, this one darker and colder. Emptier, even. The evening sun was dipping westward, its orange glow casting its good-bye kiss against the facing mountains, leaving me to wonder if I'd just missed one day or more. Noises entered through an open door to the hallway—phones rang, nurses gossiped. Shadows walked past. I felt my face where the man had touched me and reveled in a memory that would never fade. Kim came to give me comfort I no longer needed and to officially welcome me back to the world.

"Hey big guy," she said.

"Hey yourself," I answered. I tried lifting my head but couldn't. The bandages were off but the heaviness remained. I lay there in my bed and took mental stock of my body, then smiled. The weight resided solely from the neck up. My heart was light.

Kim began her routine checks, everything from my IVs to the fluffiness of my pillow. She seemed slower this time, though still deliberate. Then she rested a hand atop my bandaged head.

"You'll do anything to get out of talking to Jake, won't you?" she whispered.

"Don't tell me I missed him."

"You did."

"Well now, isn't that a shame?"

Kim smiled and said, "It is, isn't it? But he'll be back soon enough. You had me pretty worried for a while there, Andy. Thought for a minute there was a little more wrong with you than we thought."

"There was," I said. "But whatever little more that was wrong with me is better now. Promise."

"You let me be the judge of that." Kim adjusted the blanket that she herself had draped over me while I was *(gone? I thought. Was I gone? And to where?)* unconscious."I swear," she said, "these docs don't know what the heck they're doing. I tried to tell them that was too big a dose for you, and with your head injury to boot. But they've backed off now. Everything should be fine. How are you feeling?"

"I'm fine, Kim," I said. "Tired, but I'd say that was to be expected given the circumstances."

She pushed a button and raised the upper half of the bed. "Vision okay? Anything blurry?"

"I can honestly say that I've never seen things more clearly than I do right now." I smiled as I said those words, knowing the truth of that statement was something that would be lost to her even if I tried to explain it.

"Good. And I promise, no more...episodes...for you."

I knew then. Knew that to Kim and the doctors Elizabeth had been a ghost, more anesthetic than angel. Something I had conjured through the magic of medicine and a misfire of neurons. Kim had visited me through the night. She had lingered at the door on her way out with those looks of concern. I had brushed them aside, thinking they had been given for my appearance and not my actions. It had never occurred to me before that Elizabeth had never spoken to Kim nor Kim to Elizabeth. Why would they? To Kim, that chair had been empty all night. Whatever conversation she overheard from her desk or her rounds was completely one-sided. Just Crazy Old Andy, acting like himself. Kim confessed that not only had there been no one in my room, the hospital employed no in-house counselors at all. The only constant between her recollections and mine was the wooden box that sat on the table by my bed.

Someone brought it the day after I arrived, she said. Kim didn't know who, but she knew it hadn't been touched since.

I didn't believe her—couldn't—though everything I saw told me she was right.

"Who were you talking to all night, Andy?" she asked.

"I'm not sure who she was," I answered. And despite the madness Kim would believe me to be suffering and the brokenness she wouldn't know I carried within, I added, "But I loved her."

I fought the notion it had all been a lie. The human mind may be a powerful thing, but I could not believe it was so powerful as to produce something—someone—so real and so perfect. Someone so needed. No, I thought. It was more an impossibility that Elizabeth was not real than that she was. Because if Kim was right, if Elizabeth had been an invention and nothing more, than perhaps so too was the Old Man. And as I lightly touched my face, I feared that meant the man hammering upon the anvil was a mere figment as well.

I needed to believe they weren't, that they were real and that the truest things in this life were the things we could prove not with our eyes, but with the heart alone.

I needed to believe the world was not solid.

"I'm glad you're back," she said.

"Me, too." And with a wonder I never thought possible, I meant those words.

"Rest, okay? I'll be back soon."

Kim moved toward the door. Her steps weren't as clipped and purposeful as I'd seen them before. I thought that perhaps the heaviness that had fallen off of me was making its way to her.

"Kim?" I asked.

"Yes?"

I didn't know how to say what needed to be said. What I knew I should. "I always saw my loneliness as God's will. I just thought I was one of those people who wasn't supposed to find love. But it wasn't God's will that kept me away from loving someone, it was just my fear. It took me a long time to figure that out."

Kim leaned on the door. Her hand wiped at the corner of her eye. She tried to hide it by pushing her hair behind an ear in the next motion.

"Thank you, Andy," she said.

A day passed.

There were doctors and tests and orders for both rest and motion. I took walks when I could, inching my way up and down the hallway in search of the legs I once had. I don't mind saying many of those walks were taken with the hopes I'd catch a fleeting glimpse of a woman with long brown hair and glasses. I never did. Elizabeth was gone, left to wander in either a corner of my mind or a corner of heaven. I began to prefer my mind. She'd be closer there. I spent long hours listening to the television and staring at the empty chair beside my bed.

I couldn't avoid Jake any longer. He arrived that afternoon with his notebook, a pen, and a look of absolute sorrow on his face for both what had happened and what still was. He had a look of someone who had just realized that what he'd found wasn't what he was looking for. I went through everything that happened that night, leaving out only the Old Man (for obvious reasons) and Eric's last words. I figured Jake didn't need to know that, and he didn't ask. It was his turn then to fill me in on everything that had happened after. The town was scared, he said. They were all holding out for things to get back to normal, but he wasn't sure if it ever would.

"What about Taylor?" I asked him.

Jake's eyes looked from me toward the doorway. "I got the state police lookin' for him," he said, "and I'm lookin', too. My guess is they'll get him. He'll be anywhere but around town. They're watchin' his aunt's house. That's where he stayed."

"Where's he from?"

Jake shifted in his chair and cleared his throat. I wasn't sure what he was going to say, but I knew he didn't particularly care to say it. It was a surreal moment between us. Jake was interviewing me, and yet he was the nervous one.

"Happy Hollow," he said.

"Happy Hollow?"

He stared at the doorway again, and I followed his gaze. There was only the emptiness of the hallway and Kim's desk on the other side. She was on the phone. With Owen, I thought.

"Someone out there, Jake?"

"No," he said, but I thought—to him, at least—there was. "I'm sorry, Andy. About all of this. Feels like the world's just gone crazy. I'm fightin' not to think there ain't no hope left."

"I think there's always hope," I said.

He looked at my box on the table. "I see you got that, huh?"

"You bring this to me?"

Jake shook his head. "Eric's brother. Calls himself Jabber, right?"

"Right," I said.

"Called and said it was important to you and that you'd probably like it close, so I met him down at the gas station and fetched it for him. Not really procedure, but I figured I could bend the rules."

"I appreciate that, Jake," I said.

Jake tapped me on the leg with his notebook and said he'd be praying for me. "Folks say Taylor's got the Devil in him, Andy. That he's plain evil. I'm gonna get him. I swear to you I will. And I'll see that he pays for what he's done."

"I'll be prayin' for you too, Jake. Don't know why this happened, and maybe we never will. But I think everything has its reasons, however hard they may be. I hear the world's not solid."

Jake looked toward the door once more and said, "I'm hearin' the same thing."

Jake said much to me after that. Things he asked me not to share, and I will not. I suppose that's his story to tell, if he has a mind to tell it. I told him I would pray. He said he would do the same. Then he and whatever his mind saw at the doorway left me to my empty room.

35

Paper Angels

I took one last walk the night before I was to be released. I called it a victory lap to the nurses at the station, and I believed it was. I had neither conquered nor vanquished, but I had endured. Maybe that was all that mattered. It was our grip on life that spoke most of who we were.

I made my last stop the nurses' station, where Kim was still trying to catch up after arriving a half hour late for her shift. Late, she said, because Owen had driven her to work. One good-bye kiss had turned into ten, and time had a way of sneaking off and hiding when love came calling. Then I walked back into my room and stopped at the door, jarred by what I was seeing. Had it not been for the metal cart parked just inside, I would have fallen. Instead I gripped it and steeled myself at what was in front of me.

Someone was in the chair by my bed.

"Elizabeth?" I asked. Pleaded. Prayed. "Is that you?"

The figure moved from the shadows and into the light shining from above the bed. The face that appeared was a sorrowed mix of old and young.

"Mr. Andy?" it said.

I moved closer. "Jabber?"

Jabber rose from the chair. Halfway toward me he stretched out his arms. I caught him in mine and we stood there, his knees buckling against me as he let out nearly four days of grief and anger. I held him up, surprised at my strength. My eyes were open and staring not at him but at my hands resting on his back.

"Come sit down," I told him. "Come on."

We walked to my bed and I sat him down in the chair. Jabber wiped his eyes and brushed back his shaggy hair.

"How are you, Jabber?" I asked.

"Okay," he said. Then the tears began again, a torrent that rushed from him and seemed never ending. I kept my hand on him and squeezed, just as Elizabeth had done for me. "Sorry," he finally said. "Ain't right what happened. You okay?"

"I'm fine, Jabber. Promise. Doc says I'll be getting out of here tomorrow."

He nodded. "Good. Good. Sorry I didn't come sooner. Came by once. You were asleep. Things have been rough. Funeral and all."

"Don't worry about that," I said. "I know you had a lot to deal with."

Jabber's eyes said more than any words could. They seemed bigger somehow, like something had just jumped in front of him and yelled *Boo!* The boyish sparkle was gone, replaced not by a hard stare but an empty gaze. He had the look of someone who'd just lost everything. It was a look I knew well.

"Funeral was yesterday," he finally said. "Lots of people there. Kids from school, even folks from Mattingly. Was real nice."

"Wanted to thank you for bringing me this," I said, looking at my box on the stand beside me. "Really came in handy."

"I knew you liked it," Jabber said. "Sorta why I'm here. Wondering could you do me a favor."

"Sure," I said.

Jabber stared at the ground. "Wonder could you let me have his key chain. Don't know why. I got the money he owes you."

"Jabber," I said, "don't worry about that."

I reached over to open the box but found the key chain beside it. My mind raced, wondering if I had somehow sat it there or if someone else had, then handed him the key chain. "I'm pretty sure he'd want you to have it."

Jabber turned the key chain over in his hand and gripped it

like a lifeline, the one thing that kept him from being swept away.

"I loved him," he said.

"I loved him, too."

"He was the best thing in my life. He was like my daddy and my mama and my brother all at once. He was my best friend."

"How's your mom?" I asked him.

Jabber grew silent again, still studying the tops of his shoes. He shrugged. "Hasn't been home much. Said she couldn't be around me because I remind her of Eric. I think she blames me because I stayed home that night. I think she might tell me to leave."

"Why do you say that?"

"She wanted Eric and me out before. Her boyfriend doesn't like us. This might be her reason to do it."

"If you were there with us, nothing would be different," I said. "It was just his time, Jabber."

"I don't understand that."

"I don't really understand it, either. But I'm trying. I think Eric had a light to shine, and I think he shined it. And I think he did such a good job at it that God called him home."

"He'd have been a good missionary," Jabber said.

"I think he was just that. I know it. And don't you worry. I'm gonna help you out, Jabber. I'm gonna do everything I can. We'll figure this all out."

Jabber looked at me and asked the question that he both so needed and was so afraid to have answered.

"What am I supposed to do next? I feel like everything's over. Like . . . I died inside."

He looked down again. I held my words until he raised his chin. "You have, I think," I said. "But life is full of births and deaths. Things end so other things can begin. What's taken from you God will give back a hundredfold. Your troubles make your faith, Jabber. You need to find that faith now."

"I don't believe like Eric did. I went to church with him some, but not always. He said God had all the answers. Don't know about that."

"I think we'll both always have our share of questions." I stared at my box on the table beside us and knew that was true. "And I think those questions will always have a little hurt to them. But I think in that hurt is the closest thing to truth we can ever find in this life. Don't you worry. We're gonna get through this together. As long as you don't mind having to keep an eye on a bald old man."

Jabber smiled as much as he was able. "Thanks, Mr. Andy," he said. He held up the key chain. "And thanks for this."

"He'd want you to have it, Jabber. And thanks for bringing my box. It helped."

"Guess I'll head out before they kick me out," he said, though he didn't move.

There was a torment inside him, one that burned and smoked and let out tiny wisps in his speech. I wanted to reach out for him, to tell him there could never be another to him like Eric, just as there could never be another to me like my mother, but that didn't mean he couldn't find another to help bear the heavy load life had given him. I wanted to reach out, but I knew he had to reach out as well. True understanding is always met in the middle, not on the ends. I could offer my help, but Jabber had to accept it. He had to take down his wall. And the first bricks were dislodged with his next words.

"Got a ride in the morning?" he asked.

"No," I said. "Thought I'd just ask Jake."

"I'd come get you, if you want. Maybe we could talk some."

"That'd be just fine, Jabber. Just fine."

Jabber then rose to leave and gave me a hug. Even managed to slap me on the back. It was a sign he was in better spirits, at least for the time being. Still, I knew the road ahead for Jabber would be a difficult one. His life had been stripped bare of good. He could easily go the way of his mother and choose numbness over pain. Jabber needed someone who could convince him otherwise. He needed a friend. Someone he could depend upon.

He needed an angel.

Jabber left with the promise that he'd return bright and early the next day. My eyes settled upon the empty chair in front of me. I didn't know what had been real and what had been imagined, but I knew that wherever the words Elizabeth had spoken to me had come from, they had been true. I would need them. Them and more.

"Mr. Andy?"

I turned toward the door. "Yeah, Jabber?"

"Forgot to give you this. Found it stuck down in the cushion when I sat down."

Jabber dug into his pocket. Out came a folded sheet of carefully cut paper.

Elizabeth's paper.

36

The Beginning

After days of what felt like constant tears, I still found more to shed when Jabber handed me the paper and left. They dripped from my eyes and fell onto my arms, leaving me breathless and limp. It was a baptism in salty water, and I gave myself over to it. One final drowning of the old man—and the Old Man—in order to bring birth to the new.

I embraced my tears, and they became neither pain nor confusion, but joy.

Elizabeth was real.

She had sat with me by my bed. Had held and comforted me. She had looked into my eyes and seen my hidden self, and she had smiled and deemed me worthy of that smile. She had taken the brokenness of my life and pieced it together with her gentleness and had returned it remade with purpose and meaning.

Two small tabs had been cut into the front and back of the page. I grasped the ends and carefully pulled the paper apart, overwhelmed at both the design and the skill required to craft it. Stretched out in my hands were twelve paper angels joined wing to wing, each one as perfect and exact as the next. Twelve angels, one for each story I'd shared with her. One for each moment the Old Man had asked me to keep in my box.

I understood then. Perhaps not everything, but everything that mattered. My life had not been a collection of ordinary occurrences, but holy ones. I had lived not mere moments; I had lived defining ones.

And I knew this—our pasts, no matter how mangled, could be forged anew upon the anvil.

My eyes settled on the box, the book that held not all the chapters of my life, but the ones that meant the most. I took the box in my hands and walked toward the window, where I set it on the ledge. Cars moved east and west on the highway beyond. House lights and storefronts pierced the darkness around them. In the distance were the faint outlines of the mountains and the soft glow of Mattingly.

All those people, both drifting and adrift in this world, searching for their way. How many knew the truth of their lives? How many knew of the world beyond their own, a world that was hidden from them but one in which they were cast naked before it?

I looked down. A lone figure walked out of the main entrance toward the parking lot beyond. His steps were slow and staggered. A rock lying in his path was kicked to the side, then he sat on a bench to think and mourn.

Jabber.

Who better to send to a frightened young boy than someone who will understand?

At the time I thought she was speaking of the Old Man and me, but now I knew better. She was speaking of Jabber and me. And she was right. Jabber needed an angel, a special sort of angel. An angel who would understand.

I looked away from him and into the night sky. The lights from the hallway behind me shimmered then parted, only to gather themselves again into a carbon copy of my own reflection.

"That's a good boy down there," the Old Man said.

I smiled to the window and said, "Thought I was done with you."

"You are," he said. "Just came to say good-bye."

I turned to face him—or me, or at least the me that would be. The questions, the impossibility, the sheer irrationality of it all, washed over me in a wave that crashed in a sigh.

"I know," he said.

"How? How did you—did *I*..."

The Old Man shrugged. Said, "God can do whatever He wants. Whatever is good. The world isn't solid, Andy, least not all the way through. There are hollow places where the impossible shines through. Places where heaven mingles with earth and wonders abound. You know the why now. Or most of it. The how, though? I'm afraid that's not for me to say. Not because I don't know. I do. But explaining everything would be more than you could handle right now." He paused to smile at himself and added, "Besides, it would ruin all the surprise in the end. Trust what you cannot understand, Andy. Find your faith in the unanswerable."

"Elizabeth," I said. "At least tell me she was real. I have these," I said, holding the paper angels up to him, "but I need to know."

"You need to believe," he said.

"Help me believe," I answered.

He considered me and smiled. I wondered then if he had asked the same once and if someone would one day ask me. He put a hand on my box. "Open it," he said.

I lifted the latch and opened the top. All twelve pieces were there, arranged just as they'd always been. But there was one addition.

Elizabeth's hair tie.

I picked it up. Felt its smoothness in my hand, a smoothness that reminded me of her. Even the color seemed perfect— black, like the black she found me in and rescued me from. I felt it and felt her. Felt it to make sure it was

"Real," he finished for me. "See?"

The Old Man held up his wrist, and I saw for the first time the bracelet that he'd always worn, that I constantly watched him handle and caress, had not been a bracelet at all. It had been Elizabeth's hair tie.

"Good-bye, Andy," he said. "You have all you need, and you need all you have. You pray now. Pray you'll do right by that boy."